"That...shouldn't...

Jack leaned his forehead against hers. "I'll ask Declan to get someone else to go with you tomorrow. I'm not fit to be your protector."

Anne stared up into his eyes. "It's been a wild day. Our emotions are high. This could have happened to anyone." She stepped out of his arms and smoothed her hands over her shirt, her gaze anywhere but at him. "I still want you. I mean, I still want you to come with me. You've saved my life twice. I trust you to keep doing it."

He held up his hand as if swearing on a stack of bibles. "I promise not to do that again."

She held up her hand to stop him. "In case you didn't notice, you weren't the only one kissing in that scenario."

Jack couldn't erase the feeling her lips had left on his. He wanted to kiss her again. And again.

But that couldn't happen.

Anne's life depended on it.

TACTICAL FORCE

New York Times Bestselling Author
ELLE JAMES

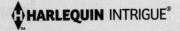

I want to thank Delilah Devlin and my daughter, Paige Yancey, for being there when I need some serious help brainstorming.

And thank you to Denise Zaza, who has been with me from the day she bought my first book for Harlequin Intrigue.

A big thank-you to my readers, who continue to buy my books. You make it possible for me to follow my dream of being a full-time author. Thank you!

ISBN-13: 978-1-335-13622-0

Tactical Force

Copyright © 2019 by Mary Jernigan

PLEASE RECYCLE

Recycling programs for this product may not exist in your area.

Printed in U.S.A.

www.Harlequin.com

Elle James, a *New York Times* bestselling author, started writing when her sister challenged her to write a romance novel. She has managed a full-time job and raised three wonderful children, and she and her husband even tried ranching exotic birds (ostriches, emus and rheas). Ask her, and she'll tell you what it's like to go toe-to-toe with an angry 350-pound bird! Elle loves to hear from fans at ellejames@earthlink.net or ellejames.com.

Books by Elle James

Harlequin Intrigue

Declan's Defenders

Marine Force Recon
Show of Force
Full Force
Driving Force
Tactical Force

Mission: Six

One Intrepid SEAL
Two Dauntless Hearts
Three Courageous Words
Four Relentless Days
Five Ways to Surrender
Six Minutes to Midnight

Ballistic Cowboys

Hot Combat
Hot Target
Hot Zone
Hot Velocity

SEAL of My Own

Navy SEAL Survival
Navy SEAL Captive
Navy SEAL to Die For
Navy SEAL Six Pack

Visit the Author Profile page at Harlequin.com.

CAST OF CHARACTERS

Jack Snow—Former Force Recon marine slack man, youngest member of the team, takes all the heavy stuff.

Anne Bellamy—Midlevel staffer for the national security adviser on the National Security Council. Former friend of the deceased John Halverson.

Shaun Louis—National security adviser on the National Security Council.

Millicent Saunders—Midlevel staffer with the homeland security adviser. Fluent in German, Russian and Greek.

Dr. Robert Browne—Special adviser to the national security adviser. Fluent in Russian. Expert on all things Russian.

Terrence Tully—White House conference room coordinator. Former army ranger.

Mack Balkman—Former Force Recon marine, assistant team leader and Declan's right-hand man. Grew up on a farm and knows hard work won't kill you—guns will.

Declan O'Neill—Highly trained Force Recon marine who made a decision that cost him his career in the marine corps. Leader of Declan's Defenders.

Charlotte "Charlie" Halverson—Rich widow of a highly prominent billionaire philanthropist. Leading the fight for right by funding Declan's Defenders.

Frank "Mustang" Ford—Former Force Recon marine, point man. First into dangerous situations, making him the eyes and ears of the team.

Cole McCastlain—Former Force Recon marine assistant radio operator. Good with computers.

Augustus "Gus" Walsh—Former Force Recon marine radio operator; good with weapons, electronics and technical equipment.

Chapter One

Anne Bellamy finished editing the document her boss had given her just before he'd left for the gym at exactly four thirty that afternoon. She'd stayed two hours past the end of the usual day in the office of the national security advisor located in the West Wing of the White House to clean up, fact-check and finish the job. The last one out of the office, she gathered her purse and checked her cell phone.

A text message had come through during the time she'd logged off her computer and collected her purse.

Unknown caller.

Curious as to who had her phone number and was texting her so late in the evening, Anne brought up her text messages and frowned down at the cryptic message.

TRINITY LIVES.

Her heart skipped several beats before settling into the swift pace of one who was running for her life. Anne hadn't heard anything about Trinity since the man who'd recruited her to spy on government officials had been murdered.

Her gut clenched and she felt like she might throw up as she returned the text.

Sorry, you must have the wrong number.

She waited, her breath caught in her throat, her pulse hammering against her eardrums.

John Halverson died because he'd got too close.

Anne gasped and glanced around her office, wondering if anyone was watching or could see the texts she was receiving. Wondering if she was doing the right thing, or revealing herself to the wrong persons, she responded to the text again.

Halverson is dead.

Again, Anne waited, afraid of the response, but afraid not to reply.

Halverson was on the right track.

Anne's heart squeezed hard in her chest. John Halverson had been a good man, with a heart as big as they came. He cared about his country and what was happening to tear it apart.

When he'd come to her, he'd caught her at a vulnerable point in her career. A point at which she'd considered leaving the political nightmare to take a position as a secretary or receptionist for a doctor's office. Anything to get out of the demoralizing, disheartening work she did with men and women who didn't always have the best interests of the nation at heart, whose careers and post-government jobs in media and lobbying meant more to them than the country's future.

Anne had kept her head down and her thoughts to herself since Halverson's death, afraid that whoever had murdered the man would come after her. If they knew her association with Halverson, and her involvement in uncovering the graft and corruption inside the office of the National Security Council, she'd be the next target.

She knew Trinity had a firm foothold in the government, and they weren't afraid to pounce on those who dared to cross them or squeal on their activities. The problem was that they were so well entrenched you couldn't tell a friend from a terrorist.

She stared at her phone screen. Was someone trying to warn her? Or flush her out into the open?

Either way, someone knew her secret. She could be the next casualty, courtesy of Trinity.

Anne quickly keyed in her message, not feeling

terribly confident she was putting an end to the communication.

I don't know what you're talking about. Leave me alone.

A moment later came a response.

Can't. They're planning an attack. A lot of people could be hurt. I need your help to stop it.

Anne pressed a hand to her breast to still her pounding heart.

No. No. No.

She wasn't the kind of person who could easily lie or pretend. Anne had always been an open book. Anyone could read any emotion on her face. She'd argued this with Halverson, but he'd insisted she could help him. She was in a strategic position, one that touched on a number of key players in politics.

If Trinity had sleeper cells in those positions, she could spot them before anyone else. *Theoretically.*

Anne hated that Halverson had paid the ultimate price. At the same time, she no longer had to report things she saw or heard, which meant she didn't have to worry that she was being watched or targeted.

Until now. Until the text warning her about Trinity.

Shooting a glance around the office and the four corners of the room, she wondered if anyone had a webcam recording her every move. She'd gotten good at discovering small audio and video recording devices stashed in telephone receiver units, lights, ceiling tiles, potted plants and office furniture.

She made a habit of scouring the room at least once a day. She'd found a small audio device once, early on, when Halverson had still been alive. They'd met at a bookstore in Arlington, where Halverson had identified the device and told her about others she should be on the lookout for.

Since Halverson's death, she'd continued looking over her shoulder. As time passed, she'd become lax. No one appeared to be following her or watching her.

How wrong had she been? And why had this person come to her now?

Instead of answering the previous text, she shoved her phone into her purse and left her office. Her heart hammered against her ribs and her breathing came in shallow pants. She was overreacting. That was all there was to it.

But who had given out her phone number? And how did they know she'd once been involved with Halverson? She'd kept that part of her life as clandestine as possible. Trying to ensure her trysts with Halverson were in as out-of-the-way a venue as she could, she'd usually met him in a public library, where running into people she worked with was highly unlikely. It wasn't a bar, and it wasn't a coffee shop. She'd thought it was the best cover of all.

How many terrorists did she know who made good use of a public library?

She'd never been to Halverson's mansion, and she'd always worn a disguise when she'd met with him at the library, never driving her own car, but taking public transportation.

Once out in the open, she inhaled fresh night air. Anne had been so busy working she hadn't realized it had rained earlier. The ground was still wet, and light reflected off the standing puddles. Her phone vibrated inside her purse, causing her heart to skip a beat. She ignored it and strode toward the Metro station, wishing she'd left while there was still some daylight chasing away the shadows. Though night had settled in, people still moved around the city. Men and women dressed in business suits, dress shoes and trench coats hurried home from office buildings, after a long day at work. Still, the number of people headed toward the train station was significantly less than during the regular rush hours.

Anne wished she'd worn her tennis shoes to work rather than the tight, medium-heeled pumps that had been pinching her feet since five o'clock that morning.

Again, the phone vibrated in her purse. She could feel the movement where her purse rested against her side. Ignoring the insistent pulsation, she moved quickly, determined to make the next Metro train headed toward Arlington, where she lived in a modest apartment.

Footsteps sounded behind her.

Anne shot a glance over her shoulder. A man wearing a black jacket and jeans strode behind her, less than half a block away. He also wore a dark baseball cap, shading his face and eyes from the streetlights he passed beneath.

Alarm bells rang in Anne's head. She increased her pace.

The man behind her sped up, as well.

Still a couple of blocks away from the train station, Anne realized the streets had become deserted. The people she'd passed earlier must have hopped into taxis or found their cars in the paid parking lots.

Alone and on the street with a man following too closely behind her, Anne couldn't move fast enough. Then she remembered there was a restaurant at the corner of the next street, which now became her new, short-range goal. Clutching her purse to her side, she sprinted for the door, her feet moving as fast as they could in heels. She didn't slow to see if the man following her was running, too. She only knew she had to get to that restaurant.

When she reached the restaurant door, she almost sobbed. It was closed—the lights were turned out and no one moved inside.

A quick glance behind her assured her the man had kept up. Whether he'd had to run or not wasn't important. He was still there. Striding toward her, his feet eating the distance between them.

Anne's gaze darted around her, searching for a pub, a convenience store or pharmacy. Anything that stayed open late and had people inside. The block consisted of still more office buildings, closed for the night. She had no choice but to continue on toward the train station and pray she reached it before him.

Starting out with a purposeful stride, she walked fast toward the Metro stop, watching the reflections in the glass windows of the office buildings beside her for the image of the man tailing her. When he appeared in the reflection, Anne shot forward, running all out.

Her breath came in ragged gasps, and her pulse pounded so hard against her eardrums she could barely hear. Rounding a corner, she spied a pub, its sign lit up over the door. With the Metro station still too far to make, she set her sights on the pub and raced toward the door.

Just as she was reaching out, a hand descended on her shoulder and jerked her back. Oh, sweet heaven, he'd caught her. She braced herself for the fight of her life.

At that moment, the pub door opened, and a group of men exited, laughing and talking to each other.

The hand on Anne's shoulder fell away.

With renewed hope, Anne dove through the men and into the pub. Once inside, she went straight to the bar.

"What can I get you?"

"Someone tried to grab me outside the bar," she gushed, her breathing catching in her throat.

The bartender leaned toward her. "You okay?" He glanced past her to a large man standing near the exit.

The man, probably a bouncer, came forward.

"This lady said a man tried to grab her," the bartender told him.

"What was he wearing?" the bouncer asked.

She shook her head. "Dark clothes and a baseball cap, I think. I don't know. I was running too fast to notice."

The bouncer nodded and left the pub. He was back a minute later, shaking his head. "No one out there fitting your description. In fact, there was no one out there at all. I walked a block in both directions."

Anne let go of the breath she'd been holding. Even if the man wasn't within a block either direction, he might be lying in wait for her to continue her progress to the Metro stop. Anne couldn't bring herself to step outside the pub.

"We're closing early tonight for kitchen renovations, lady. You got about thirty minutes until we lock up. Is there anyone I could call for you?" the bartender asked, his expression worried.

Anne shook her head. She didn't have any close friends. She had acquaintances from work. That was it. They had their own lives and she had her solitary existence. Then she remembered John Halverson giving her his phone number and telling her if ever she needed anything, she should call that number.

But he was dead.

Would anyone answer at the number? Did he still have a staff of people working for the same things he had?

Anne pulled her phone out of her purse and stared down at the icon for her text messages. She didn't want to look at them. Everything had been fine until she'd started receiving the texts.

She pulled up her contacts list and dialed the number Halverson had given her, not knowing if anyone would actually answer.

The line rang several times.

Anne was about to give up when the ringing stopped and a woman answered, "Hello?"

Not knowing what to say, Anne blurted, "I know John Halverson is dead, but I need help. He gave me this number and said to call if I ever needed anything. Please tell me you can help." She stopped and waited for a response, her heart thudding, her gut clenched.

"This is John's wife. Are you in a safe place?"

Anne nodded and then said, "For the moment, but this place closes in thirty minutes. I was being followed and I'm afraid to leave."

"Stay there. I'll have someone come to collect you."

"But you don't even know me."

"You're a human being in need of assistance. I don't

care who you are. I'll have someone see you to your home or the police station. Wherever you need to go."

"Thank you," Anne said, sagging with relief. "I'm sorry for what happened to your husband. He was a good man."

"Me, too. If he gave you his number, he would have wanted me to help you. Rest assured, I'm sending someone. Give me the address."

Anne had to ask the bartender for the address. Once she'd relayed it to Mrs. Halverson, the widow insisted she stay on the phone until the person she sent arrived.

"That won't be necessary. As long as I can remain in the pub, I'll be all right," Anne said.

"Then I'll get right on it," Mrs. Halverson said. "I'll text with an expected time of arrival as soon as I have one."

"Thank you, Mrs. Halverson."

"Don't call me Mrs. Halverson. I go by Charlie," the woman said.

"Thank you, Charlie," Anne said, correcting herself, and rang off.

A moment later, a text came across.

Jack will be there in twenty minutes.

That was a text Anne could live with, though she wondered who Jack was, what he looked like and what he'd be driving.

JACK SNOW HAD left his apartment in Arlington an hour earlier, too wound up to sit in front of a television and watch mindless shows or even more mindless news reports.

Much too jittery to find a bar and drink away the anxious feeling he got all too often since returning from deployment and exiting his Marine Force Recon unit, he climbed onto his Harley and went for a ride around the cities. He ended up in the Capitol Hill area near the war memorials. After the sun set, the crowds thinned and the lights illuminating the Lincoln Memorial made the white marble stand out against the backdrop of the black, starless night.

He'd ridden to the Korean War Memorial, parked his bike and stood near the nineteen steel statues of soldiers in full combat gear and waterproof ponchos. They appeared as ghosts, emerging from the shadows. Haunting.

They reminded him of so many operations he and his team had conducted at night, moving silently across rough terrain, like the ghosts of the men the statues had been modeled after.

His heart pinched tightly in his chest. It was as if he were looking at the friends he'd lost in battle, the men he'd carried out only to send home in body bags.

No matter how long he'd been separated from active duty, the images of his friends never faded. Often they appeared in his dreams, waking him from a dead sleep in cold sweat as he relived the operations that had claimed their lives.

He'd get out of his bed, dress and go for a ride on his motorcycle in the stillness of night, letting the wind in his face blow the cobwebs from his memories.

Tonight was different. He'd dreaded even going to bed. Tonight was the anniversary of the death of his high school sweetheart. Yet another reason to lose sleep.

He'd met Kylie in the eighth grade. They'd been together throughout high school and had big plans to go to the same college after graduation.

Though Jack had made it to graduation, Kylie had not. The weekend before the big event, they'd gone to the local mall. Kylie wanted a special dress to wear beneath her cap and gown. Jack had gone with her to help her choose.

That day, a man who'd been dumped by his fiancée days before their wedding had entered the mall, bearing an AR-15 semiautomatic rifle with a thirty-round magazine locked and loaded. Tucked into his jacket pocket was a .45 caliber pistol with a ten-round magazine. He'd come to take out his anger on his ex-fiancée working in a department store. But he didn't end there. Once he started firing, he didn't stop until he ran out of bullets in the rifle's magazine.

Jack and Kylie had just left an upscale dress shop when the bullets started flying. Before they could duck back into the shop or even drop to the ground, the gunman turned the barrel of his AR-15 on them, firing indiscriminatingly.

Jack grabbed Kylie and shoved her to the ground, covering her body with his.

When the first volley of bullets slowed to silence, he looked up.

The rifleman fumbled with another magazine for the AR-15, dropped it and bent to retrieve it.

Jack didn't stop to think about what he was doing. He lunged to his feet and charged the man before he could reload, hitting him with his best linebacker tackle, knocking him to the ground. The rifle flew from the gunman's hands, skittering to a stop several yards away.

The man tried to reach for the handgun in his jacket pocket but couldn't get to it with Jack lying on top of him, pinning him to the hard tile floor.

The mall security cop had dashed to the scene but hadn't wanted Jack to move for fear the shooter would manage to get to his feet and regain control of his weapon.

The police had arrived shortly after, taking over from Jack.

That was when he'd turned to find Kylie still lying where he'd left her, facedown and unmoving.

She'd taken a bullet straight to her heart and died instantly.

Jack had been devastated.

Her death was the main reason he'd chosen to join

the Marines rather than go on to college like many of his classmates. He needed the physical challenge to burn away his anger and the feeling he should have gotten her to safety sooner. He should have done more to save her.

Those deployment nightmares, combined with the traumatic one from his school days, had kept him moving, afraid to stand still for a moment. If he did, the memories overwhelmed him.

He stared at the shadowy figures of the steel soldiers. They were so lifelike Jack felt as if he could fall in step with them and complete the mission.

His heartbeat quickened. As he took a step forward, a vibration against his side brought him back to reality, making him stop.

He reached into his jacket and pulled out his cell phone. The name on the screen read Declan O'Neill.

Jack didn't hesitate. He pressed the talk button and pressed the phone to his ear. "Yeah."

"Dude, where are you?" Declan asked, his tone crisp.

"Downtown DC near the war memorials. What's up?"

"Got a mission for you."

"Give it to me." He needed action. Anything to take his mind off the anniversary of Kylie's death and the loss of his friends in battle. Declan's call was a lifeline thrown to him in troubled waters. A reminder that he was still among the living, and he had a team of friends to work with.

Declan gave him the address of a pub not far from where he was. "There's a female there who's afraid to leave. Someone tried to grab her on her way to the Metro station."

"What does she look like?" Jack asked.

"Long, straight black hair, blue eyes. Wearing a business suit. Tell her Mrs. Halverson sent you."

"Got it. I can be there in less than ten minutes."

"Make it five. The pub is closing. Let us know when you get her to safety." Declan ended the call.

Slipping his helmet over his head, Jack left the steel soldiers to their mission, mounted his motorcycle and commenced with his own mission. He'd hoped for something more than escorting a damsel in distress home for the evening, but at least it gave him a purpose and something else to think about besides Kylie and dead comrades.

Ignoring the speed limit signs and only slowing for the occasional light, Jack made it to the pub in four minutes. A few men straggled through the door, laughing and shaking hands.

Jack scanned the surrounding area for anyone lurking in the shadows, waiting for a lone woman to step out of the pub and into his path. When he didn't see anyone or any movement in the shadows, he parked his bike on the curb and entered the pub, passing by a large man standing near the door.

"Sorry, we're closed," someone called out from the bar.

"I'm not here for a drink. I'm here to pick up a lady."

The bartender snorted. "Sorry, we're closed for that, too. Always. Unless the lady wishes to be picked up." The man chuckled at his own humor.

A black-haired woman in a dark blazer and skirt slid off a bar stool and faced Jack. Her blue eyes narrowed, and her lips pressed into a thin line. She stood stiff, and silently maintained her distance, looking as if she'd bolt if he made a move toward her.

This had to be the woman he'd been tasked to collect. "Mrs. Halverson sent me," Jack said.

The woman drew in a deep breath and the stiffness seemed to melt from her frame. "Oh, thank God." She slung her purse over her shoulder and nodded. "Let's go."

"Hey, lady," the bartender called out. "You gonna be okay?"

She turned toward the man. "I think so." She smiled. "Thanks."

Before they left the building, the woman stopped and frowned. "I guess I should know your full name."

With a half smile, Jack held out his hand. "Jack Snow."

She took his hand in her smaller, softer one and said quietly, "Anne Bellamy."

"You want to tell me what happened?"

She handed him her cell phone with an image of a map with the directions painted in a bright blue line. "Not here. Not now. I just want to go home. That map will get you there."

He shrugged. "Have it your way. My ride is outside."

When she started to go through the door, he placed his hand on her arm. "Me first."

Anne nodded and let him go through the door ahead of her.

He stopped on the other side and glanced in both directions, taking his time to be thorough in his perusal of the buildings, alleys and every shadow. When he was fairly certain they were alone, he held out his hand.

Anne placed hers in his and let him guide her to the curb, where his motorcycle was parked.

The big guy who'd been lurking near the entrance followed them outside.

Jack shot a narrowed glance his way as he fitted Anne's cell phone into a holder on his handle bar. "Is this the guy who tried to grab you?"

"No. That's the bar's bouncer. He's just making sure we aren't attacked," Anne said. She faced the motorcycle, a frown drawing her eyebrows together. "This is your ride?" The frown deepened. "I've never been on a motorcycle before."

"Well, tonight must be your lucky night. Unless you want to wait another thirty minutes to an hour for one of my buddies to come get you, you'll have to take your chances." He swung his leg over the bike and patted the cushioned seat behind him. "Don't wait too long. You'll only be giving your attacker the opportunity to make another attempt to grab you."

Chapter Two

"How…" Anne tried to swing her leg over the bike, but her A-line skirt hampered her maneuver. Finally, she pulled the skirt up high enough to allow her to mount the cycle and settle behind him. "No judging," she mumbled.

He grinned. "Great legs. Sorry, couldn't help it." Jack handed her a helmet and helped her to adjust the strap beneath her chin. Then he pulled his own helmet over his head and cinched the strap. "Hold on around my waist."

She placed her hands on his hips, barely squeezing, amazed at how firm they were. A rush of awareness rocked through her.

"Seriously?" He took her hands and pulled them around his middle. "Now hold on tight. This beast has a powerful takeoff."

As if to prove his point, Jack cranked the engine and twisted the throttle. The motorcycle sprang forward.

Anne clenched her arms around him in a death

grip so tight she was certain Jack could barely breathe. He slowed the bike a little and drove down the street at a more sedate pace.

He looked back with a grin.

Most likely, he was happy to have startled her.

The grin disappeared and a frown replaced it in that split second he'd turned to look back at her.

Anne swiveled her helmet-heavy head and took note of headlights glaring at them. A dark sedan raced toward them at a high speed. Her heart leaped into her throat. "Go!" she yelled.

"Hold on!" Jack shouted. He made an abrupt turn, leaning hard into it.

Anne leaned the opposite direction.

Jack seemed to struggle with navigating the corner and he slowed.

"Lean with me!" he yelled, twisting his right hand on the handle. The motorcycle shot forward, putting distance between them and the vehicle turning at the corner behind them.

If Anne had any doubts they were being followed, she was certain now that the car behind them wasn't on a sightseeing trip in the night.

With the bike being more agile and maneuverable, Jack managed to weave in and out of streets, down back alleys and eventually onto the main road leading out of the city.

Anne held on, leaning when Jack leaned and in the same direction as him, making turns easier.

When she was sure they'd lost the dark sedan. Anne released a sigh of relief.

Jack settled into a smooth drive, following the altered directions on Anne's cell phone.

When they were only a block away from her apartment complex, he slowed almost to a crawl.

"Third building on the left," Anne called out as he neared the parking lot.

He drove to the location and brought the bike to a rolling stop.

Anne clambered off, her legs shaking. She smoothed her skirt down and hiked her purse strap onto her shoulder. "Thank you for getting me to my apartment. Tell Mrs. Halv—"

Jack adjusted the kickstand and dismounted.

"Where are you going?" Anne asked, her brow furrowing.

"To see you to your door and make sure you get inside safely." He cupped her elbow and walked her toward the entrance. "And to find out what this is all about."

She ground to a halt and pulled her elbow free. "I'll be fine." Already hyperaware of the man after holding him around his middle for the past thirty minutes, Anne just wanted to be free of him, and settle in with a cup of her favorite tea to soothe her fractured nerves. "Be sure to thank Mrs. Halverson for me."

"She likes to be called Charlie."

"Thank Charlie for me," Anne said and turned to walk into the building.

Jack's footsteps sounded behind her.

Anne spun to face him. "Seriously, you don't have to go up with me. I can manage on my own now."

"I've been given a mission to see you safely somewhere." He shrugged. "Although the somewhere was vague." He gave a nod toward the building. "I'll assume it was to your apartment."

"I'm here. You can go." She waved her hand as if shooing a pesky animal or child away.

"I'm not leaving until I know you're safely inside your apartment. Remember, we were followed not all that long ago."

"Yes, but you lost the trailing vehicle quite efficiently, though you scared the bejesus out of me in the process." She tipped her head toward his motorcycle. "And you quite convinced me that I don't like riding motorcycles. But thank you for delivering me to my apartment in one piece." With that parting comment, she turned and strode toward the door.

Again, Jack followed.

Anne gritted her teeth and kept going. If he wanted to follow her all the way up to her apartment…fine. As long as he didn't cup her elbow, sending crazy bursts of electrical current all the way through her body.

At her door, she fumbled for the key in her purse. Finally wrapping her fingers around it, she started to fit it into the doorknob.

Before she could, Jack grabbed her arm again.

And like before, that jolt of electricity traveled up her arm and down to her belly. She started to turn to tell him not to touch her when he gently pushed her to one side of the door and pressed a finger to his lips. He wasn't even looking at her, but at her door.

Then he released her arm and gave her door a slight nudge.

It opened without resistance. The doorjamb appeared splintered, as if someone had forced his way into her apartment.

Her heart thudding against her chest, Anne started to step inside.

Jack put out his arm and shook his head, mouthing the word *Stay*.

Too shocked to argue, Anne remained rooted to the floor outside her apartment, while Jack slipped inside.

She counted to ten, her stomach knotting and her breathing unsteady. How long could it take to look for bad guys? Just when Anne had decided she couldn't wait another moment, Jack appeared in the entryway, his mouth set in a grim line. He opened the door wider, flipped the light switch on and stood back. "I take it you didn't leave your place like this when you left for work this morning?"

Anne stepped across the threshold and gasped. "What the h—?"

Her home looked like something from a warzone. The sofa had been flipped on its back. The seat cushions had been flung across the room after they'd been ripped open and the stuffing pulled out. The artwork she'd painstakingly chosen and positioned on the walls had been slashed or painted over with a garish red spray paint.

Every drawer in her kitchen had been dumped on the floor. Knives stuck into the walls as if they'd been thrown one by one.

The photo frame containing a picture of Anne, her mother and her father had been destroyed, the picture pulled out and torn up into tiny pieces.

Tears welled in Anne's eyes as she continued through the little apartment to the bedroom. How much worse could it get? They'd destroyed practically everything she owned.

It got worse. The bedroom, like the living room, was a shambles, with the mattress dragged off the bed frame, a long gash drawn down the center. The pillows were in tatters, the filling scattered across the room. But the message on the wall was what made Anne press a hand to her chest and reel from shock.

Words written in bright red spray paint covered the wall over her headboard.

CONSIDER THIS A WARNING

Beside the words was a symbol Anne was all too familiar with. The crisscrossing Trinity symbol that might mean nothing to most but struck fear in the hearts of those familiar with the organization's history.

Anne staggered backward until her back hit the wall. Then she slid down and gathered her knees to her chest. "This. Can't. Be. Happening."

Jack dropped to his haunches beside her and took her hands in his. "I'm sorry, but it is. And you can't stay here. They know where you live and might come back."

She shook her head, her eyes glazed, her hands shaking in his. "I haven't done anything. Why would they come after me?"

"I don't know." Jack gently pulled her to her feet. "Grab the clothes you can, or better yet, leave it all here and buy new." He slipped an arm around her waist and pressed her body against his. "The main thing is to get you out of here as soon as possible."

She shook her head. "But this is all I own… My things."

"They're just things. At least you weren't here when they came in." He flung open the closet door.

Whoever had trashed her apartment had used the same red paint, spraying a thick swath across the clothes hanging in her closet.

Jack grabbed a gym bag from the floor. "They didn't get this," he said.

He unzipped it and held it open. "Find whatever you can that's undamaged, enough to get you by, and let's get the heck out of here. I don't want them to come back while we're here."

Anne couldn't seem to make her feet move. A crippling lethargy settled over her, making it impossible to think or motivate herself.

Jack dropped the bag and gripped her arms. "Anne." He tipped her chin up and stared into her eyes. "These are just things. We have to leave. I need you to be with me." He gave her a gentle shake. "Now."

Though she knew she needed to comply, she just couldn't.

"I'm not getting through to you," Jack said with a sigh. "Maybe this will work." He bent his head and pressed his lips to hers in a hard, persistent kiss.

The shock of it forced Anne's mind off the destruction and centered it on the feel of his lips against hers. She raised her hands to wrap around the back of his neck and pulled him closer. As if by kissing him, she could block out all the horror of her apartment.

When he finally set her away, he stared down into her eyes. "Are you with me now?" he asked, his tone deep, his voice gravelly.

She nodded. "I am."

He released her arms. "Then pack. You have one minute to get all the undamaged items you can into that bag. If it's nothing, so be it. You're coming with me." He left her alone in the room.

Anne shook out of her stunned haze and scrambled through her clothing, searching for panties, bras, jeans, shirts and skirts she could salvage from the items the intruders had permanently destroyed. She changed out of her skirt and heels into a pair of jeans and loafers.

She jammed what few undamaged things she could find into the gym bag and hurried to find Jack, wanting to be with him at all times. Though he was a stranger, he made her feel safer than she'd felt alone.

He stood by the open door of her apartment, looking up and down the hallway. When he heard her behind him, he shot a glance over his shoulder. "Ready?"

Anne nodded, closed the door and handed him her cell phone. "I think this has to do with the text messages I received before I left work this evening."

Jack took the phone from her and read through the messages, his face growing tighter, a muscle ticking in his jaw by the time he finished. "I take it you didn't read the last two messages."

Anne frowned. "I had other things on my mind, and I'd hoped by ignoring the texts, whoever had sent them would just go away." She snorted. "Obviously, that didn't happen."

"Read them." Jack pushed the cell phone beneath her nose.

Anne focused on the words.

Destroy your phone.

They will track you with it.

"If whoever did this to your apartment can track you using your phone, you need to ditch that phone. The sooner the better." Jack pulled his own cell phone from his back pocket and snapped pictures of the messages on Anne's cell phone. He glanced up at her. "Sorry, but it must be done." He dismantled the phone, pulled the SIM card from it, dropped the card into the kitchen's garbage disposal and ground it into oblivion. Then he placed the phone on the floor and stomped his heel into the screen.

"I need to get pictures of the message on the wall. Wait here," he said and disappeared into her bedroom. When he returned to the living room, he sent the pictures to someone and placed a call.

"We're headed your way. We could be bringing a tail... Good. See you in a few."

"What was that all about?" Anne asked.

"I sent the images to my boss. We've got a couple of computer wizzes who can do some poking around to see what they can find." He took the gym bag from her hand and led the way down the stairs toward the parking lot. He made her wait in the stairwell until he was certain the parking lot was safe.

Jack strapped the bag onto the back of the bike and went back to collect Anne. Slipping an arm around her, he shielded her body with his and walked her to the motorcycle.

Once they'd both mounted the bike, Anne leaned over Jack's shoulder. "Are you taking me to a hotel? I have nowhere else to go," she said, her heart flipping in her chest and the tears rushing to fill her eyes. She couldn't go to a friend's house. Not with Trinity looking for her.

Jack shook his head. "We're going to Charlie's."

Anne wondered whether everything would have gone on as usual if she'd ignored the first text message. Had she set the course of events by responding? And now that her phone was destroyed, the mysterious texter wouldn't have a way to contact her. Somehow, that didn't give her any sense of relief. Quite the opposite.

JACK DROVE OUT the other end of the apartment complex, choosing a circuitous route to Charlie's estate.

He kept an eye on the small rearview mirror mounted on his handlebar, searching for headlights and praying he didn't find any.

Avoiding the main roads, he wove his way through suburbs and backroads until he finally found himself on the road to the Halverson estate.

If anything was going to happen, it would happen here. It stood to reason that if they had hacked into her phone and knew she'd received messages from someone trying to stop Trinity, they would know she'd place a call to Charlie Halverson.

Since a prior attempt to break into the estate, Charlie had beefed up security and built a stronger wall to keep people out and protect those on the inside. That would be the best place to take Anne.

Getting there unscathed was the plan.

Someone else had other plans for them.

Jack turned onto the quiet country highway leading to the Halverson estate. With eight miles of curvy roads ahead, he couldn't let his guard down for a moment.

As he rounded a sharp bend in the road, a delivery truck darted out of a side road and stopped in the middle of the road, effectively blocking both lanes of traffic.

Warning bells went off in Jack's head. "Hang on," he called out.

Instead of slowing, Jack sped up, aiming straight for the truck.

As he neared, he noted men climbing out of the cab, AR-15s in their hands.

Damn. They'd brought serious weapons to the party.

He swerved at the last moment, taking the motorcycle off the road and down into the shallow ditch, praying Anne could hold on long enough to make it out on the other side.

Her arms tightened around him as they bumped

over the rough terrain. At one point he thought the bike might turn over, and then it would be all over for them. Somehow, he managed to right the front tire, gunned the accelerator and sent them popping up over the shoulder and back onto the road. A couple sets of headlights headed toward him, but there was no going back.

Jack powered forward, ready to take to the ditches again if necessary.

The trucks remained on the correct side of the road. As they approached, they slowed.

Jack's hand squeezed tighter on the throttle, preparing to twist it to make the bike go faster.

Then he saw that the lead truck was Declan's black four-wheel drive and the one following belonged to Mack Balkman. Declan passed him and turned his truck sideways, blocking one lane of the rural road, using the big vehicle as a shield to protect the two people on the motorcycle.

Mack did the same, blocking the other lane.

Jack noted there was a passenger in each vehicle. Probably Gus Walsh and Frank "Mustang" Ford. Cole was probably helping Charlie's computer guy, Jonah Spradlin, look into the texts from Anne's phone history.

A guard stood at the electric gate to the Halverson estate, armed with his own AR-15 rifle and a powerful spotlight.

When Jack rode up to the closed gate, the guard shined the light into his face.

"It's me," Jack said. "Jack Snow. And I have Anne Bellamy with me."

The guard shifted the light to the woman on the back of the motorcycle. A moment later, the gate opened and Jack drove through.

He'd never been quite so content to drive the winding road to the sprawling house at the end, knowing his team had his back, and the fence, gate and guards would see to their safety.

As he pulled up to a stop in front of the massive entrance, the door opened and Cole McCastlain emerged. Charlie Halverson stepped out behind him, followed by her assistant, Grace Lawrence, and her butler, Roger Arnold.

"I understand you've had a little excitement tonight." Cole grinned and held out a hand to help Anne from the back of the motorcycle.

She nodded and half fell against Cole. "Sorry, I'm a little wobbly after going cross-country on the back of Mr. Snow's motorcycle."

Cole chuckled. "I don't blame you. I'm always a little wobbly after riding a motorcycle. You have to ride often to build up the muscles needed to be comfortable on one."

"Good to know," Anne said. "Not that I plan on riding one ever again, if I can help it."

"Oh, honey," Grace said, moving forward with a

smile. "We never say never around here." She held out her hand. "I'm Grace Lawrence, Charlie's assistant." She turned to the older woman. "This is Charlie Halverson. John Halverson's widow."

"Mrs. Halverson, words are not enough to thank you for coming to my rescue. I don't know what I would have done if you hadn't."

"Please, call me Charlie. Mrs. Halverson was my husband's mother." She smiled and took both of Anne's hands in hers. "I'm glad Jack could help. I don't know what's going on, but you're safe now. Please, come inside."

Anne glanced back at Jack. "Thank you."

He nodded, flipped the kickstand down on his bike and joined Cole on the stairs.

Charlie led Anne and Grace into the house.

Arnold joined Cole and Jack. "Declan and the others are on their way in. They sustained some gunfire."

"Are they okay?" Jack asked.

The butler nodded. "There was some damage to their vehicles, but they're fine."

Jack shook his head. If they'd been a little slower on the motorcycle, they would have taken those bullets. Anne had been on the back of the bike. She'd have been hit first. His heart raced, and he broke out in a sweat. Anne could have died. Just like Kylie. He'd have to rethink his motorcycle if he was tasked to protect Ms. Bellamy.

With that thought came another. Did he want to protect the woman? His history with women went deeper and more tragic than with Kylie. He'd lost his mother to cancer when he was only twelve. And just when he thought he was getting over Kylie and found someone else to love, Jennifer, the nurse deployed to the same base as he was in Afghanistan, had been killed when her vehicle rolled over an IED.

No. He was bad luck to the women in his life.

Women he loved. He could protect Anne Bellamy as long as he didn't make the mistake of jinxing her by falling in love with her. The right thing to do would be to let someone else take over the woman's protection. After saving her from being run down in DC and being shot at on the road to the Halverson estate, he felt he had a vested interest in her well-being.

He couldn't get ahead of himself. If Anne stayed at the Halverson estate, she wouldn't need a personal protector. Jack wouldn't have to worry about her safety or jinxing her.

"What's wrong?" Cole asked him.

"Why do you ask?"

Cole shrugged. "You were frowning."

Jack shook his head, clearing his rampant thoughts. "I was thinking about the mess they made of her apartment and the message on the wall," he lied. Now that he did think about it, he wondered who had put it there and why they thought she was a problem.

"Halverson must have been onto something big with Trinity for them to target him for assassination."

"If they knew about Ms. Bellamy all along, why did they wait until now to go after her?"

"I assume it has to do with the person who texted her," Cole said. "Using the phone number Anne gave Snow, Jonah hacked into the phone system and is going through her call and text history as we speak. We should go to the war room and see if he's found anything."

Jack followed Cole through the house and into Halverson's study, where the trapdoor was hidden. It led into a basement painted white and set up with a conference room and a computer room with an array of monitors, CPUs and keyboards lining the walls.

Jonah Spradlin, Charlie Halverson's young computer guru, sat at a keyboard, looking up at a setup of six monitors. His fingers flew across the keys, then he'd pause and study the screen. He repeated the process several times, shaking his head, his lips pressing together each time.

"Find anything?" Cole asked, taking the seat beside Jonah. Cole pressed several keys on the keyboard in front of him and brought up a screen.

"I traced the call back to a burner phone purchased at a store in Arlington," Jonah said. "I hacked into their computer system, but the name the phone was registered to was Linda Radcliff, a woman who died five years ago."

"Did they have video surveillance at the store?"

"Yes, but I haven't hacked into that system yet. I'm working on it."

"If the phone was registered to a Linda, the person had to be female," Cole surmised. "Surely, the clerk or store owner would have denied the sale if the ID didn't match the person presenting it."

"So, we're looking for a female texter." Jack paced the length of the room and back. "What will that buy us? There are hundreds of thousands of females in this area. We have to narrow it down a little more than that."

"We're working on it. We don't have a lot to go on and now your lady doesn't have a phone for our mystery texter to send messages to."

"She figured out Ms. Bellamy was associated with John Halverson," Jack pointed out. "She's smart. She'll come up with a way to communicate with Ms. Bellamy again."

Cole glanced up. "What's your girl's plan from here?"

Jack frowned. "She's not my girl. And I have no idea. I just got her here."

"I'm going to work tomorrow, as usual." A female voice sounded behind them.

Anne descended the steps into the war room, followed by Grace and Charlie.

Jack faced her, his feet spread, his arms crossing over his chest. "The hell you are."

Anne's eyebrows rose up her forehead. "I have a big meeting to prepare for on Friday. I need to be in my office every day this week. Besides, the person who texted me wanted me to help stop Trinity from doing something. I can't help if I'm locked behind the walls of this estate."

"You're a walking target," Jack said. "It would be suicide for you to step past the gates."

Anne lifted her chin. "I can't hide away forever."

"You can until we figure out what's going on," Jack insisted.

"We can figure it out a lot faster from inside the government offices. I assume since the person texted me, I'm probably in a position to find out something. Otherwise, why would he ask me for help?"

"She," Jack corrected.

Anne cocked an eyebrow. "See? You already know more than when we started."

"Okay, she's female—" Jack threw his hand in the air "—so is half the population of the Metro area."

"I'm going to work tomorrow," Anne said. "I just need a ride in to a Metro station, and I'll take it from there."

"You can't go alone," Charlie said.

"Charlie's right," Jack said. "It's too dangerous. You're not equipped to handle armed assassins."

Again, Anne stared at him with a cocked eyebrow. "And you are?"

"More so than you," Jack shot back.

Charlie clapped her hands together. "Then it's settled."

Jack glared at the woman whose money funded Declan's Defenders. "What's settled?"

"The fact that Anne can't go to work alone." Charlie smiled as if everything was perfectly obvious. "You'll go with her."

Chapter Three

Anne frowned. "Jack can't go with me. You have to have a badge and a security clearance to get inside the office where I work."

Charlie nodded toward her computer guy. "Jonah, can you make it happen before morning?"

He nodded. "I'll do my best." He held out his hand to Anne. "Could I borrow your badge?"

Anne shrank back, her hand on the purse she still carried over her shoulder. "You most certainly cannot. I swore an oath. I could get fired."

"You could die," Jack reminded her.

Anne chewed on her lip, her gut knotting. She'd spent her entire career trying to do right by the people of her country. She prided herself on always taking the high road. Helping someone into the inner sanctum of the West Wing was almost like committing treason.

Charlie touched her arm. "Based on your informer, others could die if Trinity isn't stopped. But you have to do what you think is right."

"If it helps," Declan said. "As a Marine Force Recon team, we all had top secret clearances."

"Had?" Anne questioned. She knew what Marine Force Recon meant. They were the best of the best of the Marines.

Declan glanced at the other members of his team. "Until we were discharged from the Marine Corps."

"Discharged?" Anne tilted her head, her gaze going to Jack. "Honorably?"

Jack's lips thinned. "No. We were dishonorably discharged."

Anne reeled, shaking her head, her hand tightening on her purse. "Why?"

"For doing what we thought was the right thing," Declan said, his face grim. "Unfortunately, the powers that be didn't agree."

"Did you…kill someone?" Anne asked. "Is that why you were discharged?"

Jack snorted. "No. We didn't kill someone we were ordered to kill. If we had, a lot of innocent people would have been collateral damage. We made the decision to abort."

"I don't understand," Anne said. "I thought, as a country, we weren't in the business of killing innocent people, if we could help it."

"Someone had to take the fall for not taking out a high-powered terrorist." Declan pushed back his shoulders and lifted his chin. "My team took that fall." He spread his arms wide. "And now, because of

Charlie, we're fighting the good fight, helping people when the government can't." He stared directly into Anne's eyes. "We understand if you don't feel comfortable giving us your badge. We'll find another way to create one for Jack. He will be with you tomorrow, one way or another."

Anne chewed on the information Jack and Declan had imparted. If what they were saying was true, they'd been booted from the military because they hadn't wanted to kill innocent people. Their government had let them down.

If the informant who'd texted Anne was correct, Trinity had somehow infiltrated the government and was planning on doing something catastrophic. She couldn't let it happen. But how could she, a single midlevel analyst, stop anything from happening? It wasn't as if she could spot a Trinity operative by looking at him.

She didn't know who they were. But they knew who she was, and they didn't want her to tip off anyone as to their intentions.

By going to work, she was putting herself at risk. If she died, no one would know that Trinity was planning something big.

She might not be anyone or know anything, but she did know something was about to go down. Since the informer had contacted her, she had to be close to either the entrenched Trinity operatives or close to the people who would be targeted. Either way, she had to find out what was going down and stop it before anyone got hurt.

Anne dug in her purse, pulled out her employee badge and handed it to Jack. "I'm trusting you to do the right thing, as I hope I am by handing you my badge."

Jack took the card, holding her hand in his for a long moment. "I promise we'll do the right thing. When it comes right down to it, we love this country, despite what some individuals in powerful positions have done to us. We want what's right for the country we swore to honor and protect."

Her fingers curled around his for a moment, then he let go and handed the card to Jonah.

Jonah nodded. "I'll have that badge and your clearance entered into the system before morning."

"I don't want to know how you'll make that possible."

Jonah grinned. "It's best you don't know. Ignorance is bliss."

Anne eyed Jack. "If you're coming to work with me, we'll have to have a good cover story."

Jack grinned. "Look at you going all covert on us."

She frowned. "I'm serious. I can pass you off as the new hire coming to train in my office. I've been interviewing people for the position of my assistant for a couple of weeks but hadn't found anyone I thought could handle the workload or the stress."

She gave him a wry smile. "Guess you'll be my selection. If your clearance has come through by morning, we'll have to tell people your security clearance is in process, in case anyone noses around."

"Just what do you do?" Jack asked.

"I'm an analyst for the national security advisor who sits on the National Security Council."

Jack frowned. "That's more than a mouthful. How am I supposed to keep up with all of that?"

Her smile twisted. "Oh, man, you haven't seen anything yet. It's alphabet soup at the White House." Anne's smile turned south. "Do you have a business suit?"

Jack's frown deepened. "I haven't worn a suit since my mother passed away. And that was so long ago I don't own that suit anymore."

Declan eyed Jack. "I have a suit that might fit. We will have to take out the length on the trousers, since you're taller than me."

"My butler, besides being former military, an expert in martial arts and having amazing taste in vehicles, has been known to sew when necessary," Charlie said. "We can get that done tonight, assuming there's enough material in the hem of Declan's trousers to let them out."

Anne wanted to laugh at the deepening frown on Jack's face. "If you don't want to wear a suit, perhaps one of your teammates would prefer to accompany me to work as my assistant."

Cole looked up. "I'll do it." He grinned. "I own a suit. It's dusty, but I'm sure it will do."

Jack rose to his feet. "I'm going. Cole, we need you to help Jonah get me added to the employee database with the correct level of clearance so whatever badge you come up with works when I scan in at the door tomorrow." Jack nodded toward the leader of their team of former marines. "Declan, show me what you have, so I can get Arnold started on the alterations. We don't have much time to get things done by morning."

"Follow me. I have the suit in my closet upstairs."

Anne released a sigh of relief. She hadn't wanted another man to accompany her as her protector. Jack had proven himself twice that night. She trusted him with her life. Her niggle of doubt came because of her body's reaction to the man's touch.

Well, she'd just have to keep her distance from him and avoid bodily contact.

"It's a good thing you and Grace live here at the estate," Jack said to Declan as the two left the war room and climbed up to the study. "When did you invest in a suit?" Their voices faded as they moved through the house.

Anne turned to Charlie. "What did they mean by thanks to you, they're doing the right thing?"

Charlie glanced at the remainder of the men in the room. "I've employed Declan and his team to perform missions to right wrongs, help people and do things the FBI, CIA, state and local police won't or can't get involved in. We call the team Declan's Defenders."

"A kind of vigilante group?"

Charlie shrugged. "Some would say that."

"They're more than that," Grace said. "They saved my life and my roommate's life. I wouldn't be alive today if they hadn't come to my aid." She gave Anne a gentle smile. "You're one lucky woman to have them covering your six."

"Covering my six?"

"We'll have your back," Cole said. "Jack will be there with you at all times. If he needs additional help, we'll be there, as well. You can count on us."

Anne drew in a deep breath and let it go. "Good. This is all new to me. I'm not a spy, soldier or marine. I've never been trained in combat. I studied tae kwon do when I was a teen, but I haven't used it since I graduated high school a few too many years ago to remember how."

Grace chuckled. "I'm just now learning how to fire a handgun. Declan got me my own .40 caliber pistol. It scares me to death to think of using it against another human being." Her face hardened. "But if it's a choice between my life or the life of someone about to attack me, you bet I will pull the trigger. I refuse to be a victim, ever again. And that goes for anyone threatening someone I love."

Anne heard the conviction in Grace's voice and

wondered what her story was. What had made her so determined to protect herself and those she cared most about.

"If you knew my husband, you know he was murdered for what he knew about Trinity," Charlie said. "I might not ever find the people who killed John, but I hope I can keep others from suffering from Trinity's machinations."

Anne squared her shoulders. "John contacted me a while back, asking me to report anything out of the ordinary in the National Security Council. I wasn't sure what he was looking for, or what appeared to be out of the ordinary, but I promised I'd help him if I could. He convinced me he only wanted to expose the people who were bent on destroying our government from within. I'm still uncertain how I can help, but if this informant is on the up-and-up, and gives me some clues, perhaps we can bring Trinity down before they have a chance to attack."

"I hope we can. But we can't do it without our own people on the inside," Charlie said. "We might have to get more of Declan's Defenders inside. We'll work more on that tomorrow. Tonight, our goal is to position Jack as your protector. You can't focus on anything if you're afraid for your life."

"Thank you," Anne said. "For taking me in when I didn't know where else to go. Your husband was a good man and you're doing a great job carrying on his legacy."

Charlie's eyes filled with moisture. "He was good and kind and gentle. I miss him." She closed her eyes briefly and opened them again. "In the meantime, you need a place to stay."

"I'll show her to a room," Grace said. "Were you able to salvage any of your clothing? I saw the pictures of the destruction to your apartment. I'm so sorry."

"At least I wasn't there when they broke in," Anne said.

"I might have some clothes you can use until you can replace what you've lost." Grace led the way up the stairs to the study above.

Anne followed. "How long have you been with Charlie and Declan's Defenders?"

Grace grinned. "Since the beginning. I presented them with their first mission."

Anne shot a glance toward the pretty young woman. "Were you being targeted by Trinity?"

She shook her head. "No, but my roommate had disappeared. Declan helped me put the pieces together, and ultimately, we found my roommate. Declan saved my life in the process."

"They're as good as Charlie claims they are?" Anne asked.

Grace nodded. "The best."

Anne felt a little better about handing over her badge to the team. And she felt better knowing she didn't have to ferret out Trinity and their plan of at-

tack on her own. With Jack watching her back and
Cole and Jonah scouring the internet for clues, they
might have a chance of discovering what was going
to happen before it actually occurred.

She hoped she was right.

JACK ENTERED THE suite assigned to Declan and Grace.
They'd been together since Charlie first hired him.
It was because of the work Declan had done helping Grace stay alive while searching for her roommate that Charlie had come up with the brilliant idea
to establish a team of trained combatants to handle
situations outside of the police and federal agencies'
hands.

Declan had never been happier than he was with
Grace. After being separated from the military for
doing the right thing, he deserved to be happy.

Declan crossed the sitting room and entered the
bedroom he shared with Grace, opening a closet at
the far end. He sorted through the shirts hanging
there and dug deep into the back of the closet, eventually pulling out a white dress shirt and charcoal
gray suit. "The suit was tailored to fit me, but I think
we're about the same across the chest." He handed
the shirt and blazer to Jack.

Jack tried on the shirt over his black T-shirt. It appeared to fit just fine. The sleeves were a tad short,
but they would work. He slipped his arms into the
suit jacket and pulled it over his shoulders. It fit his

chest and waist, but the sleeves would need lengthening.

"Try the trousers," Declan said.

Jack kicked off his shoes, shucked his jeans and slipped his legs into the trousers. "They're a little loose around the waist and hips. A belt will keep them in place."

Declan patted his flat belly. "Guess I'm putting on a little weight. I might need to step up my exercise routine."

"We're just built differently." Jack looked at himself in the mirror. "If we can let out the pant legs two inches and the sleeves at least an inch, this will work." He removed the suit, dressed in his jeans and shoes and faced Declan.

His team leader handed him the hangers with the shirt and suit. "Are you up for playing the part of Anne's assistant tomorrow?"

He nodded. "I suppose so. Although I'm not quite certain what exactly all the people who support the National Security Council actually do."

"Let's see if Cole and Jonah have made any progress on that badge. While we're in the war room, we can do some research on the NSC. Since you'll be a new hire, you won't be expected to know much."

"I'll need to know how things work in order to look for potential moles or covert terrorists hiding among the people working around Anne."

"Good point. It's not like having an enemy pointing a gun in your face."

Jack's jaw tightened. "No, it's more like having an enemy smile to your face and then shoot you in the back as soon as you turn around."

"True." Declan led the way down the stairs to the kitchen, where they found Roger Arnold, the butler.

He listened to Jack's instructions and nodded. Then he took the suit and shirt. "I'll have them ready within an hour." Arnold left the kitchen.

"Let's see what Cole and Jonah have come up with." Declan motioned toward the study and descended into the war room via the trapdoor.

Cole and Jonah stood beside a printer/laminator in the corner of the room. When it spit out a badge, Jonah held it up. "Cross your fingers," Jonah said. He slid Anne's card through a reader that quickly blinked green. Then Jonah slid the new card through the machine.

Jack held his breath. When it blinked green, he let go of the breath he'd been holding. "It works here, but will it work to get me into the West Wing?"

"It should." Jonah handed him the card and shut down the machines. "I've set it up just like Anne's, with all the security access codes embedded in their database."

"You were able to access their database that quickly?" Jack shook his head, amazed at what Jonah and Cole were capable of.

"Of course. It's a government system. The Russians and Chinese aren't the only people capable of hacking into it." Jonah snorted. "It has so many back doors that anyone with a little knowledge can get in."

"I'm glad you're on our team," Jack said. "I'd hate it if you went over to the other side."

Jonah held up his hand. "Been there, done that. John Halverson recruited me out of that nightmare. I can still access the dark web, but I'm not selling secrets, and hopefully, I'm not someone's target."

Jack exchanged a glance with Cole.

John Halverson had collected a strange group of operators to staff his team. For that matter, Charlie was continuing his legacy by hiring a Marine Force Recon team that had been dishonorably discharged. Jack couldn't judge anyone, not after how their careers in the military had ended.

Cole motioned for Jack to join him in front of the monitor. "You'll need to know a little about the offices and people you'll be coming into contact with who support the National Security Council."

"Just what is the National Security Council besides the president and all of his security advisors?" Jack asked.

"Just that. The council is headed by the president of the United States. The most prominent people on the council are the vice president, secretary of state, secretary of defense, secretary of treasury, national security advisor and director of national intelligence."

For the next hour, Cole and Jack went over the names and faces of the people involved in setting foreign policy for the US government. By the time they finished, Jack's head was spinning.

"If the informant thinks Ms. Bellamy is the closest person to the sleeper agent, you need to stick with her. Pay attention to them. There are a lot of government officials, committees, directors and more in Washington. We can't begin to monitor all of them."

"That's what's scary," Jack said. "I'll send you the names of the people Anne works with most."

"We'll run background checks on them," Cole said.

"They wouldn't be in the positions they are without having been through background checks," Jack pointed out.

Jonah nodded. "True, but we'll go a step further. The dark web is a great place to go if you want the dirt on just about anyone."

Feeling a little better about the task ahead, Jack stepped outside to grab a breath of fresh air. All the talk about government positions, councils, offices and more had left him wondering how anything got done with so many people involved.

Jack left the study through the French doors leading out onto an expansive porch that wrapped around the side of the house. A garden stretched out before him, luring him away from the house. The sky had cleared, the stars shining bright and the metropolitan area glowing to the northeast.

Scents of roses and honeysuckle filled the air, calming him. He wondered if Anne was having any trouble falling asleep after the eventful day she'd had. Having been chased several times and nearly killed, she was probably lying awake, afraid to close her eyes.

As if his thoughts had conjured the woman, he saw her ahead of him, sitting on a bench in an arbor. Though her face was in the shadows, he knew it was her.

His pulse quickened and his feet carried him forward several steps before his mind kicked in, reminding him that he couldn't get involved with the woman. She didn't need him jinxing her. If this tasking was to work, he had to keep a level head and a safe distance, emotionally.

With that in mind, he didn't have to ignore the woman.

Jack announced his presence by clearing his throat softly.

Anne jumped to her feet and spun to face him, her eyes wide and white in the semidarkness.

"Oh," she said, her body sagging. "It's you."

"Sorry, were you expecting someone else?"

"No. Not at all. I'm just a little spooked." She

wrapped her arms around her middle. "Aren't you? After all we've been through today?"

He shrugged. "I've been through my share of danger."

"How do you cope? I can't even close my eyes without seeing men jumping out of trucks with scary military-grade rifles." She shivered.

"You never get used to it, but if you dwell on it, you never get any rest."

She rubbed her arms. "Well, I can't turn it off that easily. Frankly, I'm scared."

"Then call in sick tomorrow."

She shook her head. "I can't. I'm helping the national security advisor prepare the agenda for the council meeting to be conducted a few short days. I have to be there."

"What if you'd died today? Isn't there someone else to take over?"

Anne frowned. "That's supposed to be my new hire. I've been too busy to find and train someone to help out."

"The national security advisor couldn't prepare for the meeting himself?"

Anne shrugged. "He's a very busy man. He meets with many of the other directors and committees so that he's fully familiarized with the important items that will be on the agenda. That wouldn't leave him enough time to pull it all together."

"Sounds like you're what we call key personnel."

She laughed. "I guess. Though I'm sure if push came to shove, Mr. Louis could find someone to help. I like to think I'm irreplaceable, but no one really is." She lifted her chin to the sky and drew in a deep breath, letting it out on a sigh. "Why did it have to be me? I'm not the right person to spy on others. I keep my nose down and do my job."

"I'm sure you do more than that, or your informant wouldn't have tagged you."

"I'm beginning to think the informant might just be flushing out anyone who had anything to do with John Halverson. That way they can get rid of them and have open season on anything they have planned in the government."

Jack nodded. "In that case, it wouldn't hurt to find your informant. Cole and Jonah are still working on that. Tomorrow, we need to get you a new phone. We'll take a page from your texter's book and buy a burner phone that can't be traced as easily."

"If the person who sent the texts is on the up-and-up, how will she get word to me?"

"I don't know, but I'm assuming she has her methods and will find a way."

Anne nodded. "Well, I'll do my best to introduce you to the people I work with most. Then I have to get some work done. You might have to do some sleuthing on your own. I can have you deliver stuff to different departments to get you in."

"Sounds good. Does the office building have a map?"

She smiled. "Actually, I have one you can borrow. I created it when I started working for the NSA. I got lost one too many times trying to find my way around."

"It's getting late," Jack said. "Shouldn't you be hitting the sack?"

"I don't know that it will do much good. I'm too wired."

"Have you considered taking a long, hot shower?" he asked and immediately imagined her naked beneath the spray. No, this wasn't a good direction for his thoughts to drift.

"I will." Anne inhaled deeply and blew it out. "But for now, I'm trying to absorb the zen of this garden. I'm hoping between the roses and the honeysuckle, I'll calm down."

"How's it working for you?"

She laughed. "Not so great until you came out."

"Does that mean talking to me is helping?"

She tilted her head. "Surprisingly, yes."

"Why is it so surprising?"

"You're not someone I'd consider calming."

Jack chuckled. He knew he shouldn't encourage her, but he couldn't help it. "How so?"

"Well, for one, you ride a motorcycle. That screams bad boy all over the place."

"A lot of people ride motorcycles," he pointed out.

"True. Maybe I'm stereotyping, but I think of motorcycle riders as rebels." Her gaze swept over him. "And you look like a rebel. Or someone with something to hide or someone who doesn't like to get too close to anyone."

Her comment took the wind out of his sails. "It doesn't always pay to get close," he admitted softly.

"If you don't get close to people, you miss out on some of the best life has to offer, even if it's only for a short time." Anne turned away, leaving her face in profile, half bathed in starlight, the other half hidden.

"You talk like someone with experience in loss."

She nodded. "I lost my husband to cancer when I was thirty. We had four years together." She turned toward him. "I wouldn't trade those four years for anything. Who did you lose?"

Her question was so unexpected and blunt Jack reeled backward. "I don't want to talk about it." He'd lost so many. His mother, Kylie, Jennifer, Razor, Kemp, Matheson—the list went on. Getting close to someone led to pain. The faces of all those he'd lost scrolled through his mind like a movie reel.

Her hand on his arm startled him, bringing him back to the garden and the scent of roses and honeysuckle.

"Of the people you've lost, would you have avoided them had you known you were going to lose them?"

He didn't answer, his chest so tight he could barely breathe.

"Your life has been that much richer for having known and loved those people," Anne said.

Jack gripped her arms. "It hurts too much to lose someone you care about." He shook his head. "I don't ever want to feel that kind of pain again."

Her eyes rounded as she looked up into his, her lips lush and kissable. "But you miss out on the love and joy, the laughter and happiness if you're afraid to open yourself to the pain."

"I can't," he said, through gritted teeth. "I can't."

"Yes, you can." Then she did something surprising. She lifted her lips to his, and before he knew what he was doing, he'd pulled her to him, his mouth crashing down over hers.

Her body melted against his. Her hands against his chest rose to circle around his neck, drawing him closer. She opened to him, her tongue meeting his in a dance so erotic it set his blood on fire.

Jack tangled one hand in her hair, the other smoothing down her back to press her closer, the hardness of his erection pressing into her soft belly.

When he had to come up for air, he drew in a ragged breath. "That...shouldn't...have happened," he said like a runner gasping for air at the finish line. He leaned his forehead against hers. "I'll ask Declan to get someone else to go with you tomorrow. I'm not fit to be your protector."

Anne shook her head and leaned back to stare up into his eyes. "It's been an insane day. Our emotions are high. This could have happened to anyone." She stepped out of his arms and smoothed her hands over her shirt, her gaze anywhere but at him. "I still want you." Her eyes widened and she shot a look toward him. "I mean, I still want you to come with me. You've saved my life twice. I trust you to keep doing it."

He raised his hand as if swearing on a stack of Bibles. "I promise not to do that again."

She held up her hand to stop him. "Don't. Just don't. I'm not mad. In case you didn't notice, you weren't the only one kissing in that scenario." She pushed her fingers through her hair. "Let's call it a night and reboot this relationship in the morning."

He nodded and waved a hand toward the house. "Go ahead. I think I'll stay out here for a few more minutes."

Anne hesitated for a moment, then turned and entered the house.

Jack remained out in the garden, mentally kicking himself for having kissed the woman. He couldn't take it back, and he couldn't erase the feeling her lips had left on his. He wanted to kiss her again.

And again.

But that just couldn't happen.

Anne's life depended on it.

Chapter Four

Anne didn't sleep at all that night. As if being accosted outside a pub, chased on the back of a motorcycle and nearly shot wasn't bad enough, kissing Jack had completely thrown her off balance. Her mouth and core tingled well into the night. She could still feel his lips against hers and the hard ridge of his desire pressed to her belly.

Hell, the kiss took center stage in her mind, wiping out the fear of being chased and shot at. What was wrong with her? No kiss should do that.

Except the one from the man who saved her from all the bad stuff that happened that day. And he would be working closely with her until the ordeal was over.

How would she manage to function when all she'd be able to do was think about the sexy former marine on the motorcycle, storming in to save her? She had real work to finish in preparation for the next meeting of the National Security Council. Shaun Louis, her boss, the national security advisor, wouldn't be happy if she came to work distracted. He relied on her to keep everything straight, from the agenda to the types of drinks they stocked in the conference room and much more. The president didn't suffer fools. He had little patience for underlings wasting time or woolgathering about sexy marines. Shaun made certain all was in order before the president arrived.

By the time the sun came up, Anne had dressed, brushed her hair and secured it into a messy bun at the crown of her head and applied her makeup. She ventured out of her room to explore the house and maybe find a much-needed cup of coffee.

Downstairs she located the kitchen by following the sounds of clattering pans and voices.

When she entered, butterflies erupted in her stomach and her pulse leaped.

Jack stood with his back to her, talking to Declan.

For a brief moment, Anne allowed herself to study the tall, sandy-blond-haired man with shoulders so broad they made her pulse quicken. He wore jeans and a white T-shirt, and his feet were bare. He could have just rolled out of bed, but damn, he was sexy.

"Ah, there you are," Declan said, straightening away from the counter he leaned against. "Looking for coffee?"

Jack turned his gray-eyed gaze toward Anne and gave her a deep, penetrating look she could swear went all the way through her soul, rattling her normal, clear thoughts.

What had Declan asked? Anne dragged her gaze away from Jack. "Yes. Coffee would be lovely."

Declan pulled a mug from an upper cabinet, poured a steaming cup of fragrant brew and handed it to Anne. "Sleep okay?"

"Yes, thank you," Anne lied, watching Jack out of the corner of her eye. Had he lost any sleep after kissing her? Probably not. The man looked awake and ready to go.

"Charlie instructed Arnold to drive you two into DC and drop you off a couple blocks from your office building. You can walk from there."

"That's not necessary," Anne said. "If we could just get a ride to the Metro station, we can get ourselves to work."

Declan nodded. "That might be better, anyway. The fewer folks who see you in one of Charlie's limos the better."

"Right." Anne spooned sugar into her mug and followed it with cream, wondering when Jack was going to open his mouth to add to the conversation. Would he say anything about that kiss? She hoped he wasn't someone who kissed and told. He didn't strike her as someone who shared any more than he had to about his personal life.

"How soon do you want to leave?" Declan asked.

She glanced at her watch. "Fifteen minutes okay? Is it too early?"

Declan shook his head. "Arnold's been up and out in the garage for over an hour already. Any time you want to leave would be good with him."

"Then fifteen it is," she said, looking over the rim of her mug at Jack. "Can you be ready by then?"

He tipped his mug, downing the remainder of his coffee. Then he ran his hand across the sexy stubble on his chin. "I'll be ready." Jack left her drinking her coffee and disappeared into the hallway.

A man emerged from a door against the far wall of the kitchen, carrying a box of pancake mix. "Ah, Ms. Bellamy, I'm Carl, Charlie's chef. Can I interest you in a hearty breakfast?"

She smiled. "Thank you, but I won't have time."

"How about a pastry or a blueberry muffin?" he offered.

"I wouldn't mind half of a blueberry muffin," she admitted.

"Perfect. I just cut one in half for Snow."

"Snow?" she questioned and then remembered. "Oh, yes. Jack." Her face flushed with heat. "I forgot. I think of him as simply Jack."

Declan laughed. "I'm sure he'd love to know you call him simple Jack."

"That's not what I meant." She frowned. "He's smart and thinks fast on his feet. Or on his motorcycle, in my case. Was he that way in the Marine Corps, too?"

Declan glanced down at the coffee in his mug. "He was our slack man. The youngest man on the team. The guy everyone dumped on. He carried all the heavy equipment and never complained." Declan looked up. "He had our backs and we had his. You can trust Snow to protect you with his life."

The intensity of Declan's words struck Anne straight to the heart. "Knowing he will be with me today is a relief."

Carl brought her half of a blueberry muffin on a white plate with a dribble of blueberry sauce on the side and a fork.

"Thank you." Anne carried it to the table with her mug of coffee. The muffin was so moist it melted in her mouth, the blueberries so sweet they made her want to groan. Before she realized it, the muffin was gone, and she'd finished her coffee. Carrying her dishes to the sink, she passed the chef. "That was amazing."

He smiled. "Glad you liked the muffin. It's a recipe I learned in the navy."

Anne's brow twisted. "Is everyone around here prior military?"

Declan laughed. "No. Grace and Charlie aren't."

"The Halversons have a special place in their hearts for our military men and women," Carl said.

"And we have a special place in our hearts for them. God rest Mr. Halverson's soul."

"Arnold will have the car out front waiting for you when you're ready," Declan said. "If you and Jack need backup, all you have to do is call."

"Assuming I get a new phone," Anne said. The thought of receiving additional texts from her secret informer gave her chills. But she felt lost without a phone and knew she'd have to get another soon. If for no other reason than her boss liked to have a direct line to her if he needed anything.

Anne left the kitchen and waited in the entryway at the base of the stairs for Jack to join her.

The sound of a door opening and closing brought her attention to the top of the stairs.

Jack appeared, dressed in the borrowed suit, his sandy-blond hair slicked back, his face cleanly shaved. He was so handsome.

Anne's breath caught and held in her chest.

The man could have been a model on a magazine cover.

Anne had to admit she liked the blue-jean-clad, barefoot man she'd seen minutes before in the kitchen better than the man in the business suit. He was the kind of man a woman would love to wake up to in the morning.

Getting a firm grip on her thoughts would prove to be a challenge that day. Anne squared her shoulders. "The suit fits," was all she could manage to say.

"Arnold is a magician with a needle and thread." Jack tugged at the red necktie. "Haven't worn a tie in a while. Now I remember why."

"You'll live," she said and started for the door before she actually drooled on the man.

As Declan had predicted, the butler had one of Charlie's vehicles waiting at the bottom of the stairs outside the grand entrance.

Jack reached the door handle before Anne could and opened the door for her.

She moved past him, her shoulder brushing against his arm.

A flash of electricity rippled through her shoulder and south to the pit of her belly. She dove into the car and slid across the seat as far over as she could. The man had an effect on her that she couldn't fathom or control. She hadn't felt this kind of attraction since she'd fallen in love with Mason.

Jack folded his long body into the back seat beside her and closed the door.

Arnold glanced into the rearview mirror before pulling away from the house and driving down the long, winding road to the front gate.

By the time they passed through the gate to the highway, Anne was twitchy. "Are you nervous about your first day on the job?" she asked to fill the silence.

Jack shrugged. "Should I be?"

"I was." Anne stared out the window.

"How long have you been with the national security advisor?" Jack asked.

"Two years," she said.

He glanced her way. "And before that?"

"I was a staffer with the director for Europe and Russia."

"What made you go into politics?"

Anne thought back. "I guess I was a young, idealistic student in college. It bothered me that people couldn't get along. Everyone was completely polarized on the issues. I wanted to bring a level head to the table. Perhaps I could make a difference." She gave him a lopsided grin.

"How's that going for you?"

She shook her head. "Not much has changed. You either are for or against the issues, and people will either love or hate you for your beliefs."

"Sounds pretty cynical."

She sighed. "It is. But it's the direction this country has been going for quite some time."

"If you don't like it, why don't you quit?"

"I've thought about it."

"What would you do if you quit?"

She stared out the window. "I don't know. Maybe I'd join the Peace Corps and help people of underdeveloped countries pull themselves out of poverty."

"Sounds noble."

She turned to him. "What about you? Is being a part of Declan's Defenders enough for you?"

Jack turned away and looked out the window on his side of the vehicle. What he didn't know was that his expressions were clearly reflected in the window. "I never pictured myself in any other career but the military. I trained hard to hone my combat skills." He snorted softly. "When we were booted out, there weren't any jobs available that could use the skills I'd worked so hard to excel at."

"Until Charlie?"

He nodded.

"What was it you liked about being a marine?" she asked.

His chin lifted and his shoulders moved back as if instinctively. "I was part of something bigger than just me. We thought what we did meant something. We were fighting to protect our way of life, the people of our nation and the innocent people in the way of terrorists. We thought what we were doing was right."

"And now?"

His lip curled. "I still think the marines are doing what they think is right. I'm not so sure the politicians and leadership have the best interests of the nation at heart."

"Sadly," Anne said. "I agree."

"Yet, you still work with them."

"I hope that in some small way, I can influence decisions by providing the most up-to-date facts about the issues." Anne had had lofty goals when she'd gone to work for the national security advisor. The day-to-day grind had taken the steam out of them.

"In the meantime, you have a potential terrorist hiding among the politicians and staffers. That should make things interesting."

Anne chewed on her lower lip. "How do I identify someone like that? I have no idea where to begin. And I don't have the phone I did for my informant to give me clues."

"*If* your informant has your best interests at heart. What if she is setting you up to take a fall?"

"If she was, why would she have me destroy my phone?" Anne drew in a deep breath. "I'm going to take this a day at a time. I have my work to do for the meeting coming up. I need to focus on that."

Jack nodded. "I'll help you where I can. Meanwhile, I'll get to know the other players in your universe as part of my initiation into the job."

Anne hoped he could find some clue as to who might be planning an attack before the attack occurred. She didn't know at what point she should alert others of the potential. They'd been through so many drills anytime a bomb threat came across.

She just hoped she didn't wait too long.

ARNOLD DROPPED THEM off at the closest Metro station.

Jack sat beside Anne as they rode the train into

downtown DC and got off at the Farragut West Metro Station close to the White House.

As they walked toward one of the most recognizable and historical buildings in the United States of America, Jack studied the streets, buildings and alleys along the way. During the day, they didn't seem sinister, but at night, they could take on an entirely different vibe. The Metro station was a few blocks from the White House, giving a predator multiple places and opportunities to stage an attack.

Having conducted combat operations in the urban terrain of cities in Afghanistan and Iraq, Jack had a good idea of where the danger zones were.

But their first obstacle to overcome was the Secret Service guards and the ID reader they'd have to pass to gain access to the West Wing.

As they neared the building, Anne spoke in a low tone. "You aren't carrying any knives, guns or any other kind of weapons, are you?"

"You ask me now?" Jack stared at her as if she'd lost her mind.

She looked up at him, her eyes rounding. "You aren't, are you?"

He laughed. "No. Cole went over the rules of entering the White House. I'm clean of any weapons."

Anne let out a nervous sigh. "Thank God. The last thing I want is for you to be hauled off to jail for trying to bring a weapon into the building connected to the one where our president lives."

"We'll be okay," he said, in what he hoped was a soothing tone. "Just act normal."

"How?" she muttered. "This is an insane situation. I'm beginning to wonder what normal is."

He touched her elbow and led her up the steps as they entered the building and passed through a metal detector. He was glad he'd worn antiperspirant, since it was a grueling three tries before he got his card to work in the reader. But then they were on their way to Anne's office, passing men and women in business attire as they went.

He'd read that there were around four hundred employees working in the West Wing of the White House. The task would be daunting to investigate all of them for the person or persons who could be the sleepers among them.

Anne opened the door to a suite of offices. "This is where you'll be working," she said.

The first person they encountered was a staffer, a young woman with light blond hair, sitting at a desk directly in front of the door. "Good morning, Ms. Bellamy." The woman smiled up at her. Her eyes widened when Jack stepped up beside Anne.

"Gina Galinsky, this is Jack Snow. He's my new assistant. Please see that the desk in my office is set up for him. He'll need supplies, computer access and a desk phone."

"I'll get right on that." Gina jumped to her feet. "Welcome, Mr. Snow."

Jack held out his hand. "Nice to meet you, Gina." He gave her the grin he used when he used to go out carousing with the guys.

Gina's cheeks flushed a light pink and she batted her eyes. "I'll just see to your desk. Anything you might need, just ask. You'll like working with Ms. Bellamy. She's super smart and nice."

"I'm sure I will." Jack followed Anne into the office to the right of the staffer's desk. Another office door led to the left.

Once Anne was inside her office, she closed the door and pointed to a desk with papers stacked in a neat pile and a photo frame leaning on one corner. "That's my desk." She turned to an empty one on the other side of the room. "That will be yours, though I'm not sure what you will do with it."

"I'll work like I am your assistant. The more I appear to be the real thing, the less likely anyone will think otherwise."

"Good point. I'll be sure to give you assignments that will take you around to the people I interact with most." She settled behind her desk. "For now, you'll have to work with tech support to get access to the computer system and databases."

Jack sat at the other desk, pulled the keyboard forward and keyed in the log-on ID and password Cole had set up for him the night before. The computer screen came to life.

Anne left her chair and crossed the room to look over his shoulder. "How did you do that?"

He grinned. "Cole and Jonah set me up."

She shook her head. "It took my last assistant a good week to get full access." She pinched the bridge of her nose. "I don't want to know how he did it, but I want to fire all the guys in tech support and hire Charlie's team." She returned to her desk and fired up her computer. Within minutes, she was typing away, her fingers tapping the keyboard furiously.

Jack asked a few questions about the organization of the files and database and then he poked around on his own, not sure what he was looking for, but careful not to pry too hard into places that required special access or passwords.

Within a few minutes, Anne printed out a document and asked Jack to deliver it to the homeland security advisor in a room down the hallway. "Hand it directly to him and tell him I need his input by end of day."

"Yes, ma'am." Jack gave her a mock salute and left the office.

He took his time getting there, smiling and introducing himself to the staffers inside that office.

The woman at the desk blocking entry into the next suite of offices smiled up at him. "May I help you?"

She had shoulder-length dark hair, brown eyes and dark framed glasses.

"I have a document I need to deliver to the advisor for homeland security."

The woman held out her hand. "I can take it and make certain he gets it."

"Ms. Bellamy asked me to deliver it into his hands, even if I had to wait." He smiled at the woman who had to be in her midthirties, wearing a cream, black and tan plaid skirt. "I can wait." He glanced at the nameplate on her desk. "Dr. Saunders."

She blushed, pushed her glasses up her nose and straightened the papers on her desk that were already straight. "You can call me Millicent." She waved to a chair beside her desk. "Please, have a seat. Mr. Carpenter should be here momentarily. He had a meeting over an hour ago and should be on his way back soon."

As if on cue, a balding man with a wrinkled suit and a bit of a paunch hurried into the office, his face ruddy and a sheen of perspiration breaking out on his forehead. "Millie, send a note to the national security advisor's office to add the border wall as a discussion item on the agenda."

"Mr. Carpenter, you know POTUS doesn't want it on the agenda if you don't have solutions to the problem."

"He needs to know what's happening and which political action committees are in an uproar."

Millicent shrugged. "Yes, sir." She typed on her keyboard, her fingers flying over the keys. "Done."

Then she pushed back from her desk and stood. "Mr. Carpenter, Ms. Bellamy's assistant has a note for you." She waved a hand toward Jack. "If you two will excuse me, I wanted to touch base with Anthony Schuster about a matter that cropped up today." She left the office without looking back.

"Anthony Schuster?" Jack pushed to his feet.

"Director for Europe and Russia." Carpenter tipped his head toward the door Millicent had gone through. "Millie has a PhD in foreign policy, speaks fluent German, Russian and Greek. I think she would prefer to work with Schuster, but the position as his assistant was already full when we hired her on. My gain, his loss. She's brilliant. Now, if you'll excuse me, I have work to do. The NSC meets soon, and everyone is scrambling."

As Carpenter started for his office, Jack stepped forward, towering over the shorter man. "Mr. Carpenter, I have a document from Ms. Bellamy in the national security advisor's office."

"I know who Anne is," Carpenter said with a frown. He jerked the document out of Jack's hand. "The question is who are you?" He looked over the rim of his glasses at Jack.

"Jack Snow, Ms. Bellamy's new assistant."

The man shook Jack's hand. "Nice to meet you," Carpenter said. "I'm surprised she was able to get an assistant in so quickly. It can be like passing a bill through Congress to get help around here." He smirked when Jack didn't react. "That was a joke."

Jack chuckled. "Sorry. First day on the job. I guess I'm a little nervous."

"No need to be. We're all in this together and help where we can."

"Thanks," Jack said. "How long have you worked here?"

"Six months. I came in after the last guy left. I think the president fired him. But he claimed he left for medical reasons. The job can be stressful."

"I get that."

"I hope you're up for it," the homeland security advisor said. "Not everyone can handle it."

"I've been in stressful situations," Jack said, thinking back to some of the missions he'd been on, when he'd had to make life-and-death kinds of decisions. "I think I'll manage."

"Thank Ms. Bellamy for me. She's been here over a couple of presidencies. People like her are like the glue that holds us together. I'm not sure what any of us would do without her."

"Hopefully, we won't have to find out." He nodded toward the document in Carpenter's hand. "Ms. Bellamy asked that you provide your feedback before the end of day."

"I'll do that," Carpenter promised.

Jack left the office and returned to Anne's.

Gina had been in and stocked his desk with pens,

pads of paper, a leather notebook and a Rolodex. He hated to see her go to that much trouble when he wasn't going to be around any longer than it took to find the mole in the West Wing.

Having only met a handful of the over four hundred people who worked there, he had to admit he was a bit overwhelmed with the task in front of them.

Before he realized it, hours had passed, and his stomach rumbled loudly.

"I take it you're hungry," Anne said from across the room.

"I can wait," he said. "I've gone longer without food."

"I don't normally take lunch, but I could use a walk and some fresh air." She stood, stretched and looped her purse over her shoulder. "Come on. I'll take you to my favorite sandwich shop."

As they left the building, Anne made sure to introduce him to people she ran into in the hallway. No one questioned his sudden hire, nor did they ask for details about his background. Everyone appeared to be in a hurry to get work done.

Outside, Jack was almost surprised the sun was still out. He felt he'd been inside for a very long time.

"Sometimes I don't see the sun at all," Anne said, as if reading his mind. "I get to work in the dark and leave in the dark."

"That doesn't leave much time for a life."

She shrugged. "Since my husband died, my work has been my life," she said, quietly.

"How long has that been?" Jack asked.

"Three years."

"You must have loved him very much," he commented.

"I did."

Jack felt a tightening in his chest. If he'd been back in high school, he might have mistaken the feeling for jealousy. But how could he be jealous of a dead man? He'd just met Anne. She was someone way out of his league mentally and professionally. She was brilliant and admired by her colleagues. The only thing Anne and Jack had in common was the mission to discover someone who might be planning an attack.

Oh, and a couple shared kisses. But those didn't count. They couldn't.

Chapter Five

Anne didn't really have time to take a lunch, but trying to work in her office while Jack was at the desk
nearby was tantamount to impossible. She couldn't
get past the fact they'd kissed the night before. And
today, he acted as if nothing had happened.

How could he be so cool and unaffected when she
was fidgeting in her chair, having a difficult time fo-
cusing on the monitor in front of her?

By noon, she had to get up and move or climb
the walls.

The air outside was heavy, with clouds hovering
over the city. She wished she'd thought to bring an
umbrella. Hopefully, the rain would hold off until
they returned to the West Wing.

The sandwich shop was a couple of blocks from
the White House, giving her time to regroup her
thoughts and get a grip on her emotions. She should
be more worried about the person who'd texted her
and the one who'd subsequently tried to kill her.

The shop was crowded inside, with no seats available.

"We can go somewhere else, or sit outside and risk getting rained on," Anne said.

Jack glanced up at the clouds. "I won't melt," he said. "But you might not want to get wet."

"We can always leave if it starts to rain." Anne settled into a seat at one of the bistro tables and studied the menu.

Jack took the seat beside her, instead of across. He glanced around as if searching for enemy personnel.

Anne set her menu on the table and shook her head. "I really don't think anyone will try to attack during broad daylight."

"The last time I thought that, I lost a buddy of mine. The time before that, a truckload of nurses rolled across an improvised explosive device. None of them lived. And before that someone opened fire in a shopping mall in the middle of the day, killing my ex-girlfriend, a father of three children, a pregnant woman and a teenage girl." He gave her a hard stare. "Forgive me if I don't trust the daylight to keep the bad guys at bay."

He'd spoken in a low tone that only she could hear, but the intensity of his stare and the urgency of his words hit her hard. This was a man who'd seen more death and sorrow than even she had experienced through the loss of her husband.

"I'm sorry," she murmured. "You're right to be cautious."

He sat back in his chair and finally looked down at the menu, but only briefly before he laid it aside.

The waitress took their orders and disappeared.

While they waited for their sandwiches, Anne gave Jack insights on some of the people he'd met that morning.

"Gina has been with Shaun and me for the past year and a half. Her ex-husband is a lobbyist for one of the car manufacturers. She divorced him when she found out he'd cheated on her while she was attending school at Georgetown University. She's smart, reads fast and catches a lot of my editing errors. And she's a Washington Redskins fan. I can't imagine her being a sleeper spy with Trinity."

"I hadn't met anyone who worked directly with Trinity until a few weeks ago, when a woman tried to kidnap Charlie from a charity ball."

Anne leaned forward, her pulse picking up. "Seriously? You've met a Trinity agent?"

He nodded. "She'd suffered a head injury and lost her memory for a while. But she'd already left Trinity and had started to work with John Halverson before the head injury." Jack frowned. "If she's an example of the assassins Trinity puts out…"

"What?"

"Let's just say, they're highly skilled in martial arts and weapons. And they aren't afraid of much."

Anne shivered. "If the person who texted me knows all this, why did she choose me? I don't know any of that. The most violent thing I've ever done is throw my keyboard across the room when it quit being effective."

Jack chuckled and then frowned. "You had to have been chosen because of your position and your involvement with Halverson."

Their sandwiches were delivered at that moment, forestalling further discussion about Trinity or Halverson.

Once they'd finished their meal, a different waitress appeared with a dessert menu.

Anne wondered why they had a different waitress but didn't mention it. "I don't want dessert." She held up her hands, refusing to take the menu.

"I'll just leave the menu here, if you change your mind." The waitress laid the menu on the table and disappeared before Anne could say anything else.

When she glanced down at the menu, she noticed it didn't close all the way. She didn't want dessert, but she didn't like leaving the menu at an odd angle.

Anne opened the menu and stared down at what was keeping it from closing, and gasped.

Inside the menu was a cell phone. A second later, it vibrated against the menu.

Anne looked up at Jack.

He turned the phone toward him and read the text. "It's your texter."

Take the phone.
It can't be traced or tagged with a GPS tracker.

Anne stared at the phone as if it was a snake coiling to bite.

TAKE IT.
We don't have much time. Targets are being assigned.

Jack looked left and right, his gaze scanning the immediate area. "Did you get a good look at the waitress who left the menu?" he asked.

Anne shook her head. "She was a brunette. I think. But that's about all I remember."

The original waitress showed up with their check. "Can I get you anything else?" she asked as she laid the bill on the table.

"The waitress who brought our dessert menu, is she in the back?" Jack asked. "We'd like to talk to her."

The woman's brow creased. "Dessert menu?"

"Yes, this one," Jack held up the menu.

She opened it, studied it and shook her head. "That's not from here. It's from a restaurant a couple blocks from here."

Jack pulled out his wallet, gave the waitress enough to cover their meal and a tip and stood.

"What about the cell phone?" Anne asked.

"Leave it. I'd be afraid to take anything into the White House that hasn't been thoroughly checked out."

Jack jumped.

"What?" Anne asked, startled by his movement.

"Nothing. Just my cell phone vibrating in my pocket." He pulled it out and studied the message before handing it over to Anne. "It's for you."

Anne's stomach clenched as she read the message.

Very well. I'll communicate through Snow's phone.

A LIGHT DRIZZLE started as they made their way back to the West Wing of the White House.

Jack had insisted on walking around the area near the sandwich shop, hoping to find the woman who'd pretended to be a waitress and had left the phone on the table.

He couldn't believe he'd been so nonchalant about her. She could have been carrying a gun or a knife and killed either one of them, had she really wanted to.

"I don't know about you, but I'm not feeling very comfortable about any of this," Anne said as she hurried to keep up with him.

Jack hadn't realized he was walking so fast. He slowed his pace to match Anne's. "I'm sorry. That was my fault. No excuses. I shouldn't have let her get that close to you."

"You couldn't have known she would walk right up to us."

"No, but I should have been ready for anything." He cupped her elbow and drew her closer. "I promised to protect you. I've failed."

"You did a great job last night. I'm not ready to consider you as having failed," Anne argued. "Apparently, my contact wants to continue the conversation about the pending attack. I should take this information to my superiors. I'm afraid that if what she's said is true, it would only warn the attacker and he'd continue to hide until another opportunity came up. But I feel like I need to let someone know."

"You already have. You've let Declan's Defenders know. We'll work this out. Cole and Jonah have to come up with something soon."

"In the meantime, she's going to contact us through your phone." Anne moved closer. "I hate that she's so vague at this point. *Targets are being assigned?* What does that mean? We have no idea where to start looking. Did she say anything else?"

Jack pulled his phone out of his pocket. "No. You saw for yourself."

Anne read the words again as if hoping to read more into them than she had before. "She said she would communicate, but so far, she hasn't given us anything substantial to go on." Anne glanced back at the sandwich shop in the distance. She shook her head. "Leaving the phone was the right thing to do, wasn't it?"

He nodded. "I wouldn't have trusted it."

"Yeah. You never know if someone could load it with some explosive device. Or it could be set up as a listening device."

"I don't like that she so easily tapped into my phone. Where did she get the number? I wonder if she's hacked into Charlie's computer or phone."

"Cole and Jonah have managed to hack into the White House security system," Anne pointed out. "Why not this woman who insists she's trying to stop an attack?"

Jack's thoughts had already gone down that path. Whoever this woman was, she had some skills in hacking into phones and making herself semi-invisible. Why hadn't she done what Jack had and infiltrated the White House herself?

He glanced at Anne. Why would she when Anne was well known by everyone in the West Wing? She was the perfect person to snoop around right under everyone's noses. A stranger, like the woman texting them, or even Jack, would be more noticeable if they were caught in the wrong places.

A siren sounded nearby. Then another. A fire truck raced past, followed by an ambulance, heading toward the White House.

Jack shot a glance toward Anne. "Do you think the target has already been acquired?"

Anne's eyes widened. "I hope not." She turned with Jack and hurried toward her office building.

A block ahead, the ambulance and fire truck had pulled to a stop, blocking traffic on the usually busy road.

"What's happening?" Anne asked, craning her neck to see over the gathering crowd of emergency personnel and rubbernecking tourists, who were snapping photos of the first responder vehicles.

Jack stood on the tips of his toes to see over the heads of others. "They're performing CPR on someone. A woman, I think." Then he noticed the cream, black and tan plaid fabric of the person's skirt and his heart slid to a stop. "Millicent?"

"What did you say?"

Jack gripped her hand and pushed through the throng to get a closer look.

The police had arrived and were holding the people back to give the emergency personnel room to work. A couple of them were asking questions.

"Anyone here see what happened?" an officer asked loudly.

A woman covered her hand with her mouth, stifling a sob, before she said, "I s-saw it all."

The officer pulled a notepad and a pen out of his pocket and stopped in front of the woman. "Can you tell me what happened?"

"The car. It came out of nowhere." A sob made her body tremble. "The driver didn't even swerve.

He sped up and hit her as if he was actually aiming for her." The woman buried her face in her hands. "It was horrible. She slid up over the hood of the vehicle and fell to the side."

"Could you describe the car?"

She shook her head. "It all happened so fast. The car was a dark sedan. Maybe a four-door." She wrung her hands as tears spilled from her eyes. "I don't know. It all happened so fast."

"Did you happen to see the license plate?" the policeman asked.

"No. I didn't. I wish I had."

A hand on Jack's arm made him look down at Anne's face.

"Can you see the woman?" Anne asked.

He nodded, his jaw tight. "I recognize her skirt."

"You recognize her skirt?" Anne's brow furrowed. "I didn't know you had friends in DC. You knew her?"

He shook his head. "No, I met her this morning in the West Wing."

Anne pressed her hand to her lips. "One of our own?"

He nodded.

"Who?" Anne asked, her voice not much more than a whisper.

"Dr. Millicent Saunders."

"Millie?" Anne started to push forward. "I just had lunch with her the other day. We promised to get together to go to a museum. Can you tell if she's all right?" She clung to his arm. "Please tell me she's all right."

"They're loading her into the ambulance right now. They have an IV hooked up and they've strapped her to a backboard." Jack dropped down from his toes. "The ambulance is leaving." He stared at the buildings on the corners, the street signs and the names of the businesses. "Let's get back to the West Wing."

"But what about Millie?"

"The EMTs will do their best." Jack fished his phone from his pocket and called Declan. "One of the staffers from the West Wing was a victim of a hit-and-run. Millicent Saunders."

"You think it had anything to do with our mystery woman's warning?" Declan asked.

"I don't know, but it wouldn't hurt to investigate." He gave Declan the address of where the incident had occurred and names of some of the businesses nearby. "A witness reported it appeared as if the driver deliberately hit the woman."

"I'll see if Cole and Jonah can pull video recordings from the businesses or street cameras," Declan said.

"Anything to report on the technical front?" Jack continued talking in a low tone that wouldn't carry far as he walked alongside Anne, his gaze scanning the street, the sidewalks and the vehicles coming and going.

"Nothing so far," Declan said. "Jonah's tapping into the dark web for any message traffic involving Trinity."

"Good luck."

"Same to you and Ms. Bellamy," Declan paused. "If that woman was targeted because she works in the West Wing, you will definitely need to watch your backs."

Jack ended the call and slipped his cell phone into his pocket. He cupped Anne's elbow as they crossed the street, his body tense, ready to run if someone drove a car at the two of them. He didn't relax until they were on the other side and headed toward the West Wing.

The Secret Service agents were all abuzz about Dr. Saunders's accident. Word had traveled fast from the street to the White House. Even though they passed through the metal detectors with no problem, Jack and Anne were stopped to be scanned with wands.

"Have there been any threats to the White House?" Anne asked.

The agent waving the wand over her arms and down her torso shook his head. "No, but when one of our employees is run down in the street, we take a few extra precautions. Tours of the White House have been suspended for today until the incident can be investigated."

Jack was glad that the security had gotten a little tighter, but not completely reassured, since he suspected the threat might also come from inside the walls of the nation's capitol building.

With all the Secret Service personnel, how did someone from one of the most dangerous covert organizations get inside the West Wing?

Jack studied every person he passed in the hallway, wondering if he or she was a Trinity-trained assassin. Was it the guy in the glasses whose pants were two inches too short, wearing white socks with his black suit? Or the woman with her hair pulled back into a tight ponytail, wearing a sleek black pantsuit, looking like she could throw a side kick and render him unconscious in the blink of an eye?

More than four hundred people worked in the West Wing of the White House. What if the Trinity mole was one of the Secret Service agents with access to every room? If that were the case, why hadn't he made the move yet? What was he waiting for?

If Millicent Saunders had been targeted for some reason, what was the reason? What had Carpenter said about Dr. Saunders? She was fluent in Russian, German and Greek and would have been a better fit for a position with the director for Europe and Russia. She'd left her desk that morning to pay a visit to that office. Had she stumbled upon something that could have revealed the mole?

Hopefully, Declan and his crew would find something that would give them a place to start. Jack felt like he was striking out and, based on the texts, they were running out of time to locate and neutralize the Trinity assassin.

When they reached Anne's office, she waited until he'd entered and closed the door to the outer office and leaned against it. "I'm not cut out to do this," she said. "I'm not trained for this kind of thing."

Jack went to her, placed a finger over her lips and leaned close to whisper in her ear. "We don't know if this place is bugged. We should probably limit our conversations to your work."

She stared at him, wide-eyed, and nodded. "You're right. We should keep it…professional." Her voice faded and her gaze shifted from his eyes to his lips.

Jack should have moved away at that point, but he was so close now he could feel the heat of her body and smell the herbal scent of her hair.

Her tongue swept out to slide across her bottom lip. "We should get back to work," she whispered.

"Yes, ma'am." Still, he didn't move but leaned closer, his lips hovering over hers. "What is it about you that makes me want—"

A knock sounded on the door. "Ms. Bellamy, you have a visitor," Gina called out.

Jack backed away, cursing himself for losing control, yet again.

Anne's hand fluttered against her throat and then smoothed her hand over her jacket and skirt. "I'll—" she said, her voice coming out in a squeak. Clearing her throat, she tried again. "I'll be right out." Then she turned, yanked open the door and smiled at the visitor. "Dr. Browne, what brings you to see me?"

Remembering his duty to protect, Jack hurriedly stepped up beside Anne. "Dr. Browne, is it?"

The older man nodded, his brow puckering. "And you are?"

"Jack Snow, Ms. Bellamy's new assistant."

"My apologies, I should have introduced you two. Mr. Browne is our Russian special advisor. Please, come in." Anne stepped to the side, allowing Dr. Browne to proceed into the room. "It's a pleasure to see you."

Dr. Browne entered the office and paced across the room before he turned. "I came as soon as I heard about Dr. Saunders."

Anne nodded. "We heard, as well, and we're hoping she has a full recovery."

"As am I," the older gentleman said. "But I'm here because she was on her way to see me when she was struck down."

"Dr. Browne, you can't blame yourself for what happened to Dr. Saunders." Anne took the older man's hands.

He shook his head. "I'm not blaming myself. I'm concerned. She contacted me just before lunch. She said she had something she wanted me to look at, something that could have a direct impact on the upcoming NSC meeting."

Jack stiffened. "Did she say what it was?"

"No. She wouldn't tell me unless we could meet in person." Dr. Browne scrubbed his hand over his face. "I had scheduled another meeting for lunch. I was to meet her immediately following that, at the same restaurant." He hung his head. "She never made it. When I called her office, I heard what had happened and came immediately."

Chapter Six

Anne promised Dr. Browne she'd do her best to find out what Dr. Saunders had wanted to discuss with him. The man was so distraught he left the building, heading for his home in Arlington.

"What would Dr. Saunders have wanted to discuss with Dr. Browne?" Anne paced across her office and back.

"She was just leaving her office when I delivered the document to Carpenter," Jack said. "But she didn't say anything about meeting with Dr. Browne. If I recall correctly, she was heading to the director for Europe and Russia's office."

"I used to work in that office." Anne ran her finger down a list on her desk, lifted the phone and punched several keys. "I'd like to speak to Dr. Schuster."

Jack stood in front of her desk, waiting to hear her one-sided conversation.

"Dr. Schuster…"

"Oh, Anne, did you hear about what happened to Millicent?"

Anne nodded. "Yes, I heard. That's what I'm calling about. I understand she paid you a visit before lunch."

"Yes, yes, she did," Schuster said. "I asked her to come by. I had a message from the American ambassador to Russia that I'd hoped she could help me decipher."

"And what was that message, if you are at liberty to share?" Anne asked, looking up at Jack as she spoke. She met his gaze, holding her breath while she waited for the other man to speak.

"It was a short message the ambassador received from a Russian aid worker. But it didn't make much sense."

"Why didn't the ambassador clarify with the Russian aid worker?" Anne asked.

"He said he got the message via a social media photo. It was in Russian and cryptic. He said he normally didn't respond to social media, but the photo concerned him."

"Did you get the photo and the message?"

"We did, but that's what has us stumped. We had it, then it disappeared out of our emails."

"But Millie saw it before it disappeared?"

"Yes, she did. Then we heard about her accident. When we looked back at the email, it was gone. As if it never existed."

"Did you happen to print a copy of it?"

"We did, but Dr. Saunders took it with her. She couldn't make heads or tails of it, either, and wanted to meet with someone else who was an expert in Russian to see if they could figure it out."

"Do you remember what the message said?" Anne asked.

"Sure. Millicent translated it to *XC-16 Bringer of Death*."

"And can you tell us what the image was of?"

"The Russian aid worker took a photo of himself and a village behind him." Schuster paused. "It appeared as if there were bodies lying on the ground. The aid worker's eyes were bloodshot, and he was bleeding from his nose. I'm not sure what it was all about, but he didn't look well at all."

Anne shivered. "Did the ambassador know where the photo was taken?"

"He did not."

"Did the Russian aid worker identify himself?"

"No, he did not. He had a social media name, but it wasn't a typical name. He might have used it to disguise his identity. Posting the wrong thing on social media can get you in trouble in the US, but it can get you killed in Russia."

"If you hear anything else from the ambassador, or you think of anything else Dr. Saunders might have said about the message, will you let me know immediately?"

"Sure. You don't think the message had anything to do with Dr. Saunders's hit-and-run, do you?" Schuster asked.

"I really don't know. But it doesn't hurt to check into this message." She ended the call and went over the information with Jack. Then she called the office of Chris Carpenter, the homeland security advisor. "Chris, Anne Bellamy here. What hospital did they take Dr. Saunders to? I'd like to send her some flowers."

He gave her the name of the hospital. "We haven't heard anything about her condition. I've asked the nurse in ICU to notify us of any change."

"Let me know what you find out. And thanks." She placed the phone in the cradle, pushed to her feet, looped her purse strap over her shoulder and headed for the door.

Jack fell in step beside Anne as they left her office and walked down the long hallway to the exit. "Let me guess, we're going to the hospital to see Dr. Saunders, aren't we?"

She nodded. "I hope she's okay. If she's conscious, we need to ask her a few questions."

"If she's not?" Jack asked.

"We need to go through her belongings and see if we can find that printout."

Jack's lips twisted into a wry grin. "Now you're getting the hang of investigations."

"I don't like sneaking around, but I also don't like my friends being targeted by assassins." She stepped out smartly. "We have to determine what's so important people have to die to keep the secrets."

At a street corner, Anne raised her hand to hail a cab.

Jack slipped an arm around her waist and pulled her away from the street. "Let me. I don't want anyone aiming two tons of steel at you."

"What about you?" she asked.

"I can move a little faster." He tipped his gaze toward her feet. "I'm not wearing heels."

Anne liked the playful wink he gave her before he turned to wave down a taxi.

The taxi drove them to the hospital where Millie had been taken.

Once inside, they learned she'd just come out of surgery and was in a room in ICU.

Anne and Jack rode the elevator up to the ICU floor and stopped at the nurses' station. "We're looking for Millicent Saunders."

The nurse glanced at the computer monitor in front of her without looking up. "She just got out of surgery and hasn't woken yet. Only relatives can visit. Are you relatives of hers?" At that point, she looked up, her eyes narrowing slightly.

Anne opened her mouth, but Jack jumped in before she could say anything.

"Yes, we are. Actually, Anne is Millie's first cousin, and I'm Anne's husband. The rest of Millie's family is in Georgia. They asked us to come check on her. They're arranging transportation to get here as soon as possible."

The nurse's brow lifted, and she smiled. "You're welcome to sit with her in her room. She won't wake any time soon. She suffered a concussion as well as internal injuries. They're keeping her under to give her a chance to heal." The nurse gave them the room number.

"What did they do with her personal effects?" Anne asked. "We might need to take her clothing home and have them cleaned or bring in fresh items. Did they bring her purse up with her?"

"All of her things are stored in a cubby in her room." A beep sounded behind the counter. "If you'll excuse me, I need to check on another patient." The nurse left her station and hurried to the room with a light blinking over the door.

Jack took Anne's hand and led her to the room the nurse had indicated.

Millicent Saunders lay comatose in a hospital bed covered in crisp white sheets and a blanket, with wires and tubes running from her arm and chest. The machine beside her bed emitted a steady beeping sound to the rhythm of her heart.

Millie's face and arms were scraped and bruised. As Anne stared down at her friend, her chest tightened and her fists clenched. "Whoever did this needs to pay."

"Agreed." Jack slipped his arm around Anne's

waist, bent and pressed a kiss to the top of her head. Then he stepped away and searched the cubby where personal items were stored. "Here's her purse. Do you want to go through it?"

"Sorry to be digging into your things, Millie, but we have to find out who's responsible for what happened to you." Anne dragged her gaze away from the woman on the bed and joined Jack at the cubby.

After a few minutes of going through Millie's purse, they couldn't find anything suspicious or even interesting. Despite the purse having been flung with Millie across a road, it was still neat and organized. "Nothing."

Jack was searching through her pants pockets and then her trench coat. He pulled out a folded sheet of paper and smoothed it flat. "Bingo."

Anne looked over his arm at the grainy image of a man with red-rimmed, bloodshot eyes. In the background were bodies lying on the ground.

At the sound of wheels rolling to a stop in the hallway, Jack quickly slipped the printout into his pants pocket and Anne shoved the purse and clothes back into the narrow closet and closed it.

A nurse entered the room and smiled. "Are you relatives of Ms. Saunders?"

Anne's first instinct was to tell the truth, but she bit down hard on her lip and her cheeks filled with heat.

"Y-yes, ma'am," Jack answered.

"I'm just checking her vitals and IV. Can I get

you two anything? Afraid all I can offer is a cup of ice water. There is a coffee machine in the lounge area down the hall."

"Thank you," Jack said. "We have to leave for a few hours, but we hope to be back soon. If she wakes, tell her that her loved ones were here."

"I probably won't be here." The nurse checked the IV drip, updated the chart on her laptop and looked up. "My shift ends in an hour."

"Will she be okay?" Anne asked.

"I'm not the doctor," the nurse said. "You'll have to ask him when he makes his rounds in the morning." She touched Anne's arm. "All I can say is that time will tell."

Anne and Jack left the hospital and flagged a taxi that took them back to the White House. By the time they entered her office, many of the West Wing employees were already on their way out, heading home.

"I need to check my emails and gather a few things, and I'll be ready to go."

"Take your time. I'll get our team moving on locating the guy." He unfolded the paper and spread it out on his desk. Then he took a photo image of the picture and texted it to Declan.

Anne logged into her computer and checked her email. She might as well have been gone a week, if the number of emails in her box was any indication. She stared at dozens of unread messages, most of them about the traffic accident involving Dr.

Saunders, with a reminder to look both ways before crossing busy intersections. Anne quickly deleted those and searched for a message from Chris Carpenter. Though Millicent belonged to his department, he had promised in an email to get back to her with his input for the NSC agenda by the end of the day.

After a thorough search of her inbox, she sighed, finding nothing from Chris. Anne turned to the telephone on her desk, keyed Chris's number and waited for a response, hoping he was working late and that was why he hadn't gotten back to her.

His voice mail picked up after five rings.

"Chris, this is Anne Bellamy, I still need your input for the agenda. We finalize in the morning. Have a good evening." She ended her call, brought up the agenda, checked it against the messages that had come in, made minor changes and saved. Then she logged off the computer, looped her purse over her shoulder and turned to Jack. "I'm ready to leave when you are."

Once they were outside the building, Anne squared her shoulders. "I need to do something about my apartment. I can't just leave it like it is."

"Charlie has a lot of connections. Let's talk to her when we get back to the estate."

"We should have called the police and filed a report last night. I was just too shocked to think straight."

"After being chased and shot at, we couldn't stick

around and wait for someone to pick you off." He gripped her elbow. "As it is, we're way too out in the open for my liking."

"I'm glad we left the office while there's still daylight."

"Daylight didn't help Dr. Saunders. It just made it easier for her attacker to hit her."

Anne's gaze darted left then right as they approached a crosswalk that would lead them through a busy intersection. They waited with a dozen other people. When the walking man sign lit up, everyone shuffled forward.

Anne hesitated.

Jack leaned close to her. "Just move quickly and be aware." With his hand at the small of her back, he hurried her through the intersection to the sidewalk on the other side. "Are you okay with the subway? We can stop at a café and wait for Arnold to collect us."

"No. The Metro makes more sense. I don't wish the traffic on anyone." With Jack at her side, Anne felt more confident they would make it back to the Metro station close to the estate unscathed. As many people as were riding the train heading out of the city, an attacker wouldn't have a chance to get to them or get away.

At least, that was what Anne hoped.

JACK STAYED ALERT throughout their walk to the Metro station, his gaze sweeping the crowd surging toward the mass transit. He watched for any-one who might be carrying a gun, a knife or any other kind of weapon. If someone stared too long at Anne, Jack was sure to block their access to her as they passed.

The Metro station posed more of a challenge as people crowded onto the platform and waited for the next train headed in their direction. As the crush move forward, Jack kept Anne in the curve of his arm, using his body as a shield as much as he could. He liked how she fitted perfectly in his arms, not too tall or short, but just right. With her forehead level with his mouth, he could easily have pressed a kiss to her temple.

Thoughts like that would get him killed. Not be-cause Anne would hurt him for taking advantage of their nearness, but because it meant he wasn't pay-ing close enough attention to his surroundings and the people populating it.

After all that had occurred the night before and what had happened to Dr. Saunders, Jack was sur-prised they made it into the train with no problems.

For the first several stops they stood, holding on to overhead straps. As people exited the train, they were able to find seats.

Jack pulled his cell phone from his pocket and texted Arnold the approximate time they'd be at the Metro station for him to collect them.

As he sent the message, another came in from an unknown caller.

Saunders was no accident.

Anne leaned over his arm and read the message. "It's her, isn't it?"

Jack nodded.

You're being followed.

Anne drew in a sharp breath.

Jack's glance shot up and he scanned the train car.

For the most part, the people appeared to be tired commuters on their way home.

The only people who stood out as different were the guy wearing a headset with a hooded sweatshirt pulled up over his head and an old man with a scraggly beard, wearing a Fedora hat and carrying a cane. A woman with shoulder-length blond hair, wearing a classy gray suit, stood by the door, her head down as she thumbed the screen on her cell phone, probably catching up on her texts, email or social media. Another woman sat close to the exit door, her purse clutched beneath her arm, her gaze looking out of the train, her face reflected in the window. The rest of the people on the train wore business suits or business casual clothing and carried briefcases or satchels.

Jack leaned close to Anne and took her hand. "Be ready to move."

She nodded, her fingers squeezing his gently.

Keeping a close watch on the people in the train car, Jack rose to his feet, bringing Anne with him. He positioned Anne in front of him and they headed toward the car next to them, crossing through the connection.

As the train pulled into the station, Jack waited while everyone who was getting off did. Then, as others climbed aboard, he nudged Anne. "Get off."

She did and Jack followed right behind her. They walked alongside the train for several yards as if heading for the exit.

The man with the headset and hoodie had exited the train, as well as the old man with the cane and a dozen businessmen and women.

The signal that the train was about to leave the station sounded.

He leaned close to Anne's ear. "Ready to jump?"

She nodded.

"Go," he whispered. With his hand tight around hers, he stepped onto the train with Anne. The doors closed immediately behind them.

As the train pulled out of the station, Jack took note of the old man with the cane moving toward the exit. The young guy with the hooded sweatshirt stood next to the train, his narrowed gaze on the windows as they passed out of the station.

Anne held on to a metal pole, staring out the window until they'd left the station. Then she turned her gaze to the people in the car. "Do you think we shook him?" Just then, Jack's phone buzzed with a text.

Jack and Anne leaned over Jack's phone to read the text.

Good. You lost your tail.

Jack glanced around the train car and through to the next car.

Some of the same people were still on the train, including the blonde by the door and the woman clutching her purse.

Jack responded to the message.

Headset and hoodie or old man?

He watched the blonde staring at her cell phone. Her fingers didn't move.

The train pulled into another station and the blonde left the train. The reply came.

Neither. Man in dark suit, black running shoes.

"I didn't see him," Anne said, shaking her head.

Are you still with us? Jack typed.

For another long moment, she didn't answer.

Jack assumed she had been the blonde who'd gotten off the train and she was busy walking home, or to her next stop.

Still with you, but not for long.

Jack and Anne both looked up as the train slowed at their stop. They scanned the few remaining people going on to the next station along the line. But they didn't have time to study everyone to make a determination.

They had to get off.

Jack slipped an arm around Anne's waist and guided her off the train and to the exit.

Arnold was there with the car to collect them.

As he sat in the back seat, Jack closed his eyes, trying to recall the faces of the people on the train.

"Could she have been the woman sitting by the door with her purse clutched to her chest?" Anne asked, her thoughts running along the same lines as Jack's.

"Maybe she was the bearded man with the tweed jacket and thick glasses," Jack said. "She could have worn a disguise."

"Hiding in plain sight," Anne concurred.

"I'm not doing such a good job of protecting you if I can't figure out who the good guys are, much less the bad ones." He sighed. "We might have to switch this up and put one of the other members of my team with you."

Anne curled her arm through his. "I don't want someone else. I'm just starting to get used to having you around."

"Yeah, but I can't risk losing focus. I should have seen the man following us before our anonymous spy pointed him out."

"How could we have known?" Anne asked. "A man in a black suit is like so many other men in black suits walking the streets of DC."

They pulled into the Halverson estate and wound through the trees to the sprawling mansion.

Declan met them on the stairs. "Charlie had a function to attend tonight. But you might want to see what we've found."

Jack was tired and would have liked something to eat, but the excitement in Declan's voice was hard to ignore. "Show us."

Declan led him through the foyer into the study and down the steps into the basement war room.

The rest of the team and Grace were gathered around Cole and Jonah, staring at the array of monitors. They glanced up when Declan, Jack and Anne entered the room.

"Look what we found on social media from a couple of days ago," Cole said, his face grim. He tipped his head toward the six monitors.

In one image, a woman wearing a dark headscarf held her lifeless child in her arms, her face contorted in grief.

In another photo, several bodies were laid out side by side on the ground.

At the same time as Jack saw the man in the third image, Anne gasped. "Isn't that the man in the photo Millicent was carrying?" She pointed to the screen with the picture of a man wearing an aid worker's shirt, giving a child a shot in the arm. A line of men, women and children waited their turn behind the child.

"It looks like him," Jack said. He pulled the folded paper from his pocket and held it up to the screen.

Declan nodded. "We did a facial scan of the image you sent and found this man's photo taken in a small Syrian village a couple days ago. The time stamps on the others are a day or two after the image of him giving shots to the villagers."

Anne shook her head as she stared at the last three monitors. "Are all of those people dead?" she asked.

Declan nodded. "It appears so. And I don't see any sign of a bombing."

"Do you think the aid worker poisoned them?" Jack asked, studying the people in line for the shot. "He appears to be vaccinating them."

"We have a name for the man—Aleksandr Orlov. He's a Russian aid worker. We traced him to the village in Syria. We also found a report by the World Health Organization that they quarantined the village until they can determine why every person in the village died."

"An epidemic?" Anne asked.

"I spoke with a WHO rep late this afternoon," Declan said. "They don't know, and they're not taking any chances."

"We found something else." Cole touched a few keys and an article appeared. "We searched for Aleksandr Orlov and found a connection between him and this article about a new cancer vaccine being co-developed between a Russian pharmaceutical company and one here in the US."

Cole moved his mouse and highlighted the US company's name—Waylon Pharmaceuticals.

"And get this," Jonah said. He clicked on his mouse and a city map overlaid the dead bodies. "Waylon Pharm is here in the metro area."

"Isn't it a stretch to think Orlov was testing a cancer vaccination on a Syrian village?" Jack asked.

"Probably," Declan said. "But if it's true, that's a good reason to stop Dr. Saunders from sharing the information with the NCS, which is due to meet in two days—if someone from the drug company wants to influence Russian sanctions, that is."

"That doesn't explain why someone was after Anne—Ms. Bellamy," Jack said. "She didn't know anything about the deaths in Syria until today. She was attacked yesterday."

Declan tapped his chin and stared at a far corner. "True. The two incidents seem unconnected. Ms. Bellamy's getting texts from someone who knows something about Trinity. That in itself is enough to trigger Trinity. They don't like it when they're outed. From what Jasmine says, they kill people who leak information. There are no second chances in their organization."

"Who's Jasmine?" Anne asked.

Jack nodded toward one of his teammates. "Gus Walsh's significant other. She's had some dealings with Trinity."

Anne frowned. "And lived to tell about it?"

Gus's lips twisted. "Sort of."

Anne's frown deepened. "What do you mean *sort of*?"

Jack shook his head. "It's a long story and one that can wait until we figure out what happened to Dr. Saunders, and the reason behind someone going after you." He turned back to the monitors. "What do the Saunders and Bellamy incidents have to do with each other?"

Declan sighed. "At this point, we don't know."

"Why would a Trinity dissident contact Ms. Bellamy?" Cole asked softly, as if to himself.

"Remember, the original message was her reaching out because Trinity was planning an attack that could impact a lot of people," Jack pointed out.

"Who are they attacking?" Declan asked.

"I assume since the message came to me," Anne said, "the attack has something to do with the national security advisor, the National Security Council, which includes the president and vice president, or anyone in the White House."

Gus snorted. "That narrows it down."

Jack tipped his head. "Now we're dealing with a hit-and-run of one of the people working with the Department of Homeland Security."

"Who was, by the way, chasing down something outside her area's responsibility," Anne reminded them.

"She was working with the director for Europe & Russia," Jack said.

Anne's lips twisted. "And she had scheduled to meet with a subject matter expert on Russia."

"About an incident that occurred in Syria," Declan added.

Cole tapped the monitor with Orlov's image. "An incident involving a Russian aid worker."

Jonah pointed to the article on the monitor. "And a potential cancer vaccination."

"And a whole lotta dead people," Jack finished, his tone flat. "Sounds like a lot of loose dots that may or may not be connected."

"I say we contact the pharmaceutical company and find out what their part is in the cancer vaccination," Anne said.

"I'm betting they won't tell you anything," Declan said. "Especially if their drug has caused the deaths of an entire village in Syria."

"Doesn't hurt to ask," Anne said. "What have we got to lose?"

"It'll have to wait until morning." Jack glanced at his watch. "They won't be open for business at this hour." He stepped away from the monitors. "Might as well have dinner and call it a night."

Cole and Jonah remained seated. "We'll dig into Waylon Pharmaceuticals and look for more about the XC-16 vaccine."

With the information they'd just received roiling around in his mind, Jack turned toward the exit to find Charlie descending into the basement war room.

"What did I miss?" she asked.

Chapter Seven

Anne stood back and listened as Declan's Defenders explained to their benefactor, Charlie, what they'd found and their plan for continuing their search through the internet and a proposed trip to Waylon Pharmaceuticals the following day. Her mind and heart felt bruised as she contemplated what they'd learned. Unscrupulous people were willing to test an anticancer vaccine on innocents. Cancer—it had killed her husband. She knew more than most the tantalizing hope a vaccine or cure could bring to millions. To have that hope twisted into this perversion was more than wrong. It was evil.

Charlie nodded. "Chef Carl has dinner prepared for you all. Please, come eat."

Anne's belly rumbled. The food they'd eaten at lunch had long since been converted into fuel and burned.

As they started up the stairs, Charlie waited for

Anne to catch up to her. "What's on the agenda for the National Security Council this week?"

Anne stiffened. "I don't normally discuss the agenda with people outside work."

"Then answer this...is there an issue that could be directly impacted by recent events?"

Anne shrugged. "Almost anything can be directly impacted by the recent events. But I'll review the agenda once more to see if there is anything that is so controversial it warrants trying to kill a staffer in the West Wing."

"Good." Charlie said with a firm nod. "Politics can get downright bloody if you let them get out of hand."

Anne hid a smile. Charlie was opinionated, but she really cared about people, and wanted the best outcome for them.

"How did Mr. Halverson get involved with Trinity?" Anne asked.

Charlie shook her head. "I don't know. He wanted the best for the people who worked for him and he got involved with the political arena in Washington, DC. I think he was frustrated with the corruption and the fact politicians could be bought. I'm sure that when he discovered Trinity played a part in our country's leadership, he probably took it as a personal challenge to expose and eliminate their influence."

"I don't know why he asked me to keep an eye out for people who might be involved with Trinity."

Anne laughed, though she saw no humor in the situation. "I work hard at my job and try to do things right for our leadership. I want what's best for our country."

Charlie draped an arm over Anne's shoulder. "That's why John chose you to help him. Your heart is in the right place. That's not always true for other members of our government."

"Why would this person who's texting me think I can help stop something horrible from happening? I'm not a trained military person. I don't know martial arts and I don't carry any kind of weapon."

"You're smart and you notice things. My husband obviously trusted you, and this person knows it. And you have the right people around you now who can have your back and provide that support you need when things go south." Charlie tilted her head back toward the war room. "Declan's Defenders are all good men. They fought for the country as Marine Force Reconnaissance and now as private citizens concerned for the well-being of their nation."

Anne nodded. "I don't know what I'd do if I didn't have Jack and his team helping me with this situation. Thank you for that."

Charlie hugged Anne briefly. "My husband would have wanted me to carry on his legacy. I only wish he'd involved me before his death. I'm playing this by ear. I have no idea how deeply he dug into Trinity. I assume it was deep enough to get him killed.

Which leads me to think he struck a nerve. Someone in a position of power might have connections with Trinity and my husband was getting too close to the truth." Her lips formed a tight line. "I want to find the one responsible for putting a hit out on my husband. And when I do, I'm bringing him and his entire organization down."

Anne could feel the determination in the older woman's hold on her shoulders. If anyone could find the leader of Trinity, Charlie Halverson was the woman for the job. She had the right people working for her. It could be nothing more than a matter of timing, hard work and a little luck.

The entire team gathered around the enormous table in the formal dining room of the Halverson mansion, along with Grace. Three other women joined them.

"Anne, you haven't met some of the other members of our little family here," Charlie said. "Riley Lansing is Grace's former roommate."

A petite woman with black hair and hazel eyes held out her hand to Anne. "I understand Snow is working with you to figure out who is texting you about a potential attack. I assume the target is the White House or the West Wing, since that's where you work." She shook her hand. "If there's anything I can do, let me know."

"Riley works at Quest Aerospace," Charlie said.

"And she was trained to be a sleeper agent for the Russians."

Anne's eyes widened. "A sleeper agent?" She wondered if being in the same room with the woman compromised her own job.

Riley smiled. "My parents raised me that way, but I was a lost cause because I grew up in America. This is my country. Not Russia. I'm raising my brother here and want only the best for this place I call home."

"And you might not have been formally introduced to Mack Balkman." Charlie continued. "He's one of the Declan's Defenders who helped Riley recover her brother when he'd been kidnapped."

"Hi, I'm Emily Chastain." A pretty young woman with strawberry blond hair and blue eyes held out her hand. "I'm with Mustang. I teach Russian at the university. Mustang helped me when there was an incident at the Russian embassy. I wouldn't be alive today if he hadn't come to my rescue." She smiled up at the former marine with brown hair and brown eyes.

Mustang held out his free hand. "Frank Ford. But you can call me Mustang."

"I'm Gus." A black-haired man with deep brown eyes stepped up to her. He brought with him a woman with equally black hair and brown eyes. "This is Jasmine. Can we eat now?" He winked.

Jasmine held out her hand. "He's only this rude when he's hungry."

Anne shook the woman's hand, taken aback by how firm her grip was and how strong she seemed. "Are you the one who had dealings with Trinity?"

Jasmine shot a glance toward Gus, who held out a chair for her to sit.

He nodded silently and tipped his head toward the seat.

Jasmine shrugged and sank onto the chair. "Yeah."

The rest of the group took their seats.

Anne sat next to Jack, across from Jasmine and Gus. She unfolded her napkin and spread it across her lap before she looked directly at Jasmine, curiosity pushing her to speak. "Jasmine, would you have any idea why this woman who is texting me won't just come out and meet me face-to-face?"

The other woman's lips thinned. "If she's a former member of Trinity, her life is on the line. Usually, the only former members are dead members."

A chill rippled down Anne's spine. She reached for Jack's hand beneath the table and held on to it. No wonder her texting woman remained out of sight or in disguise. "How would she know what's going to happen at the White House if she's left Trinity?"

"From what Gus has told me, she doesn't know exactly what's happening, or if what was planned has changed," Jasmine said. "She could have been the one assigned for the attack and decided she didn't

Dear Reader,

Since you are a lover of our books, your opinions are important to us... and so is your time.

That's why we made sure your **"FAST FIVE" READER SURVEY** can be completed in just a few minutes. Your answers to the five questions will help us remain at the forefront of women's fiction.

And, as a thank-you for participating, we'd like to send you **4 FREE THANK-YOU GIFTS!**

Enjoy your gifts with our appreciation,

Pam Powers

To get your
4 FREE THANK-YOU GIFTS:

✱ Quickly complete the "Fast Five" Reader Survey
and return the insert.

"FAST FIVE" READER SURVEY

1	Do you sometimes read a book a second or third time?	○ Yes	○ No
2	Do you often choose reading over other forms of entertainment such as television?	○ Yes	○ No
3	When you were a child, did someone regularly read aloud to you?	○ Yes	○ No
4	Do you sometimes take a book with you when you travel outside the home?	○ Yes	○ No
5	In addition to books, do you regularly read newspapers and magazines?	○ Yes	○ No

YES! I have completed the above Reader Survey. Please send me my 4 FREE GIFTS (gifts worth over $20 retail). I understand that I am under no obligation to buy anything, as explained on the back of this card.

❏ I prefer the regular-print edition
182/382 HDL GNTY

❏ I prefer the larger-print edition
199/399 HDL GNTY

FIRST NAME   LAST NAME

ADDRESS

APT.#   CITY

STATE/PROV.   ZIP/POSTAL CODE

HI-819-FF19

READER SERVICE—Here's how it works:

▲ If offer card is missing write to: Reader Service, P.O. Box 1341, Buffalo, NY 14240-8531 or visit www.ReaderService.com ▲

BUSINESS REPLY MAIL
FIRST-CLASS MAIL   PERMIT NO. 717   BUFFALO, NY

POSTAGE WILL BE PAID BY ADDRESSEE

READER SERVICE
PO BOX 1341
BUFFALO NY 14240-8571

NO POSTAGE
NECESSARY
IF MAILED
IN THE
UNITED STATES

want to be a part of it. In which case, she knows they're going to make a move, but they would have changed when, where, how and who, based on her defection."

Anne nodded. "That makes sense. But why would someone come after me? I don't know anything."

"You're receiving texts from someone who might be a former Trinity assassin." Jasmine stared across the table at Anne. "They have a vested interest in finding your informant. They're probably hoping you can lead them to her."

Anne shivered.

Jack's hand tightened around hers.

Carl, the chef, brought out tray after tray laden with food. He'd prepared roast beef, potatoes and carrots along with freshly baked yeast rolls, asparagus and a pasta salad.

Talk about what had happened to Millicent and the close call on the Metro filtered around the room until everyone had a chance to fill their plates. Silence fell over the table as they ate the delicious meal.

When Carl returned to the table with crème brûlée, a collective groan sounded from the people gathered around.

When Jack passed her the dish, Anne stared at the dessert longingly but held up her hand. "I wish I could, but I can't. I'm completely full. I need to walk off what I've already eaten."

"Me, too." Jack's glance swept the gathering.

"Please excuse us. We're going to get some air and then call it a night."

Declan nodded. "I don't blame you. It's been an eventful day."

Jack stood and helped Anne to her feet, his hand settling at the small of her back.

She had to admit she liked how warm and comforting it felt. Even more, it caused a spark of desire to grow deep inside. A spark she hadn't thought she was capable of since her husband's death. Jack had changed that in just the day she'd known him.

As they started out of the room, Declan called out, "Gus and I will visit the pharmaceutical company tomorrow and let you know what they have to say as soon as we're done."

"Thanks," Jack said. "Good night."

Jack led the way to the study where a French door led out into a rose garden.

As soon as she stepped out of the house, Anne drew in a deep breath and let it out slowly. "Wow, Charlie has a great chef." She patted her belly. "I'll have to work out twice a day for the next month to make up for that."

"You don't have to make up for anything. You look like you need to put some meat on your bones."

She snorted softly. "Most women on Capitol Hill think you have to be model thin."

"You already are, and most people are wrong."

She laughed, the sound catching in her throat as a sob escaped. Anne pressed a hand to her chest. "Why is this happening to me? And poor Millicent…she didn't do anything."

He turned her to face him. "Did you think that it might be that you were meant for this mission?"

"But I'm not like you. I've never hit anyone in my life. I don't even like to squish bugs."

"If you didn't care, you'd have quit before we got started."

"How do you know? These people who are after my informant might have come after me anyway." She shook her head. "I can't help but feel I'm the wrong person for this job."

"I wish you weren't in this position." He cupped her cheeks in his palms and tipped her chin up. "Because it's so dangerous, not because I don't think you can handle anything thrown your way. I think you've held up remarkably well under the circumstances. No one knows how they will react when things go wrong, until those things go wrong. You're amazing. Taking it one step at a time…one breath at a time." He bent and pressed a kiss to her forehead. "I'm impressed."

She covered his hands with hers and turned her face into his palm, pressing her lips to his skin and loving the heat and strength of him. "I couldn't do it without you."

WHETHER IT WAS her soft cheek against his palm or the starlight shining down on them, Jack couldn't say which was more potent. Either or both had him lowering his face to hers, touching his lips to her soft mouth.

And he drank in her essence, filling his soul with her in his arms. He'd tried to resist, but he couldn't. She didn't realize just how strong she was. To every curve ball thrown her way, she'd reacted with speed and agility. This woman might not think she could handle what was happening, but she'd already proven she could. She was smart, pretty and determined.

Jack skimmed the seam of her lips with his tongue. When she opened to him, he swept in, took her in a long, sensuous caress.

Anne's hands slipped up his chest and into the hair at the back of his neck, pulling him closer.

She felt so warm and soft against him he could barely breathe.

He explored her mouth, then her cheek and the long line of her neck down to where it connected to her shoulder.

Jack wanted more, but they were out in the open. Anyone could look out the window and see them standing in the garden. This wasn't right. He shouldn't be kissing her. He was supposed to protect her, not take her to bed. But that was where he wanted her. In bed, naked and moaning his name.

Finally, he broke away and stepped back until his

arms fell to his sides. "We should call it a night," he said, his voice husky, his heart pounding against the wall of his chest as if it was trying to escape.

She pushed her hair back from her face, her blouse stretching over her chest as she moved. Then she nodded. "You're right. We should." She turned toward the house.

Jack didn't move. He knew he should let her go to her room alone. That was the right thing to do.

When she turned back to him, she asked, "Aren't you coming?"

"I'm going to check on something before I hit the sack."

She nodded, her gaze lingering on him. Then she left him standing there in the starlight. Alone.

Jack waited until she was inside and safe before he turned his back to the house and closed his eyes. What was he thinking, kissing her? Didn't he know how this would end? If he got involved, she'd end up like the other women in his life he'd ever cared for. He could not let that happen to Anne.

Giving her a good ten-minute lead, he entered the house and retreated up the stairs to his bedroom, grabbed a pair of shorts and crossed the hallway to the bathroom.

After a cool shower that did nothing to quell his desire, he gave up and left the bathroom to return to his room.

As he reached for the door handle, the door beside his opened.

Anne stood in the doorway wearing an oversize T-shirt that came down to the middle of her thighs. Her eyes flared as she took in the fact he was only wearing shorts and carrying the clothes he'd changed out of.

She drew in a deep breath, stepped out of the doorframe and came to him. "Jack, I have no right to ask this… We've only known each other for a short time…" She stared down at her hands twisting together and then looked up into his eyes, her kiss-swollen lips parting. "What I'm trying to say is—"

Footsteps sounded on the stairs below.

Anne's eyes widened. She reached out, grabbed his hand and dragged him through the doorway into her room. Once they were both inside, she closed the door and leaned against it, staring up at him. "I really don't want to be alone tonight."

She stood before him, in that damned T-shirt, looking so vulnerable and sexy Jack couldn't think straight. If he had a functioning brain cell, he'd step past her and leave.

But he didn't…have a brain cell…he didn't leave.

He couldn't pull his gaze away from her long legs peeking out from under that T-shirt. "You don't know what you're asking," he said, his voice choked with desire.

A smile curled the corners of her lips. "Oh, I think

I do." She held up her hands. "I'm not asking for forever. I don't expect commitment. I just don't want to be alone."

"You could ask one of the ladies to stay with you for the night," he suggested, though he really didn't want her to choose that option.

"I don't want one of the ladies to stay with me." She stepped toward him. "I feel safest when I'm with you." She took the clothes from his hands and dropped them on a chair. Then she laid a hand on his bare chest, her gaze following her fingers as she curled them into his skin. Her voice lowered. "But that's not all I feel." Then she lifted up on the tips of her toes and pressed her lips to his. "I feel warm… no…hot." She laced her fingers behind his head and pulled him down to her. "I can't unfeel that heat. It won't go away with a cool shower. I tried." She shook her head. "I can only think of one thing that will help."

His groin was so tight. His shaft pressed against her soft belly. He clenched his fists by his sides, afraid if he placed his hands on her, he'd be a goner. There would be no going back. "What will help?" he murmured against her hair.

She took his hands and wrapped them around her waist, shifting them lower to cup her bottom. "Just say you don't want me, and I'll leave you alone."

He chuckled. "Isn't that what I'm supposed to say?" Jack dug his hands into her flesh. She was so soft, but firm. As if of their own volition, his arms tightened around her, pulling her closer, crushing her slowly against his body.

"You...me...whatever feels right." She pressed her lips to the pulse beating wildly at his throat. "This feels right." She kissed his throat and traveled lower to press her lips to his collarbone. "And this."

Jack moaned. "You're killing me, Bellamy."

"As long as you let me, I'm going to do a whole lot more," she murmured against his skin.

"And I thought you were a proper business-woman, all stiff and starched." He slid his hands lower, cupped the backs of her thighs and lifted her.

Anne wrapped her legs around his waist and rested her arms across his shoulders. "I'll take this as a yes."

"Yes, I'll stay with you. No, you don't have to commit. And maybe I'm interested in the whole lot more you alluded to." He kissed her lips, her eye-lids and her cheeks as he walked her toward the bed. Then he leaned over, depositing her on the mattress, her legs draping over the side. Then he stared down into her eyes. "How far are we going?"

Anne pushed up on her elbows, a half smile lift-ing one side of her mouth. "All the way?"

He straightened.

Her brows dipped. "Am I being too forward? It's been a long time since I seduced a man."

"Let me guess...since you were with your husband?" He shook his head, turned away and reached for his pants. He prayed he had protection stored in his wallet. He hadn't been with a woman since he'd left the military. Hell, he hadn't wanted to be with a woman until now.

He fumbled with his wallet, flipped it open and let out a sigh of relief when he found the little packet tucked into one of the hidden pockets.

Hands circled him from behind.

He hadn't heard her move from the bed, but Anne stood behind him her front pressed to his back, and if he wasn't mistaken, she'd removed the T-shirt.

With a groan rising up his throat, he turned in her arms and held up his find. "We might be heading into wild and crazy territory, but not without firm roots in reality."

"Whew," she said on a sigh. "And I thought I'd blown my chances."

"I thought I was blowing mine, if I couldn't find one." He tossed the packet onto the bed and angled her chin upward. "Now, where were we?"

"You're overdressed," she whispered, her fingers sliding beneath the elastic of his waistband, pushing the shorts over his hips.

Jack took over and stepped out of his shorts, his shaft jutting forward.

Anne stood before him, wearing only a pair of lacy pink panties.

He raised an eyebrow. "Now who's overdressed?"

Anne slid her fingers beneath the elastic of her panties and dragged them very slowly over her hips and down her thighs. Then she kicked them to the side, lifting her chin at the same time.

With a beautiful, naked woman standing before him like a gift, all of Jack's patience flew out the window. He scooped her up in his arms and carried her to the bed. Depositing her on the mattress, he crawled up her body and leaned on his arms over her. "Who'd have thought you were a beast beneath that straitlaced suit?"

He bent to nibble on her earlobe.

"You should never judge a woman by the clothes she wears," she said, her hands sliding up over his shoulders to weave into his hair.

He claimed her sassy mouth with his and kissed her until he was senseless and eager to move on to tastier parts of her body. Starting with the long, slim line of her neck. He kissed a path over her collarbone and down to the swell of her right breast. For a long moment, he paid homage to the nipple, flicking it with his tongue and then rolling it between his teeth.

Anne arched her back off the bed. Her fingernails dug into his scalp every time he touched his tongue to the tight little bud of her nipple.

His shaft hardened, throbbing with his own need. But he wanted her to lose herself first. With that goal in mind, he moved to the other breast and treated it to equal torture and pleasure until Anne moaned softly beneath him.

With Anne thrashing against the comforter, Jack moved down her body, tonguing each rib and leaving a trail of kisses down to the tuft of hair at the juncture of her thighs.

As he cupped her sex, her fingers curled into the blanket and she drew her knees up, digging her heels into the mattress.

Jack loved that she gave herself with such abandon, her soft moans making him even hotter and eager to consummate their first time together. Parting her folds, he thumbed the strip of flesh between.

Anne sucked in a sharp breath, her body rocking with each stroke of his hand.

Replacing his thumb with his tongue, he swept across that nubbin of nerves and then flicked and swirled until she writhed beneath his mouth.

Her body grew rigid and she remained steady, her breath held and her fingers digging hard into his shoulders.

Then she was dragging him up her body, her hands sliding over his backside, feverishly stroking him. "Don't make me wait another minute," she growled. Her hand reached out to her side, slapping at the mattress until she found what she was searching for. She grabbed the little packet, tore it open and pulled out the little piece of protection.

Without missing a beat, she slid it over his staff and down to the base. "Now," she said. "Do it. Now."

Jack chuckled, though it cost him. He was so hard he could barely draw in a breath. He settled himself between her legs and nudged her with the tip of him. "Are you sure about this?"

"Oh for Pete's sake." She gripped his hips and pressed him into her, not slowing to accommodate his size, or to give herself a chance to get used to him. She slammed him all the way in, and held him there, her hands tight on his buttocks.

"Is that how you like it?" Jack bent to kiss her forehead as he pulled back.

Again, she brought him home. Then she settled into a rhythm, pushing him back and pulling him in.

Jack let her for a short time, holding back his own release. Then he took control, pumping in and out, loving the feel of her channel constricting around him. He made love to her until he pitched over the edge, his body stiffening, sensations rocking him in waves until he collapsed on top of her and rolled to the side.

For a long moment, he lay with her in his arms, his hand smoothing over the soft skin of her hip. "Wow," he said when he could get his vocal cords to respond.

"Wow," she echoed.

Then he laughed and she joined in, snuggling close to him, their connection unsevered.

Jack held her close, ignoring the nagging thought

in the back of his head. He cared for her. And by caring for her, he'd doomed her, just as he had the other women he'd dared to love.

Chapter Eight

Anne slept soundly through the night, held close in Jack's arms, her body sated from the most incredible lovemaking she'd experienced in many years. Maybe ever. When her husband had fallen ill, their sex life had faded to nothing as he battled fatigue and worse. She hadn't realized how much she'd missed the passion, the heat. Not a single bad dream disturbed her slumber, and she didn't have to fight off any bad guys invading the room. When morning came, she opened her eyes, a smile on her face.

As she stretched, she realized that the body that had been spooned around her throughout the night was no longer there.

All grogginess disappeared, and she sat up, pulling the sheet up over her naked breasts. "Jack?" she whispered.

There weren't any places to hide in the room. It didn't have a connecting bathroom or a huge walk-in closet. Still, Anne rose from the bed, wrapped the sheet around her body and padded over to open the closet and look inside. He wasn't there.

Jack was gone.

Irritation warred with disappointment and a hint of fear.

Why had he left before she'd awakened? She would have loved snuggling a little before getting up for the day. Or, worse…had he been dissatisfied with her performance in the bed?

Anne found the T-shirt she'd tossed to the floor the night before and slipped it over her head. She gathered clothes and toiletries and hurried across the hallway to the bathroom. After a quick shower and even quicker work with the blow-dryer, she felt more like her stodgy self, dressed in a boring business suit, ready to go to the White House and get the rest of the agenda pulled together for the national security advisor to review and approve.

When she had that done, she'd meet with the police at her apartment and get that report filed. She couldn't live in Charlie's house forever. Eventually, she'd have to go home.

Home.

Her apartment had never felt less like home than at that moment. She wished Jack was there to wrap his arms around her shoulders and make her feel better instantly.

Convinced Jack had ducked out to avoid the awkwardness of the morning after, Anne left the bedroom where she'd had the most blissful sex she could remember. She cast one last glance at the neatly made-up bed that had been so beautifully used the night before.

With a sigh, she descended the sweeping staircase to the foyer and followed the sound of voices into the kitchen.

There she found Declan, Grace, Charlie and the chef, Carl. But no Jack.

"Jack went out for a run earlier. He should be back soon," Declan said. "We promised to keep an eye out for you."

"Thanks." Anne went directly to the coffeepot and poured a cup.

"It's Carl's day off, so we're fending for ourselves for breakfast," Charlie explained as she put two pieces of bread in the toaster. "I've been known to cook an egg or two. Can I interest you in an omelet?"

Anne shook her head, amazed that her billionaire hostess would offer to cook eggs for her. "I'll stick to coffee."

"Gus and I will go to the pharmaceutical company around ten this morning," Declan said. "We'll let you know what we learn when we do."

Anne nodded. "I need to file a police report about my apartment. I should have done it the day I found it. But better late than never."

"I'll call my contact in the police department and

have them help you out," Charlie offered. "What time can you be there?"

"A little before noon. I want to be back at my desk after lunch. We have the council meeting tomorrow, and I need to be sure I've tied up all the loose ends."

"Are you at liberty to say what you'll be discussing?" Grace asked.

Anne shook her head. "The council can disclose that information if they choose in a news conference. It's not up to me."

Grace smiled. "I understand. I just thought maybe whatever will be decided in the meeting might have something to do with why Trinity feels the need to cause trouble."

Anne stared at Grace, wondering if what she'd just said held the key to what had been happening with the texter who'd tried to warn her there would be trouble. If the agenda was the reason for the attack, what did Trinity hope to gain?

She'd have another look at the schedule and try to read between the lines of what would be under discussion. How could something on the slate make Trinity desperate enough to stage an attack? But then she hadn't received all the agenda items as of the end of yesterday.

Anne checked her watch. They needed to get going if they wanted to catch the Metro into the city.

"Arnold has the car out front," Charlie said. "He's ready to go whenever you and Jack are."

"Thank you." Anne set her coffee mug in the sink. "I just need Jack, and we'll be on our way."

"It's nice to be needed," a man with a deep voice said behind her.

Anne spun to face Jack, neatly dressed in his suit and tie, his hair damp from a shower and slicked back from his forehead.

Her heart beat hard in her chest and heat rushed up her neck into her cheeks.

His gaze met hers without mercy, a smile quirking one corner of his mouth.

Anne dropped her gaze first and looped her purse over her shoulder. She turned to Charlie with a smile pasted on her face. "Thank you for all you've done. I'll do my best to get my apartment in order. I can't keep taking advantage of your hospitality."

Charlie waved a hand in her direction. "Don't be silly. You're welcome to stay as long as you like or need. After all the damage that was done, your apartment won't be livable for a while. Speaking of which, I can have my handyman help you out."

"Thank you. That would be great. And I'll pay him to do the work. Again, I can't let you do everything for me."

"Humor this old gal." Charlie hugged Anne. "I'm being selfish. I get to have people around. It beats an empty house."

"You're not old." Anne smiled at the woman, grateful beyond words for what she'd done for her.

"Thank you." She left the room ahead of Jack, headed for the front entrance, with purpose in her steps.

Jack caught up with her at the door and opened it for her. "In case you didn't hear me while you were sleeping, good morning, beautiful," he said, his tone rich, deep and sexy as hell.

Anne wanted to hang on to her irritation at being alone in the bed when she'd awakened.

As she passed him, he leaned closer, speaking in a tone only she could hear, "I had to go for a run. I get stiff if I don't exercise at least every other day." He tapped his thigh. "This old war injury gives me fits. And you were sleeping so well I didn't have the heart to wake you."

And like that, he wiped away her irritation. All she had left to cling to was her fear she'd somehow not measured up. After all, he'd left the bed before she'd known it, even if it was to go for a therapeutic run.

Anne didn't comment. What would she say? *Was I any good? Have you had better? What could I do different...assuming we were to make love again?*

She'd been the one to guarantee he'd have no obligation following that night. No commitment. Jack had been quick to agree.

Oh, hell, she didn't have time to worry about what a man thought about her sexual prowess. She had a life-and-death situation to contend with. If she lost her focus, she could end up run over by a vehicle like

Millicent had been. Or have her neck snapped in a back alley by a Trinity assassin.

That thought shook her enough to bring her focus back to where it belonged. On the job ahead, not the man behind her.

As promised, Arnold was waiting at the bottom of the steps with Charlie's SUV.

Jack opened the back door for Anne and waited while she got in. Then he rounded the vehicle and climbed in beside her.

Arnold pulled away from the curb and started down the long, twisting driveway to the highway beyond.

Anne sat on her side of the vehicle, her hands in her lap, her gaze out the side window, trying to ignore how incredibly turned on she was by the man sitting beside her. And how nervous she felt about seeing him again after their incredible lovemaking. Well, it had been incredible for her.

She was so intent on looking out the window that she didn't actually see anything.

A hand closed over hers and squeezed gently. "Did I say something to make you mad?"

She started and would have pulled her hand free, but he held on. "No," she murmured.

He turned her hand over and traced the lines in her palm. "If I did, I'm sorry. You have no idea how hard it was to leave you in bed. I wanted to wake you up and make love to you all over again. But you were sleeping so well I couldn't do it."

Anne's heart swelled. "I wouldn't have minded missing a few minutes of sleep," she said softly, finally looking at him.

He sighed. "You had me worried. I thought you were going to hold me to the no-commitment, no-obligation theory when all I want to do is find the nearest hotel room and get naked with you."

Anne shot a glance toward Arnold.

Charlie's butler never glanced back in the rear-view mirror. His gaze remained on the road ahead as they passed through the estate's gate and turned onto the highway.

For the rest of the ride to the Metro station, Anne clutched Jack's hand, her thoughts along the same lines as Jack's. Heat burned through her, coiling around her core. If she didn't get her act together, she'd end up in the hospital or the morgue.

But she couldn't bring herself to let go of Jack's hand until they arrived at the station.

Jack emerged from the vehicle first and looked around before he opened the door for Anne.

After being followed on their Metro ride the day before, Anne made a concentrated effort to study everyone standing at the platform waiting for the train.

When the train arrived, Jack held Anne's hand as they boarded the car and found a place to sit for the ride into the city. They exited at the Farragut West station and walked the rest of the way to the White House. Thankfully, though the clouds hung heavily over the city, the rain held off, allowing them to arrive dry at the West Wing of the White House.

Anne made it a habit to arrive thirty minutes to an hour early for work. The extra hour gave her time to determine where she'd left off and make her list of tasks to accomplish that day. By the time the majority of the White House staff arrived, she had her head on straight and was ready to tackle any problem that might crop up during the day.

She checked her computer inbox for Chris Carpenter's input for the NSC agenda. As he'd promised, his email was waiting for her. She opened it and transferred his changes to the official agenda. When she'd adjusted it to the correct format, she spent a few minutes going over the outline of what was to be discussed with the president, vice president, secretary of state, secretary of defense, secretary of treasury, national security advisor and director of national intelligence.

The usual border control issues, upcoming foreign dignitary visits and military deployment decisions were listed along with discussions concerning various nations that might impact national security. They would hear from the director for Asia on the changes to trade agreements. The director for Europe and Russia would speak on imposing sanctions on

Russia for human rights violations in Crimea, Syria and other countries Russia had a presence in.

The agenda didn't appear much different from the last time the NSC had met. Some problems never seemed to go away or get resolved.

After going over the document three more times, Anne printed a copy and carried it to the office next to hers, where Shaun Louis, the national security advisor, worked. She glanced at Gina, the staffer seated at the desk in front of the NSA's office. She was the first line of defense to keep people from interrupting Shaun. "Is he in?"

She nodded and held her fingers up to her ear, indicating he was on the phone.

Knowing he wanted the slate as soon as it was ready, Anne tapped softly on the door and poked her head through.

Shaun was still on the phone.

Anne held up the document and waited for him to acknowledge her.

He waved for her to enter.

She handed off the paper and left the room. Barring any major changes, the slate was ready for the next day's meeting of the National Security Council.

Anne hurried back to her office, closed the door and went to work. It wasn't until later she remembered to call the police.

When she did, they put her on hold.

"I take it you're ready to deal with your apartment?" Jack asked quietly. He'd removed his jacket and rolled up his sleeves to work at the computer, digging through whatever files he could tap into.

She nodded. "I have to get started on the cleanup. I don't like relying on others as much as I have with Mrs. Halverson."

"Ms. Bellamy? This is Detective Hutcheson. Mrs. Halverson gave us the heads-up that you'd be calling. I've been assigned to your case. What time would you like to meet?"

"Within the next thirty minutes if at all possible," Anne glanced at her watch, surprised at fast the morning had flown. "I'll take a long lunch, but I need to get back to work."

"That's perfect. I was going that direction for a meeting after lunch. I can be there in thirty minutes."

"Thank you." Anne ended the call and stared at Jack. "We'll need to get moving if we want to catch a train that direction."

Jack had already rolled down his sleeves and buttoned them. He shrugged into his jacket and smoothed a hand over his hair. "Let's go."

Anne led the way from the office down the hallway to the exit.

They didn't take long getting to the Metro station and a train happened along at that moment, going in the direction they needed.

Once on board, Anne stood near a door, her hand

on a pole to keep her balance. She leaned close to Jack. "See anyone suspicious?"

He smiled. "I'm not even sure I could pick out the bad guys at this point."

Anne snorted. "Me, either."

Fortunately, they weren't accosted, and they arrived at the station close to her apartment complex. Once off the train, Anne hurried along the sidewalk.

As they reached the building, an unmarked dark sedan pulled into the parking lot. A man stepped out, wearing a charcoal gray blazer, black polo shirt and trousers. He pulled a notepad out of his pocket and looked down at it before glancing up at the building.

"Detective Hutcheson?" Anne asked, closing the distance between them.

The man turned and held out a hand. "That's me. You must be Ms. Bellamy."

She shook his hand. "This is Jack Snow, my…"

"Boyfriend," Jack interjected and shook the detective's hand. "Thank you for coming on such short notice."

"It's not a problem," Hutcheson said. "Mrs. Halverson has been such a help to the department I'm only happy to return the favor." He nodded toward the building. "I understand the break-in happened two nights ago?"

Anne nodded. "It did. I haven't had time to do anything about it. Work has taken up most of my time."

"Understandable. But the longer you delay the investigation, the harder it is to find the culprit," the detective said. "Show me."

Anne led the way to her door and unlocked it. Then she stood back and let the detective enter. The place was as she'd left it two nights ago. And she had the same reaction to the destruction as she had the first time she'd seen it. She rested a hand over her belly, feeling as if she'd been sucker punched. Her place of solace was now chaotic and destroyed. She began to think she would never feel safe there again.

Jack slipped an arm around her waist and pulled her against him.

They spent the next half hour answering questions for the detective. Anne told him about the man who'd followed her from work that night and how she'd ducked into the pub and waited for Jack to come get her. She didn't mention the text she'd received that day or the ones she'd received since.

After the detective left, Jack took her key from her and locked the door to her apartment. "Why didn't you tell him about the texts?"

"If our informant doesn't want to be identified, I'm not going to bring her up. She was there for us on the train last night. I could be wrong, but I feel like she's a bit of a guardian angel looking out for us."

"What if she's the one causing all the trouble?" Jack asked.

Anne shook her head. "I don't think she is. Call it intuition, or stupidity. I don't think she's the one who tried to grab me the other night, nor was she the one to destroy my apartment. I think whoever has been bothering me might want to get to her."

Jack took her hand and squeezed it gently. "I really hope you're right."

Anne prayed she was, too. She didn't want either one of them to be hurt because she'd trusted someone she had never seen or met.

Chapter Nine

Just as they reached the Metro station, Jack's phone buzzed in his pocket. He pulled it out to read Declan's name in the caller ID screen. He hit the talk button. "What did you find?"

"It took some finagling, but we finally got in to talk with the director of research and development who is overseeing the cancer vaccination project."

Jack came to a stop inside the station, his gaze searching the platform and the people standing there waiting for the next train. "And?"

"He said he couldn't go into too much detail about the XC-16 vaccine. They'd been working on it for the past two years, getting closer than they've ever gotten before. The vaccine triggers the immune system to kill cancer cells, which was a great step forward. But experimenting on mice proved to be deadly for the mice. Even at extremely low doses, the mice died within hours of receiving the vaccination."

"So the serum killed cancer, but killed the patients, too?"

"Exactly. The drug was deemed too dangerous to experiment with on human subjects. They made some changes to the formula and they had some better results. The mice didn't die as suddenly. They lived at least a week before they started showing signs of decline. Ultimately, the experiments were thought to be a failure, as the mice died anyway."

"What did they say about the man in the picture? Do they think the man in the photo might be using one of their vaccines?" Jack asked.

Declan snorted. "The director said no one had authority to test the XC-16 vaccine on humans. They're using nanotechnology to deliver the vaccine into the patient's system and it's considered unstable at this time. In fact, the program had been put on hold until they could figure out what was killing the mice they'd used as test subjects. The researcher in charge of the program was laid off until further notice."

"Did you get the name of the researcher?" Jack asked. "Maybe we can learn more from him. He might be more likely to spill information since he's been laid off."

Declan chuckled. "We did. His name is Leon Metzger." He texted the man's address to Jack. "We planned on going there next."

"Hang on while I look at the location." Jack pulled the phone away from his ear, put it on speaker and stared down at the text. The address came up and he clicked on it, bringing up the map on his phone.

Anne leaned over his shoulder. "That's not far from here. It's close to the next stop. I almost rented a condo in that area."

Jack glanced at his watch. "Do you have time to swing by there?"

Anne nodded. "As long as we get back to my office before two o'clock."

"I think we can make it. Did you hear that, Declan? We're only about a five-minute train ride to that location. We'll swing by."

"Good, because it'll take us at least thirty minutes fighting traffic. Let us know if he's there and we can meet you there."

"Roger," Jack said and ended the call.

The train rolled into the station and they boarded.

When they got off at the next stop, Jack used the GPS directions on his phone to get them to the row of condominiums where Metzger lived.

"Fourth door on the left," Jack said.

Anne pressed the doorbell.

Jack could hear the echo of the bell inside the hallway. No one came to see who was there.

Anne pressed it again.

Jack heard another sound coming from the garage attached to the condo. He stepped close to the garage and pressed his ear to the overhead door. The hum of an engine sounded inside. Why would someone have his car engine running with the garage door closed? As soon as the thought entered his head, he knew something wasn't right.

Jack tried the front door, but it was locked. He ran around to the back of the building and counted to the fourth back door and tried it. Not wanting to leave Anne alone for too long, he hurried back around to find her standing on her toes, looking into the window of the condo.

"I don't see anyone moving around inside."

"I think it's because whoever lives here is in the garage, with the car running," Jack said, his face grim.

"That would be stupid. He could die of carbon monoxide poison—" Anne's eyes widened. "Oh, dear."

"Call 911. I'm going to break a window to get inside."

"Calling," Anne said. "Hurry,"

Jack grabbed a landscaping brick and threw it into a window on the first floor. The glass shattered, leaving a large hole.

Using a stick, Jack broke away the remaining shards of glass, ducked through the window and ran through the kitchen to the door leading into the garage.

He could smell the sulfurous smoke before he opened the door. A white sedan stood where the owner parked it, the engine running. Inside, slumped over the wheel was a man in a gray T-shirt, his face pale and waxy.

Jack pulled his shirt up over his nose, slammed his hand onto the garage door opener and yanked open the car door.

The man behind the wheel slumped sideways. If Jack hadn't been there to catch him, he would have fallen out of the car.

Grabbing beneath the man's shoulders, Jack dragged him from the car and out of the fume-filled garage into the open air and laid him on the grass.

"The fire department is on the way," Anne said, slipping her phone back into her purse. Her brow pinched. "Is he…"

Jack felt for a pulse at the base of the man's throat. "I don't feel a pulse and he's already cold. I'd say he's dead."

SIRENS SOUNDED IN the distance, getting louder as they moved closer. A red truck pulled into the condo driveway, red lights blinking from its roof. Emergency medical technicians jumped down from the truck, grabbed their gear and ran toward where Jack and Anne stood. The first one there dropped to his knees, felt for a pulse and frowned. He pulled out a stethoscope and pressed it to the man's chest. He shook his head, folded his stethoscope and stuffed it into his pocket.

Anne held her breath, wishing the man would find a pulse, knowing he wouldn't.

A police cruiser pulled to a stop beside the fire truck and, a minute later, an ambulance arrived.

For the next thirty minutes, Jack and Anne answered the questions they could, and waited for the police to clear them to leave. Eventually, Leon Metzger's body was loaded into the ambulance and carried away to the morgue.

Anne had her own set of questions, but Jack had stepped away while the techs worked on Metzger and called Declan, who assured him they'd look into this incident immediately. For the time being, they had to be patient.

Anne and Jack walked to the Metro station and caught the train back to the Farragut West station. They found seats near the back of the car and sank into them.

"You think it was suicide?" Anne asked softly.

"We won't know until they do the autopsy."

Anne wasn't sure, but her gut was telling her it wasn't suicide. "He didn't look like someone who was going to commit suicide. He looked like he was going for a date or something."

Jack nodded in agreement. "Metzger didn't look like he was ready to die. He was dressed in his best, with the scent of cologne lingering on his skin, like he was trying to impress someone." He lowered his voice. "And I noticed something on his kitchen calendar when I ran through there. He had a vacation coming up. Bermuda in big capital letters. He was looking forward to the future."

"Why would someone want to kill a research scientist?" Anne asked.

"Better question is—" Jack glanced toward her "—who had something to lose if he talked about his research with the cancer vaccine?"

Anne's eyes narrowed. "The company developing it?"

"You heard what the program director said," Jack said. "They put the project on hold until they could figure out what was killing the mice. They went as far as laying off some scientists."

"You think he took his research elsewhere?" Anne asked.

"It's possible. But he'd have to take it a lot farther than in the same country where the scientific community speaks the same language." Jack's brow furrowed. "You have to know they talk to each other."

Anne stared at the back of the seat in front of her. "Some place like Russia? And they used the vaccine on the people in that Syrian village, because they would trust anyone to help them when they needed help most." She shook her head, her stomach roiling at the senseless murders. "They experimented on those people." She pressed her knuckles to her lips. "They killed everyone in that village, including the children."

"We don't know that for certain. This is all circumstantial at this point. Until the World Health Organization can get in there and test some of the bodies, we won't know anything."

Anne nodded. "You're right. At this point, all we can do is guess at what's happening. In the meantime, I have tomorrow's NSC meeting to prepare for. I should be getting the finalized agenda back from the national security advisor. Then I need to update the briefing slides and stage them for tomorrow morning. The president hates to be kept waiting on technical glitches."

"Then we just have to make sure there are no glitches. Are you in charge of the audiovisual equipment?"

"No, but I help the guy who is. Terrence Tully is our conference room facilitator. He makes certain the conference room is in perfect order, there are seats for everyone invited to speak and drinks for everyone. He sets up the audiovisual connections and loads the briefings. I'll be there to make sure all the images come across correctly."

"That means we have to be at the office early tomorrow." He didn't ask the question. He stated a fact.

Anne was always extra early on NSC meeting day. "Right. I'll want to be even earlier than we were this morning."

"I can do early," Jack said.

The train came to a stop at the Farragut West. Jack

took Anne's arm and helped her out of the train and through the exit into the late afternoon sunshine. "We missed your two o'clock deadline," Jack said as they entered the West Wing.

"I'm not sweating it. I only set the hour as something to aim for. I can stay as late as I need to. We'll see how many changes Shaun came up with. That will determine how late I'll be here."

"Anything I can do to help…let me."

She gave him a weak smile. "I will." Anne paused outside the door to the NSA office suite, hesitating before diving in. "I admit I've never seen a dead body up close and personal like that."

"You never get used to it," Jack said. "It's hardest when you knew the guy."

Anne shot him a glance but didn't question him. He didn't need her forcing him to relive something as catastrophic as losing a friend in battle.

As soon as she stepped through the door, Anne was hit by one request after another.

Shaun had her in his office going over the last-minute fixes to the agenda and the images he expected to use for his portion of the briefing.

"Who put the question of Russian sanctions on the agenda?" he asked.

"Chris Carpenter."

"We settled that a couple months ago. Why does he insist on rehashing it?"

Anne didn't speculate. Chris had his reasons.

It wasn't her place to question them. The council would decide what was important and assign taskings to different government bodies to accomplish what they wanted done. She sat in the meetings on rare occasions if they wanted someone to clarify an issue. Normally, she was simply moral support. But sometimes she provided valuable background information if members had questions.

Anne checked the entire slate and researched all the issues in order to advise the NSA so that he might brief the president. Shaun didn't necessarily need her advice, but he liked to bounce ideas off her. She figured it was one of her job duties to listen to her boss's thoughts and ideas. He was the one who had to present to the president, vice president, the chief of staff, and other members of the council.

Once she had all the changes incorporated on the slide presentation, she saved a copy to her desktop as backup and moved another copy into a file they used specifically for the council meetings. Terrence would know where to go to get the presentation and Anne would be there to double-check the right document was loaded.

Once she'd completed setting up the agenda and the supporting documents that Shaun might need, she poked her head back into her boss's office. "Do you need anything else?"

He was on his feet, slipping into his suit jacket.

"No, thank you. I have another meeting to attend tonight. I'll be in early tomorrow morning."

"Have a good evening, Mr. Louis," she said.

"And you." He paused as he passed her. "Anne, is there anything else going on with you?"

She looked at him in surprise. She'd been working hard every day to get this meeting arranged. Anne prided herself on keeping her emotions to herself. She didn't like weak or whiny women, and in keeping with that, she refused to be one of them. "No, sir. Why do you ask?"

"You seem to be distracted. I hope you aren't experiencing any problems outside of work."

Anne bit down hard on her tongue to keep from telling her boss everything that had gone wrong over the past few days. But she stopped herself in time. Shaun didn't need to know her life was getting more complicated by the minute and that she had an assassin after her. "No, sir. Everything is perfect." A perfect mess. She pasted a smile on her face. "Have a good evening."

"You'd tell me if something isn't right in your world, wouldn't you?" he persisted.

"Yes, sir," she said, holding up her hand as if swearing an oath, though she was lying through her teeth. She didn't like telling untruths, but sometimes a person didn't need to share even a small portion of her life with her colleagues. Her boss had much bigger issues to concern him. The safety of the nation was far more important.

The text messages she'd been receiving could be hoaxes, for all she knew. She had yet to identify the person who'd sent them. Not one of the Secret Service staff had received anything indicating a threat to the president, vice president or any other member of the council. If they had, the meeting would have been postponed and everyone in the White House would have been warned.

Should she have raised an alarm when she'd received the first volley of messages?

Her boss continued on toward the door.

"Mr. Louis," Anne blurted out.

"Yes, Anne?" he said and turned to face her, his eyebrows cocked.

The words she knew she should say lodged in her throat. Finally, she forced air past her vocal cords. "Have a nice evening, sir."

Shaun's eyes narrowed slightly, and for a moment, he looked like he wanted to say something, but he didn't. "Thank you," he said and left.

Anne let go of the breath she hadn't realized she'd been holding and walked back into her office. Once she shut her door, she paced the length of the room.

Jack rose from where he'd been seated and crossed the room to stand in front of her. "What's wrong?"

She shook her head. "I'm not cut out to be a spy."

"You don't have to be." He held open his arms.

Anne sucked in a deep breath, fighting the urge to take advantage of his offer to comfort her. She had been at this job long enough to know right from wrong. At that moment, she was almost convinced she'd been wrong to keep a potential threat from the others working in the West Wing. "I should tell someone that something bad might happen soon."

He dropped his arms to his sides. "Do you know for certain when and where?"

"No." She huffed out a frustrated breath and held out her hand. "Give me your phone. It's about time we got some answers from our text woman."

JACK HANDED OVER his cell phone and waited while Anne keyed in a text to the mysterious woman who'd been less than helpful in their search for answers.

Anne hit the send button and looked up. "Now we wait and see if she actually responds. Telling someone there's going to be trouble without giving any specifics is almost worse than letting them be surprised."

"I disagree. At least we're not blind sheep being herded over a cliff. We are aware and watching." Jack wished he'd found more information through his search of the West Wing database he had access to. Nothing had seemed to stand out.

Cole and Jonah were in a better position to cyber-snoop. With the ability to hack into many different government and corporate databases, they could get in and get out without being detected.

As the new White House staffer, Jack would be easily detected. He suspected that anyone in the White House with connections to Trinity would be extra careful about contact with them. They wouldn't use their government computers or the cell phones they used for work. That kind of sloppiness could get someone killed.

He looked over Anne's shoulder at the words she'd typed to the woman who'd been texting.

Tomorrow is a big day, lots of targets in the NSC meeting. Need help. Can you give us any more specifics?

After a minute passed, Jack began to think their texter wasn't online. After three minutes, he shook his head. "We might as well call it a night. Tomorrow will be an early day."

Anne nodded and stepped close to Jack. She reached around him and turned on a small desk fan before she spoke, creating noise to drown out her words. "She might not contact us while we're here. We don't know what kind of surveillance equipment is employed within these walls."

Jack nodded, inhaling the fragrance Anne used.

Or was it the fresh scent of her shampoo? Whatever it was, it was intoxicating.

She stepped away and gathered her purse.

Jack slipped into his jacket and they left the office and the West Wing of the White House.

The evening crush of people hurried toward the Metro in their mad rush to get home.

Jack kept a close watch on Anne, afraid someone would make a move while she was buried in a sea of humanity. If someone was to attack, now would be the time. It was too dangerous. He gripped her arm and pulled her into one of the cafés along the way.

She looked up at him, a questioning expression on her face.

"I couldn't protect you from everyone," he whispered. "We'll wait until the crowd thins out before continuing on."

Anne nodded and looked around at the little restaurant. "We could go ahead and have dinner here. By the time we get back to the estate, it will be late."

"I'm all for it." He grinned. "We were so busy at lunch we never stopped to eat."

Anne pressed a hand to her belly. "That must be why I'm so hungry."

They waited to be seated by the hostess and looked at the menu.

Jack studied Anne across the table. He could imagine this as a real date. They sat in companionable silence, comfortable in each other's company.

He wouldn't consider her unconventionally beautiful with her straight black hair and blue eyes. But her true beauty came from her intelligence, compassion and life experiences. This was a woman who, despite the trying circumstances, forged ahead and went to work, instead of cowering in a corner, afraid to live because someone was after her.

As they waited for the waitress to return, Jack reached across the table and captured Anne's hand. "You amaze me."

She appeared clearly startled by his touch and words. A smile quirked upward on one side of her mouth. "Why do you say that?"

"You've been nothing but a trouper through this whole ordeal."

She snorted softly. "I'm only as strong as the man who's been by my side practically from the start." Anne squeezed his hand. "I couldn't do this without you."

He shook his head. "I believe you could."

"Well, I'm glad I don't have to." For a long moment, they held hands across the table.

Like a couple.

For the first time in a long time, even though he knew it put Anne in jeopardy, Jack wished this relationship would continue after they resolved the danger.

His phone vibrated in his pocket, jerking him back

to reality. He dug it out and stared down at the text from their informer.

Be at the movie theater on 6th and H Street for the 7:35 showing.

Along with the text was an attachment with two tickets to *Godzilla*.

Chapter Ten

They didn't have a moment to digest the information before the waitress arrived with their order. Having barely touched her salad, Anne felt bad that she'd left so much of the delicious meal on her plate. The thought of meeting with their informer face-to-face for the first time had her stomach knotted and her anxiety level at a fever pitch.

Jack leaned toward Anne. "I have to admit I'm worried."

"You're worried?" She laughed, the sound fading off. "Me, too."

"All the what-ifs are going through my mind." He pulled his phone out of his pocket and hit a button.

"Who are you calling?" she asked.

"Declan." He waited for the connection. "Hey. We have a situation." He gave his team lead the information they'd been given and the location of the theater, speaking in a soft tone that wouldn't be overheard. "No, it's the first time she's offered to meet with us.

We need more information than what we're going on. We're going." He nodded.

Anne wished she could hear what Declan was saying. If they weren't in a public place where someone could eavesdrop on their conversation, she'd have Jack put the phone on speaker. But there were still too many people around. People who could be waiting for the opportunity to catch their informer. She stared at the man sitting alone at a table in the corner, reading a newspaper. Anne's eyes narrowed. Or was he?

"Thank you," Jack was saying into his phone. "We'd appreciate the ride." He ended the call. "Declan's coming with Arnold to give us a ride back to the estate after our rendezvous. They'll be here in forty-five minutes or less and wait for us to signal for them to come."

Anne let out a long breath. "It's good to know they'll be here as backup."

He looked at her through troubled eyes, his brow creased.

"What?" she asked, knowing something was bothering him.

"I want Arnold to take you back to the estate. I'll handle this with the team."

She stiffened. "No!" Her heart beat fast at the possibility that Jack might be going into harm's way, and she wouldn't be there with him. "The informer expects to see me with you. If I'm not there, it could go wrong."

"It could go wrong regardless. And I won't let you get hurt," he said, his voice tense.

She touched his arm. "I know you won't. I know you'll protect me. But if we don't do this right, I could be in danger for a lot longer." She squeezed his arm. "Let's just get this over with and see what happens."

"I don't like it," he said.

"I'm sure you don't," Anne said, her jaw firming. "But I'm going. With or without you."

THEY STAYED AT the café until just before time for the designated movie showing. Thankfully, the theater wasn't far from where they were. They could walk the few blocks and arrive in time for the movie.

Jack walked alongside her, his hand protective at the small of her back. Darkness settled in around them. The streetlights flickered on, one by one. "Is this what it would feel like to go on a date with you?" Jack asked. She suspected he was trying to ease her tension.

Anne laughed, the effort helping to calm her nerves only slightly. "I hope not. I'd like to think going on a date with me wouldn't include the threat of being mugged, shot, or run over by a vehicle." She glanced around, looking for any of the threats mentioned. "Why? Are you going to ask me out on a date?"

"The thought crossed my mind," he said, his tone light, his gaze scanning the street, sidewalk and alleys all around them.

Warmth filled Anne's chest. In all the craziness, this man was thinking about asking her out. "If you did ask, I might say yes." She slipped her hand through his arm. It almost felt like they were going on that date. Except for the nagging fear of someone watching them, possibly lining them up in their crosshairs.

A shiver rippled down the back of Anne's neck. That feeling of being watched increased until she felt as if she needed to spin around, run or throw herself on the ground, out of whatever line of fire.

But nothing happened. No one jumped out to nab or stab her. Bullets didn't fly out of the darkness and they arrived in time for the movie at the designated theater.

Using the digital tickets that had been sent to them via text, they entered the theater and Jack walked her past the theater room listed on the ticket.

"Why aren't we going in?" Anne asked in a hushed tone.

"I wanted to make sure no one was following us." He entered the next door, paused just inside and waited.

When no one followed, Jack took Anne's hand.

"Okay, let's meet our text girl." He left the wrong theater and entered the correct one. Once inside, he glanced up at the seats. The lights had already been dimmed for the advertisements. There was enough of a glow from the screen to see which seats were filled and which were empty.

"Let's sit in the seats near the top." Anne liked the idea of having her back to the wall, from where she could see everyone entering and leaving the theater.

"Though I like the idea of having my back to the wall, I'd feel better if we sat near the exit, closer to the middle."

Anne agreed with his logic and they chose a couple of seats on the end of a row, near the exit. As she walked up to her seat, she counted the number of people in the theater. Since it was a weeknight, there weren't many. Most of them were probably tourists who didn't have to go to work the next day. A family of six sat near the back of the room, while several older couples sat in a group near the front. A young couple sat close together, holding hands and sharing a bucket of popcorn. There were more people, who appeared equally innocuous.

Where was their texter girl?

Once Anne took her seat, she couldn't watch the people behind her, which made her feel exposed.

Jack sat a little sideways in his seat, as if looking at her. Anne did the same, looking at him. That way they could see a little to the side and back of them and cover each other's blind spots.

As the time for the movie grew closer, more people drifted in. Some climbed to the top, while others took seats in the middle and lower rows.

A family of five entered the theater and chose the row directly in front of Jack and Anne. They all moved to the center, except the teenager wearing a baseball cap, his shoulders slumped. He sat a couple seats away from the rest and hunkered down. It put him directly in front of Anne.

Anne glanced around. Why had the teen chosen that particular seat? Their informer might come in, see someone too close and move on, afraid of being overheard.

She couldn't do much about it and it was too late to move. The film credits rolled onto the screen and the movie started. The teen chose that moment to stand and walk to the back of the theater, probably to get even farther away from his family, as teens were like to do.

Anne breathed a sigh and relaxed, or tried to, beside Jack, her attention on the people in the room as the giant monster proceeded to crush and destroy everything in its path.

Twenty minutes into the movie, Anne had begun to give up hope that her informer had actually shown up.

Then the images on the screen turned dark until

the theater was almost pitch-black. The moviegoers all seemed to be holding their breath, waiting for the monster to jump out and scare them. When it did, people in the theater screamed and laughed at their own jitteriness. The monster roared, and noise filled the auditorium.

"Anne." A soft voice sounded next to Anne's right ear. When she started to turn to see who it was, the voice continued. "Don't look. I don't have much time. They followed me into the theater. It's only a matter of time before they find me."

"Who followed you?" Anne asked.

"Trinity."

A cold shudder shook Anne's body.

"Why are they after you?" she whispered between the roars of the monster.

"I was one of them. But I'm not anymore."

"I thought they didn't let anyone leave," Jack said, keeping his gaze forward on the screen.

"They don't. You're in for life. I'm trying to avoid the other alternative." She touched Anne's shoulder. "I'm sorry I got you into this. They're after you two now because of me."

"What does finding you have to do with what's happening at the White House?" Anne asked.

"I caught wind of some of their plans."

"What plans? Who are we dealing with? Should I shut down the White House until it's cleared?"

"No," the woman said. "They want the White

House closed. We need to let things happen so we can identify the sleepers. If you shut down the White House, we won't find them before it's too late."

"But if we just let things happen, it might be too late for some," Jack said.

"We can't let Trinity call the shots. Not anymore. They have to be stopped. The security of our nation is at risk."

"Why me? Why us?" Anne asked. "I need to let the Secret Service know what's going on so they can be prepared."

"I know something is going to happen, but I don't know what."

"Can you identify the Trinity agents inside?" Jack asked.

"No. After a certain stage in our training, we aren't allowed to mix and mingle with the others. Knowing other agents allows you to see them when they're coming after you. Trinity doesn't want us to know when the target is one of its own."

"You've given us this warning. What can we do with it? We don't know who we're up against or what their plan is. It's an impossible situation. And the NSC meeting is tomorrow."

"I know. The attack will be after the meeting begins."

"With what?"

"I don't know. But be ready to get out when it goes down."

"Where will you be?" Anne asked.

"Nearby."

"How do we know you aren't one of them?"

"If I was, you'd be dead by now."

Movement behind her made Anne turn. "Wait." She managed to snag the woman's arm.

"Why meet? Why not text us?" Anne couldn't help it. She was suspicious of everyone now and didn't trust the woman who wouldn't show her face.

"Too much texting can be captured. I've endangered you as it is," she whispered before shaking free and rushing away.

In a flash, the woman was halfway down the steps on the other side of the theater, heading for the exit door on that side. She was dressed as the teen with the baseball cap and a hoodie pulled up over the hat.

A couple of dark figures entered from the door close to Jack and Anne.

Anne slid lower in her seat.

The men spotted their informer across the auditorium and ran after her.

The woman slipped through the exit. A few moments later, the two dark figures followed.

"Shouldn't we help her?" Anne asked.

"She's a trained assassin. You're not." Jack texted Declan, then rose, gripped her arm and helped her to her feet. "Come on, we're getting out of here." Then he grabbed Anne's hand and led her out the way they'd come in. Once out in the lobby of the theater,

Jack pulled Anne against the wall, sank his hands into her hair and kissed her long and hard.

A man in dark clothing ran past them and entered the theater they'd just left.

Anne barely noticed. With Jack's mouth crushing hers, all thoughts flew out of her head. She gripped his shirt collar and returned the kiss.

When Jack finally raised his head, he took her hand again and hurried out the door.

Arnold had the car waiting at the curb, with Declan in the passenger seat.

Anne slid in and scooted to the far side of the seat to make room for Jack.

He bent his long frame and dropped into the seat beside her. "Go, Arnold. The sooner, the better."

Arnold jabbed the accelerator. The car lurched forward.

Anne slammed back against the seat and immediately buckled her seat belt.

"What just happened?"

"We had a narrow escape," Jack said.

"Don't speak too soon," Declan said. "We have a tail."

Arnold stepped on the accelerator and made a sharp right turn. The car fishtailed, the rear end sliding across the pavement until the tires engaged and the vehicle straightened.

"We still have them," Declan called out.

Something crashed through the rear window of the SUV, shattering the glass.

"Get down! They're shooting at us." Jack called out. He shoved Anne's head down in his lap and leaned over her with his body.

Arnold picked up speed and then rounded another corner, taking it fast, slinging them sideways.

Anne couldn't see anything but Jack's legs. The safety restraint and Jack's arms kept her from being flung out of her seat. After several more turns, Arnold slowed.

Jack sat up and looked out the window. "I think we lost them."

Anne sat up and pushed her hair out of her face. She glanced back at the hole in the rear window and shivered. Had the bullet hit a few more inches to the left or right, someone in the SUV could have been killed.

Arnold drove them back to the estate, choosing a more circuitous route. It took longer, but they didn't pick up another vehicle with people shooting at them.

When they arrived at the front steps of the Halverson mansion, Charlie, Grace, and the rest of the team came out to greet them.

Anne was glad to have their support. Mostly, she was glad to have Jack at her side throughout the ordeal. She couldn't begin to repay him. She probably wouldn't be alive if not for him.

Jack emerged from the vehicle and helped Anne

to her feet. "Guys, we have to come up with a plan. I have a feeling tomorrow is going to be a rough day."

THE TEAM MET in the war room.

Cole and Jonah had their computer screens up with a variety of images displayed, including a street image of the men getting out of a dark van and entering the theater a few minutes before Jack and Anne left.

"That was close," Cole said. "We had just brought up the theater's webcam when the van pulled up."

"Did you get a license plate on that van?" Declan asked.

"We gave it our best shot. It had what appeared to be a temporary tag on it," Jonah said. "We tried to trace it, but it was a tag from over two years ago."

"What did you get from your informer lady?" Declan asked.

"Not enough." Jack's lips pressed together tightly. "She confirmed our suspicions that she was a trained agent for Trinity."

"Which means they're out to kill her," Gus said. "You know the only way out—"

"—is in a box." Jack nodded. "We know."

"That's why she hasn't come out in the open to meet with us face-to-face up until now," Anne said. "I kind of forced her to do it. I asked for more specifics on what Trinity is planning. I hope she made it out of the theater safely."

"She thinks whatever's going to happen will take place tomorrow," Jack said. "That's the only new info she passed along."

"And tomorrow is the National Security Council meeting," Anne added. "I think we should warn the president and Secret Service."

Jack's brow furrowed. "As our informer said, it will just postpone the inevitable and the sleeper Trinity agents will still be working there until the next attempt is made."

"By holding back the information, we put our president and the people in the White House at risk," Charlie said. "How can we even consider not alerting them?"

Anne nodded. "Security will be extra high during the council meeting. I can't imagine anyone getting into the session who hasn't been thoroughly screened."

"What about the rest of the building?" Jack asked. "What if they create a diversion?"

"There will a full contingent of Secret Service personnel on hand for tomorrow's meeting," Anne said.

"One of which could be a Trinity plant," Declan pointed out.

"We need to have the team inside the White House." Declan turned to Charlie. "Are you okay with us getting past security and inside however we can?"

She held up her hands. "I'm all for the team being there. Whatever methods you deem necessary, short of killing. Although, if it's a Trinity operative, you know what to do." She nodded toward Jonah. "Can you make it happen?"

"I'll do the best I can." Jonah turned to his computer and started keying furiously.

Cole settled in the seat beside him. "We'll need someone with the Secret Service. Some of us can come in as tourists visiting the White House. Tours have resumed since Millicent's incident." He waved a hand in the air. "We've got this. We'll have what we need in place by morning. Get Arnold in here. We might need help getting uniforms and equipment."

"What can I do to help?" Anne asked.

"Get a good night's sleep," Charlie said. "You might be in for a helluva day tomorrow." She took Anne's arm and led her up the stairs. Over her shoulder, she called out, "Let me know if you need anything from me. I'm afraid I'm only good for contacts."

"Thanks, Charlie," Declan called out.

Jack's gaze followed Anne up the stairs. He wanted to go with her but needed to be in on the planning for the day ahead.

Jack turned back to the operation planning. "Bring up a schematic of the White House. This operation could even be more dangerous than some we've conducted in the Middle East. We won't be able to take weapons inside."

Chapter Eleven

Anne lay awake well past midnight, listening for the sound of Jack's footsteps. She'd purposely left her door unlocked, hoping he'd come up and check on her. Maybe she was selfish, but she wanted a repeat of the night before. If things went south the next day, she wanted to have the memory of making love with Jack to be with her no matter what happened.

She must have fallen asleep because the next thing she knew, something was tickling her lips. She opened her eyes to find Jack leaning over her, a smile curving his lips.

"Hey," he said.

She blinked open her eyes.

He wore a pair of running shorts and nothing else.

Anne moved over in the bed, making room for him.

He slipped beneath the sheets and pulled her into his arms. "Go back to sleep. I just wanted to hold you."

"Mmm," she murmured, pressing her lips to his bare chest. He smelled of aftershave and man musk. Anne committed that scent to memory. She felt tomorrow would be a turning point. Whatever happened could set the course for her career, her life and perhaps her relationship with this man. "Promise me," she whispered.

"Promise you what?" he asked, smoothing her hair off her cheeks, tucking a strand behind her ear.

"You won't get hurt." She slipped her arm over his chest and held on tight. "I don't know if I can go through that again."

"Go through what, darlin'?" He kissed her temple and the tip of her nose.

"Losing someone I care about." There, she'd admitted to something she'd tried hard not to do since her husband's death. Care about someone so much it hurt. And a man who was a stranger mere days before. Was she insane? She scooted closer, until her body was flush with his. Yes, she was insane, but she didn't care. For the first time since Mason's death, she wanted someone else in her life and was willing to risk losing her heart again. To a man who risked his life in the work he performed.

His arms tightened around her. "You know, you were supposed to be the job. Nothing more."

"What do you mean, the job?"

"I wasn't supposed to get involved." He tipped her

chin up so that he could stare into her eyes. "But I'm failing at that miserably."

"Miserably?" Her lips twisted. "That doesn't sound good." She tilted her head and pressed a kiss to his chin.

Jack turned his head and captured her lips in a soul-defining kiss that left her breathless and wanting so much more.

"I promised myself I wouldn't love another woman," he said. "But I'm afraid I might be falling for you."

Her heart pounded hard in her chest. "And that's a bad thing?"

"Yes. I'm bad luck to the women in my life."

"How so?" She shook her head. "You've been nothing but good luck for me. I could have been dead twice over if you hadn't come along and scooped me up on the back of your motorcycle."

He held her close, crushing her to his chest. "I'm afraid for you, Anne."

"I'm willing to take the risk," she said.

Jack rolled her onto her back, pressing her into the mattress with the weight of his body. "I'm not sure I'm willing to risk your life, because I want you so badly."

"It's my life. Doesn't that make it my decision?" she said staring up into his eyes. She wrapped her arms around his neck and pulled him down to her. "Make love to me, marine. Whatever this is we're feeling can't be all bad, and we can figure it all out after tomorrow. Let's make the most out of what's left of tonight."

"Tonight, then," he said and proceeded to fulfill all the fantasies she'd had about him before she'd fallen asleep.

They didn't get much sleep, but they made memories into the wee hours of the morning. By the time her alarm went off, Anne was already awake, staring at Jack as he caught a few minutes of sleep. She wanted to remember him so relaxed and sexy, lying naked in the bed beside her. If all went well that day, they might have more nights like this. If not, she'd have her memories to hold close.

The alarm blared. Anne turned it off and pressed a kiss to Jack's lips.

He opened his eyes and smiled. "Is it that time?"

"I'd rather not go to work today at all," Anne said.

He pulled her into his embrace. "If only we could stay here and forget the world outside."

Anne kissed him again and leaned up on her arm. "It's like a bandage that needs to be removed. Let's rip it off and get it over with."

"Then we can pick up where we left off here?"

Anne nodded. "That's the plan." She rose from the bed and padded naked to retrieve her T-shirt from where it had been tossed in the night. After she pulled it over her head, she grabbed her toiletries and paused with her hand on the doorknob.

Jack had risen from the bed and stood looking out the window.

His body was magnificent, all muscle and sinew.

Her core heated again with desire. If only they didn't have to go to work. If only they didn't have to save the world…

With a sigh, she left the room, crossed to the bathroom and got into the shower.

A few moments later, the shower curtain shifted to the side and her handsome former marine stepped into the shower with her. He held out his hand. "Soap."

She gave him the bar and watched in shivery anticipation as he worked up a lather and then spread it over her shoulders and downward to cup each breast and tweak the nipples with his sudsy fingers.

By the time he cupped her sex, she was past ready. When he lifted her by the backs of her thighs, she swallowed the moan rising up her throat and lowered herself over his shaft.

They made love until the water cooled.

Then they dried each other off and dressed quickly, aware of the hour and the fact they had to get to the station in time to catch the early train into the city.

Combed and dressed, they made their way down to the kitchen where the rest of the team had gathered.

"Arnold is driving you two into the city this morning, so you won't have to catch the train."

Anne glanced at the clock. They were still early enough they would miss the worst of rush hour. "Thank you. At least we won't have to worry that there might be bad guys on the train in."

Jack nodded. "Right. Let's save the confrontations for later."

"We can hope there won't be a confrontation at all," Charlie said.

"Then we wouldn't smoke out the Trinity assassins entrenched in the White House," Declan said.

"True," Charlie conceded. "I hate to be a downer, but we'll only be scratching the surface of the organization by identifying and eliminating some of the pawns in their game. Until we find the leader and take him out, we won't hear the end of Trinity."

"You have a point," Declan said. "We'll work on that. Hopefully, we'll recruit Anne's texter to join our team. Between her and Jasmine's help we might have a shot at finding their leader and bringing him down."

Carl had breakfast cooked and laid out on the table. They all took their seats and dug in, not knowing what the day would have in store for them.

Anne could imagine the marines eating like it might be their last meal for a long time. In the desert, they probably went for long stretches without decent meals as they prepared for and conducted battles.

Today would be like that, only in a falsely civilized theater of operations. Even though they'd be in the heart of the city, they would be up against some of the most ruthless opponents they'd ever contended with.

Anne prayed they all came out of it alive.

IF JACK HAD his way, he'd leave Anne at the Halverson estate where she'd be safe. Knowing her like he did, he didn't even suggest it. She wouldn't stand by and let things happen to the people she worked with. If there was any way she could help, she would. Staying home from work wasn't an option, and if he insisted, he worried she'd find a way in, no matter what, without his protection.

With that in mind, Jack held open the door to the SUV Charlie had provided for her to climb into, glad she'd chosen to wear a pantsuit and sensible shoes. If there was any running involved with the day's events, she'd have a better chance in flat shoes than the heels she normally wore with her skirts.

Declan, Mack and Cole were getting into the White House as tourists and would be close by if needed. Arnold and Charlie had pulled some strings and secured a Secret Service uniform for Gus. Jonah had hacked in and had Gus added to the Secret Service roster for the day. Gus had already reported to the Secret Service Office in the West Wing of the White House. Hopefully, he hadn't had any difficulties assimilating. Mustang would enter the West Wing as a new staffer assigned to fill in for Dr. Saunders in the national homeland security advisor's office during Saunders's recovery.

Declan's Defenders would be in or near the West Wing during the National Security Council meeting. They would be able to monitor for anything unusual and be there to help out if something bad were to happen.

Not knowing who would initiate the event or what would transpire had Jack on edge. After spending time in the West Wing, he found it unsettling that some in the building might be Trinity assassins planted over time. He might have passed them in the hallways.

He handed an earbud to Anne.

"What is this?" she asked.

"Radio communications."

She shook her head. "Not that I even know how to use them, but how would we get them past security?"

"Put it with your cell phone when you go through the scanner. If they ask, it's a Bluetooth earbud for your cell phone. The worst they can do is set it aside and hold it until you leave for the day. The best would be if they let it pass and you have it in case you get in a tight situation and you need to communicate with one of us."

She stared at the device as if it might bite her.

Jack chuckled. "It won't hurt you."

Arnold dropped them off a block away from the West Wing. He would find a place to park and remain close by throughout the day. As a prior military man himself, he could provide backup in case they needed him. If nothing else, he would be there to provide transportation should they need to get somewhere quickly.

With a practiced eye, Jack surveyed the surroundings, searching for anyone who seemed out of place or looked as if they might initiate an attack. He kept Anne close to him as they walked to the West Wing and entered. As usual, they passed through the metal detectors, dropped their cell phones and earbuds into a dish to go through an X-ray machine and scanned their IDs. They reached Anne's office without any undue delays. Since it was early, there weren't as many people in the building yet, although there were more than Jack expected.

"Is this usual for this many people to be this early?" he asked.

Anne laughed. "The NSC meeting is a big deal. We like it to go smoothly. Most areas have someone come in early to make sure there are no loose ends remaining to be tied."

"Dedication."

"Some major decisions come out of these meetings," Anne said.

He moved closer and lowered his voice. "Anything dealing with the major pharmaceutical companies?" Jack asked.

"I don't think so," Anne responded. "Why do you ask?"

"I'm trying to connect the dots between the Russian aid worker in the dead Syrian village, the pharmaceutical company experimenting with cancer vaccinations and the potential attack on the National Security Council. None of it's adding up."

"I know what you mean."

"Would the NSC be interested in a pharmaceutical company performing unsanctioned drug testing on humans in Syria?"

Her brow puckered. "That might be something that would be discussed. And the word *sanction* brings up another thought. Imposing sanctions on a country known to conduct biological warfare on populations." Her eyes widened. "Do you think Trinity is working with the Russians and the big pharmaceuticals? Maybe they don't want the NSC to shut down trade between the US and Russia. It might cut into their profits."

Jack pulled his cell phone from his pocket and called Jonah. "I need you to check into members of the NSC and who might have connections to Waylon Pharmaceuticals. Text me with anything you might find as soon as you get it. Thanks."

A knock sounded on the door to Anne's office.

Jack, being closest, opened the door.

Gina poked her head inside. "Mr. Louis wants to see you, Anne."

"Thank you, Gina. I'll be right there."

Gina left, closing the door behind her.

Anne glanced at Jack. "Be careful today."

"Same to you." He winked. "I'm counting on seeing a lot more of you."

She crossed to where he stood, leaned up on her toes and pressed a kiss to his lips. "Me, too."

Jack pulled her into his arms and kissed her hard, his tongue pushing through to slide along hers in a long, sexy caress. Then he set her away from him. "Do you still have your earbud?"

She patted the pocket of her suit jacket and nodded.

"Don't forget to use it."

"I won't." She gave him one last glance before he opened the door and stood back.

"Have a good day, Ms. Bellamy," Jack said. He prayed she would have that good day.

Anne left the office and went to the one next door.

While Anne met with her boss, Jack fitted his earbud in his ear and switched it on. "Testing," he said quietly. "Snow here."

"Gus here. Stationed outside the NSC room as sentry."

"Declan here with Cole and Mack, waiting to get into the White House tour. Close by, if you need us."

"Mustang at Dr. Saunders's desk, awaiting computer access. Deliver me from boredom."

"We can only pray for boredom," Jack said softly.

"Amen," Declan responded.

"Arnold?"

"On a park bench, feeding the pigeons. Here if you need me."

"Is Ms. Bellamy wired?" Declan asked.

"She has the gear," Jack said. "Whether she chooses to use it is up to her."

"Gotcha. Stay cool," Declan said. "And call if you need us."

"T minus two hours and counting." Jack said. "See you at close of business."

Unable to sit still for long, Jack paced the length of the office, turned and paced back. The NSC meeting wasn't for another two hours. What would he do until then? He sat at the computer and thumbed through what little data he could tap into. As a new staffer, he still didn't have access to much. Not that there would be anything on the White House database that could incriminate any of the president's advisors. They'd have to be completely stupid to put anything on the shared databases that could compromise their careers.

He did find a draft copy of the NSC agenda Anne had worked on until it was finalized.

Jack glanced through the topics and yawned, until he got to the line listing the scheduled address by the director for Europe and Russia. He was to speak on Russia's most recent involvement in the Middle East and move for sanctions.

Had he been close when he'd speculated that some folks on the council would not want sanctions imposed against Russia? Would some people do anything to stop the sanctions from being invoked?

Leaving the office, Jack strode through the halls of the West Wing, too wound up to stay in one place. He was back in his own hallway when Anne emerged from the national security advisor's office.

She smiled as she walked toward him, a stack of paper in her hand. "Can't stop. Have to get to the conference room to help with setup," she said as she passed him.

"Can I help?" he asked.

Anne shook her head. "Sorry. Just me and the conference room facilitator, Terrence Tully."

He tapped his ear with a pointed look as a reminder that she had an earbud for communications, should she need it.

She gave a brief nod and continued down the corridor toward the conference room.

Jack's gaze followed her until she disappeared around a corner. He wanted to go after her and be with her every second of the day but knew he couldn't. She had a job to do, and he couldn't follow her everywhere.

It didn't make it any easier knowing someone might make a move that day.

The wait was excruciating. But the longer they waited, the longer the people in the building remained unharmed.

Chapter Twelve

Anne hurried to the conference room where the NSC meeting would take place. A Secret Service agent was in the room with a K-9.

The dog had its nose to the floor, sniffing. After a complete circuit of the room, the Secret Service guy nodded toward Terrence Tully, the conference room facilitator, who stood in the corner. "It's all yours." And the agent left.

"Hey, Terrence." Anne smiled. "How've you been?"

He moved about the room straightening chairs and setting out water glasses for the attendees. "Good. You?"

"Great," she answered, lying through her teeth. Anne laid a paper copy of the agenda on the conference table in front of each chair.

"Long agenda today?" Terrence asked.

"The usual," Anne responded. "Missed you at the last meeting."

He shrugged. "I've been traveling a little. Had to burn some use-or-lose vacation."

She nodded, familiar with the life of a staffer at the White House. Too often they lost vacation time because they couldn't take the time off. Or, in her case, had no reason to take the time off.

Alone since her husband's death, she had no desire to travel. Without someone to share the beauty of the places visited, there didn't seem to be a point.

Her thoughts drifted to Jack. Traveling with him could be fun. She could imagine lazing on a beach beside him, soaking up the sun. Or hiking a mountain trail in Colorado.

Shaun stuck his head in the door. "It's almost time. POTUS is on his way."

Her heart skipped several beats and she stepped to the door where Shaun stood. "Let me know if you need anything. I'll be in my office."

Shaun's eyes narrowed. "No, you won't."

Anne frowned. "What do you mean?"

"You're staying here. I want you here. You'll stand in the back of the room in case I need you to answer any questions."

"Are you sure?" Anne asked.

"Absolutely. Unless you had other plans."

If anything was going to happen that day, the target had to be the National Security Council meeting, where all the key players were present. Again, she worried that she should have warned the Secret

Service of the potential attack. At the very least, she would be in attendance, watching for any preemptive signs from any of the staff or supporting staff. She could be there to help get people out, if things went south.

Anne squared her shoulders. "I'd be honored to attend."

"Good, because it's time."

The vice president arrived, followed by the secretary of state, secretary of defense, secretary of treasury, director of national intelligence, director for Europe and Russia, the director for Asia, director of foreign policy and others.

Anne moved to the back of the room, out of the way, as the advisors to the president assembled in the room and stood behind a chair, waiting for the president. Each person wore his best suit, and was clean-shaven and perfectly coifed.

A Secret Service agent entered the room first.

The vice president stood at attention and announced, "Ladies and gentlemen, the president of the United States."

Everyone stood at attention as the chief executive walked in and took his position at the head of the conference table. "Please, take a seat," he said.

The meeting began with reports from the various advisors as they worked their way down the agenda. When they reached Chris Carpenter's agenda item on Russian sanctions, Anne tensed.

Chris cleared his throat and plunged in. "As you are aware, the Russian bombing of a base in Syria was investigated and found to be deliberate and catastrophic, with over three hundred civilian casualties and twice that many injuries. The Russian president has no comment. We stood by while Russia waged war on Crimea without lifting a finger. I move that we, as a nation, impose sanctions on Russia until they cease waging war on civilians."

Immediately, the other members of the National Security Council jumped in, everyone talking at once.

"One bombing is not sufficient grounds to impose sanctions," Anne's boss said.

"Maybe not, but how about Russia allowing one of its largest state-owned pharmaceutical companies to secretly test drugs on human subjects in Syria?" Chris's comment was met with stunned silence.

Anne held her breath, wanting to jump in with what she knew. She waited for Chris to explain his statement.

"As you all are aware, a member of my staff was injured by a hit-and-run driver in the street right outside this compound. You could put it down to an accident, but I say it was deliberate. She had just met with Dr. Schuster, who I've asked to join us today." He waved a hand toward the director for Europe and Russia. "Dr. Schuster, what did you share with Dr. Saunders?"

Dr. Schuster nodded toward the screen on the wall. "If you could bring up the image…"

The screen flickered and the grainy image of the Russian aid worker came into focus. "Our ambassador in Russia received a communication from this man, whom we later identified as Aleksandr Orlov, a Russian aid worker deployed to a small Syrian village, where he was supposedly giving regular vaccines to the local population. The World Health Organization has since found that the vaccine administered was a drug called XC-16, designed to eliminate cancer."

Anne held her breath. This was exactly what they'd discovered.

"The drug had only been tested on mice and found to be unstable and potentially dangerous. If released, it could decimate a population." He waved toward the image on the screen. "That entire village and the Russian aid workers are dead. Given the company that sent the drug to Syria is owned by the Russian government, we contend the Russians knew the potential harm and still tested it on humans, without getting their consent or informing them of what they were getting into. The vaccines were probably passed off as something innocuous, like the ones for measles, mumps and rubella. We can't know, since the entire population of that village is unable to answer questions."

"That, Mr. President," Chris said, "along with the bombing and the crimes against Crimea, are sufficient justification to impose sanctions on Russia."

The president glanced around the room at his advisors. "Although I agree the charges are egregious, imposing sanctions against Russia is a big step with lingering ramifications." He looked around the room at his other advisors. "How many of you agree with Mr. Carpenter's proposal?"

Anne looked at the faces of those present, trying to read into their expressions.

"Sanctions could disrupt the balance of power throughout Europe," the secretary of state said. "Many Europeans rely on the Russians for many of their products and there are many US corporations that would suffer if they were unable to do business with Russia."

Out of the corner of her eye, she saw Terrence back into a corner, close his eyes and cover his ears.

Alarmed, Anne turned to face him when an explosion rocked the building and sent her crashing to her knees.

People yelled, women screamed, chaos ensued.

The president's bodyguards scooped him out of his chair and rushed him from the room.

The remaining members of the council scrambled from their chairs and ran for the door.

A Secret Service agent grabbed the vice president's arms and hurried him toward the exit.

"Ms. Bellamy, come with me." Terrence Tully gripped her arm and helped her to her feet. "We have to get to somewhere safe."

Shaken and disoriented, her ears ringing from the concussion caused by the explosion, Anne let him guide her toward the door, following the vice president and his bodyguard.

They ran down the hallway and entered another door that led to another, and finally ended up at a side door marked Emergency Exit Only.

They burst through, out into the open, near a street.

Sirens wailed, emergency vehicles screamed around corners in the distance and people ran from the building.

Once outside, Anne slowed, digging her feet into the soft ground. "Wait. We have to help the others out of the building."

"No, we don't." Tully bent, slung her over his shoulder in a fireman's carry and ran toward a white van.

Anne, her ears still ringing and her world turned upside down, fought to free herself of his hold. "Let me down!" she yelled.

Her cries could barely be heard over the wailing sirens converging on the White House. Anne screamed louder when she caught a glimpse of a

Secret Service man angling toward the van, with a gun held to the vice president's head.

The man shoved the vice president alongside Terrence.

"Let us go!" Anne shouted. "You can't get away with this. That's the vice president of the United States."

Tully didn't answer, just carried her to the van.

The door opened before they reached it and a man jumped out.

As Tully stood her upright, the man from the van slung a large gunnysack over her head, trapping her arms inside.

Anne jerked free of his hands and ran. Unable to see, she tripped and fell,

Someone landed on her back, knocking the air from her lungs.

She fought, kicked and yelled for help, but no one came.

Again, she was lifted off her feet, then deposited on the floor of the van. The sound of the door sliding made Anne twist and struggle against the sack. She rolled to the side and ran into something hard and unmoving. The door slammed closed and she had no way to escape.

JACK HAD BEEN pacing in Anne's office when the explosion sent him sprawling against the tile floor. He rolled to his feet and ran toward the offices, touching a finger to his earbud. "Declan, did you hear that?"

"Roger. Tourists are being ushered out. I tried to dodge the security staff, but there's no getting by. We're heading out on the White House lawn."

"Mustang?" Jack queried as he pushed through the rush of people running for the exit.

"Still in the West Wing," Mustang said in Jack's ear. "Secret Service is herding people out. I've managed to duck them by hiding in a closet."

"Gus?" Jack murmured as he passed several of the men and women that were scheduled to be in the NSC meeting.

For a long moment, Gus didn't answer.

Jack listened for Gus's response, worry eating at him when he didn't see Anne among those rushing down the corridor from the conference room where the meeting was to be held.

"Gus?" Declan queried.

"Sorry," Gus said, the sound of heavy breathing coming through the connection. "I'm sitting on the guy who set off the explosion. Caught him with his hand on the detonator, dressed as Secret Service personnel."

"Jack," Declan said into Jack's ear. "What about Ms. Bellamy?"

Jack arrived at the door to the designated conference room. Everyone had made it out. The room was empty. "I'm here. In the room they were sup-

posed to meet. No president. No vice president…"
His stomach sank as he made a clean sweep of the
room. "No Anne."

"Did you give her the earbud?"

Jack exited the conference room and ran in the
opposite direction from where he'd come. "I did.
Bringing up the GPS on my phone now." Thank
God, the earbuds were also equipped with a GPS
tracking device. As long as she didn't lose it, they
could find her.

Still dashing down the corridor, searching every
room along the way, Jack brought up the application on his cell phone and held his breath, waiting
for the reassuring green dot to appear on the map
grid.

When it did, he stopped running. "Damn." His
pulse pounded so hard he couldn't hear himself think
and his knees grew weak.

"What?" Declan's voice came through as if in a
tunnel.

"She's not even in the building."

"Not in the building?"

"No." Jack performed an about-face and ran
back through the corridors of the West Wing. "She
must be in a vehicle, because she's moving quickly
through the streets, heading for the highway."

"We're almost to the exit of the West Wing," Declan said. "Meet you there."

"Arnold?" Jack said. "Can you make it to the street with all the emergency personnel in the way?"

Arnold gave them a location a couple of blocks away.

Jack caught up with Mustang on his way out of the building. They were delayed briefly by the Secret Service staff but made it out to find Declan, Cole and Mack waiting for them.

"Gus is staying to make sure his guy doesn't get lost in the shuffle. Needless to say, the man isn't talking. Gus said he had the Trinity tattoo on the inside of his wrist, beneath the watch he wore. He's definitely one of the sleepers."

Jack didn't wait around to ask or answer questions; he took off at a sprint, pushing past people who stood on the streets, staring at the White House, wondering what had happened. He didn't have time to stop and fill them in. Anne was moving farther away by the second. If they didn't catch up with her soon...

He couldn't think what would happen to her if they discovered she had a tracker on her. Hell, even if they didn't, what were their plans for the White House staffer?

Jack was first to arrive at the corner where Arnold was just pulling to a stop.

He jumped into the front passenger seat.

Declan, Mack, Cole and Mustang dove into the back seats of the big SUV.

"Go! Go! Go!" Jack urged. He held his phone in

front of him, watching as the green light crossed the Potomac into Arlington. "They're getting away."

Declan leaned over the back of Jack's seat and touched a hand to his shoulder. "Not as long as she has that tracker on her."

Jack's heartbeat slammed against his chest. He willed the SUV to move faster, but the traffic held them at nearly a standstill. They inched forward, crawling through downtown toward the 14th Street bridge. Once they reached the major highway, they would gain some speed. In the meantime, Anne's signal showed them blowing through Arlington, heading west.

A call came through on his phone from their informer.

Though he didn't want to switch applications, Jack had to.

"Go ahead," Declan said. "I've got Anne's tracker up on my phone now."

Jack answered the call.

"Did everyone make it out?" The voice he recognized from the movie theater sounded in Jack's ear.

"No," Jack gritted out. "Someone has Anne. We have them on a tracker, but we don't know how long it will be before they figure out she has one. They're heading into Virginia."

"On my way," she said.

Jack gave her the route they'd taken and the direction the tracker was headed.

"I'll catch up," she said. "Let me know if things change. You can reach me at this number for now."

Jack wanted to throw the phone out the window, he was so mad at the woman for putting Anne at risk.

Anne didn't have a cell phone on her. She wouldn't be able to call them. If they were going to use her to negotiate a trade for their informant, how were they going to get in touch? And would their defector agree to the trade to save Anne's life?

She by God better. The Trinity-trained woman was in a much better position to defend herself than Anne. Anne didn't have any skills in self-defense, a situation Jack promised he would remedy as soon as he got her back.

Assuming they got her back alive...

He couldn't think that way. Anne was a fighter, even if she didn't have combat skills. She was smart and could figure out a way to survive. She was strong and determined.

Jack brought up the tracking application and held his breath until the green light appeared again. They had to get to her before anything bad happened. And when they did save her, it was all on for bringing down Trinity. No organization should be able to pick off someone like Anne, just because she'd had contact with one of their defectors. And no covert organization should be able to infiltrate the US government so thoroughly. Trinity had to be stopped.

Arnold proved to be an excellent driver, weaving

his way in and out of traffic, slowly closing the gap between them and Anne's location. At the rate they were gaining, they might actually catch up to them before they pulled off the main road. As it was, the goons were only ten miles ahead of them.

As long as the police didn't try to pull Arnold over for exceeding the speed limit by thirty miles an hour, they had a chance.

Jack leaned forward in his seat, willing the SUV to go faster. At some points, they were flying down the interstate at over one hundred miles per hour. Already, they were a danger to other vehicles on the road.

Arnold handled the vehicle like a professional race car driver, cool, calm and collected. It was just as well he was doing the driving. Jack was anything but calm and composed.

Five miles between them. Five miles away from Anne. They had to catch up to them before they turned off onto smaller roads. That would slow their speed significantly and make it harder for them to catch up.

If anything horrible happened to Anne...

No, he couldn't think that way. He couldn't allow his past to shape his future with Anne. For her sake, he had to let those thoughts go or he wouldn't be effective. And she needed him at the top of his game, not dragged down by memories. He was more than capable of finding her and helping her. And meting out justice to her abductors.

Jack shook his head. The black cloud that hung over him could not affect her. She would not be the fourth victim of his bad luck.

His mother's death had been because of the cancer. Not him.

Kylie had been a victim of a shooter.

Not Jack's bad luck.

And Jennifer, the nurse he'd met while deployed, had died because of an IED explosion.

None of those had anything to do with the fact he'd loved them. None. Of. Those.

Then why did he feel he was responsible for their deaths? He was the one factor in common with those three women. He'd loved them. And he was falling in love with Anne. Holy hell. He was falling in love with her.

His chest was so tight he could barely breathe.

The vehicle they were following was now only three miles ahead of them. Then two.

"Go, go, go," Jack murmured. Slowly, the distance reduced until only one mile of road stood between him and Anne.

Jack stared ahead, his gaze searching the vehicles in the distance. Which one was Anne in? Then he saw it.

A white van hogging the left lane swerved right

and left, trapped between the vehicle in front of him and the one in the right-hand lane.

"There." Jack pointed. "That has to be them." He looked down at his phone.

The car in the right lane exited the highway.

The white van whipped into the right lane and sped past a truck that had been blocking the left lane.

Arnold increased his speed.

As they approached the truck, it moved to the right lane.

Arnold passed it and caught up to the white van.

"That's them," Jack said, his lips pressing into a thin line. "Now what?"

Chapter Thirteen

Once she was bagged and dumped into the van, Anne had been secured by being wrapped in what she imagined was duct tape. They'd sat her up and circled her body, gunnysack and all, several times with tape, making it impossible for her to move her arms. Thankfully, the sack was made of a loosely woven material. She could breathe and even see shadowy forms through the gaps between the threads.

Once they were out of the city, the driver increased their speed, weaving in and out of traffic. Every time he swerved, Anne rolled across the floor of the van and bumped into someone she assumed was the vice president.

The entire time, she wiggled and shifted, trying to work the sack and the tape up her body. It was a slow process and she didn't know if she was being watched, but she couldn't do nothing. She thought about the earbud she'd put in her pocket. By now, they were well out of range of the two-way radio.

And it didn't matter because she couldn't see where they were going.

If she was going to get out of the situation, she had to do it on her own. And she had to do something. She couldn't stand by and let these people hurt the vice president of the United States.

After a while, a voice sounded from the front of the van. "We're being followed."

More promising words could not have been spoken.

Hope swelled in Anne's heart.

"How did they find us?" someone else said. "Check them. One of them might have a phone or tracking device on them."

While the van driver increased his speed and swerved between vehicles, the other two men in the vehicle worked over the other captive first.

"You won't get away with this," Anne heard the vice president say. "By now they will have launched helicopters. Every law enforcement agency will be on the lookout for you. They'll set up roadblocks."

"Shut up." A loud smack sounded, followed by a grunt.

Anne bunched her legs up and kicked hard at one of the shadows she could see squatting in front of her.

The man fell over, cursed, righted himself and punched her in the side of the head.

Pain knifed through her temple and she saw stars.

"VP's clean," a man said.

"Check the woman."

Something sharp nicked Anne's arm and the tape around her was cut loose.

With her arms somewhat free, Anne scrambled to shove the gunnysack off her head.

When she managed to free herself, hands reached out and grabbed her from behind. The man wearing the dark suit of a Secret Service agent knelt before her and ran his hands over her body.

Anne kicked at him, landing a heel in his gut.

He grunted, grabbed her ankles and yanked her hard, laying her flat out on the floor of the van, and threw his body over hers. He straddled her hips and continued his search.

The man holding her arms gripped her wrists and pulled them up over her head.

She thrashed and twisted her body, but she was pinned by the weight and strength of her captors.

He found the earbud in her pocket and held it up. "What's this?"

"It's my earbud. I use it to listen to music," she said, praying he wouldn't take it. If by some slim chance the vehicle following them contained Jack or any member of his team, she could use the communication device to contact them.

"Give it to me." Terrence Tully, the driver, held out his hand.

The man sitting on her slapped it into the man's palm.

A moment later, the earbud flew out the window.

Anne's heart sank, but she refused to give up hope.

"That's all the electronics I found."

"Cufflinks?" Tully asked.

"None."

"Ditch their shoes," the man holding her wrists said.

The man sitting on her twisted around, yanked off her shoes and handed them to Tully. They flew out the window, as well.

"Lose the tail," commanded the man sitting on her.

The driver turned sharply, sending the van off the nearest exit.

Anne couldn't see where they were headed, but the vehicle slowed.

Good. Slow was good. The people following them might have a chance of catching up.

The man sitting on her reached for a roll of duct tape and wrapped it around her ankles.

Though she fought, struggled, bit, kicked and cursed, they sat her up and secured her wrists behind her back. She tried her best to leave a gap between them to give her a chance to work her way out. Alas, they cinched them tightly and shoved her onto the floor.

One of the men sat near the rear of the van, looking out the back window; the other two looked out the front. Rain started falling, slowing them down as they wound through curvy back roads, hydroplaning as puddles built on the road.

"Turn here," the man who'd moved to the passenger seat said.

The driver cut sharply to the right, slinging Anne over onto her side again.

"I think we lost them," the man in the back called out.

After another short burst of speed, Tully turned to the left. The new road was bumpier, and water splashed up against the side of the vehicle. Had they turned onto a dirt road?

Again, Anne tried to sit up and look out the window. The rutted road made it difficult. When she finally managed to sit up, she braced her back against the side of the van and stared out at what she could see from the floor of the van.

Tree limbs drooped over the road, brushing against the sides of the vehicle. The rain and the tunnel of greenery blocked out the sun, making it appear dusky outside.

If they'd lost whoever was tailing them, they'd never find them out in the backwoods.

Anne glanced over at the vice president. "Are you okay?" she whispered.

He lay on his side, his wrists and ankles bound much like hers. He nodded. "They will mobilize the military and deploy all the law enforcement agencies."

The man peering out the back window snorted. "By then, it'll be too late."

"What is it you want?" the VP asked.

The dude looking out the back threw a glance toward Anne. "Ask her."

She frowned. "I'm nobody. What do I have that you could possibly want?" She knew, but she wanted to hear them say it.

The man in the passenger seat turned and snarled at Anna. "A connection to her, the woman who betrayed us."

"Who are you talking about?" the VP asked.

Passenger-seat guy jerked his head toward Anne. "Ms. Bellamy knows. She's known all along. If she hadn't hired someone to look out for her, we'd wouldn't have had to go to so much trouble."

Anne dropped all pretense. "For one, I don't even know who she is. All I know is you are all part of Trinity. And she wanted out. I've never even seen her face."

Passenger-seat man's hand snaked out and slapped her hard across the cheek. "You lie."

Anne flinched, her chin going up. "It's true. She only talks to me via text."

"You met with her in the movie theater. We almost had her then."

"You saw more of her than I did," Anne said. "She was behind me."

"Doesn't matter. You are our bargaining chip."

"Do you really think she'll hand herself over to you in trade for me?" Anne snorted.

"If not you—" passenger-seat guy tipped his head toward the vice president "—then the VP."

"Trinity trained her to be ruthless," Anne argued. "She's probably halfway across the country by now."

"That's not her style," Tully said. "She's hung around the DC area for over a year. We just couldn't catch up to her. She's a master of disguise and an expert at technology. She wouldn't have involved you if she didn't feel like she could save the world."

"Well, her plan backfired. She didn't save anyone," Anne said. "She'll be long gone."

"If you hope to live," the guy in the passenger seat snarled at her, "you better hope she's not."

The van lurched to a stop.

"Everyone out," Tully said.

The two not driving exited the van. One reached in and pulled the VP out, bent forward and threw him over his shoulder. The other man waited until they were out of the way, then reached in for Anne.

She scooted across the van floor, trying to get away.

He grabbed her ankle and yanked her to the edge of the floor and then flung her over his shoulder and marched toward a little white farmhouse that had seen better days. The windows had been boarded up and the front porch drooped as if the posts it was built on had rotted through.

Tully parked the van as far beneath a tree as he could, got out and hurried to the house.

He tried the door handle. When it didn't open, he cocked his leg and kicked the door hard. It flew open, crashing against the wall inside. The roof over the porch shuddered.

Anne twisted and struggled. With her wrists and ankles bound, she couldn't do much.

The man carrying her entered the house and dropped her on the floor.

She hit feetfirst but couldn't get her balance and crumpled to the floor, hitting her hip and then her shoulder. "That's going to leave a bruise," she muttered. Bruises were the least of her worries, though. Trinity recruits were trained assassins. From what she'd learned from John Halverson, they were very secretive and didn't like anyone knowing who they were.

The fact Anne and the VP had seen their faces could be bad news. They didn't let people live who could recognize them. Another reason to kill their defector.

Even if they got Anne's informant to agree to trade herself for the release of Anne and the VP, they wouldn't be good on their word. They'd kill the defector, Anne and the VP, too.

Anne had to find a way out of this mess and get the VP out, as well. She wasn't ready to die.

She glanced around the room, searching for anything she could use to cut through the tape around her wrists.

Whoever had abandoned the house had left little in the way of furniture. But there was an old wooden crate in one corner and a stack of yellowed newspapers.

After the Trinity assassins dumped their captives, they stepped out onto the porch.

Through the open door, Anne strained to hear what they were saying.

From what she could tell, they were checking for cell phone reception.

"It should be enough to get through to him," Tully said. He entered the house and stood in front of Anne. "What's the phone number of your boyfriend?" he demanded.

"I don't have a boyfriend," she said, her chin rising. She wished Jack was her boyfriend, but they barely knew each other. Hadn't she insisted they weren't obligated to a commitment just because they'd slept together?

Tully pulled a gun from his jacket pocket and pointed it at the VP's head. "What's your boyfriend's phone number?"

Anne struggled to remember, her heart slamming hard against her chest. She told him what she thought it was and held her breath, praying it was correct.

He dialed the number, hit the call button and

touched the screen again to put it on speaker. The phone rang once.

"This is Snow."

Tully smirked at Anne. "Got your girlfriend and the VP. We want to make a deal with you."

"Are they alive?"

"Yes."

"I want proof."

Tully nodded toward the man closest to Anne.

He reached down, grabbed Anne by her hair and yanked her head back.

Tully shoved the phone close to her face. "Say hello to your lover."

JACK HELD HIS breath, waiting for the sound of Anne's voice.

"Jack." Anne sounded scared but strong.

He let go of the breath lodged in his throat. "Anne, are you okay?"

"We're fine," she said. "For now."

"We'll find you." Jack's free hand clenched into a fist. "And when we do, we'll kill every last one of the bastards."

A man laughed on the other end of the connection. "Won't do you much good to find them, if they're already dead. Keep your shirt on and get in touch with our traitor. Tell her it's her for these two. You have one hour before I start shooting. I don't care who goes first." His tone grew sharper. "Maybe you do." Then he ended the call.

"We have to find them," Jack said.

"They can't be far. We had them up to the last turn."

Jack knew they'd found and ditched the tracking device when they'd passed the location of the green dot and the van they'd been following was still way ahead of them.

Then the van had veered off the highway onto an exit and taken to back roads. They'd managed to keep up for several miles. Then the van seemed to disappear.

The fact that it had started raining didn't help. And the deeper they went into the backwoods, the narrower the roads became and the denser the vegetation. The van could have gone off the road and been swallowed up by trees and bushes.

Arnold had pulled off the highway onto a dirt road and stopped the vehicle.

Jack had nearly come apart. "We can't stop now. They might be right around the next curve."

"Or we could have passed them already," Arnold argued. He got out of the SUV.

"Where are you going?" Jack asked, preparing to take the driver's seat if Arnold wasn't willing. "You can't quit now."

"I'm not quitting. I'm getting something that will help us get a better view."

That was when the call had come through.

While Jack had been on the phone with Anne's captors, Arnold carried what appeared to be a remote-control drone to the front of the SUV. The others had gotten out, as well. Arnold laid the drone in the middle of a dirt road and reached into the back of the SUV for the controls. In less than a minute, he had the drone rising into the air, the images it recorded showing up on the video display.

After the assassin ended the call, Jack leaped out of the SUV and ran to Arnold, who stood staring at the monitor while maneuvering the joystick on the controls.

"See anything yet?" Jack asked.

"Not yet," Arnold said, his head down, concentrating on the screen in front of him.

"You'd better contact your Trinity informer," Declan said.

Jack redialed the number of the woman who'd gotten Anne into this mess in the first place, anger and frustration making him want to hit someone. Preferably the people holding Anne hostage.

"Sitrep," their informer said as she answered.

"They want to make a trade."

She sighed. "I was afraid it would come down to that. Current location?"

"I don't know where they are but hang on." He texted her a pin drop of their location and then got back on the phone. "How soon can you be here?"

"Three minutes, tops. I'd almost caught up with you when you left the highway. Then I lost you."

"Sounds familiar. We lost the white van we were following, but our guy is looking for it with a drone."

"Good thinking."

Two minutes later, a motorcycle pulled up behind the SUV and a woman climbed off, pulled off her helmet and shook out long, auburn hair.

She walked straight up to him and held out her hand. "Jack Snow, I'm CJ Grainger."

He recognized her voice, even if he didn't recognize her face. "You got her into this, what are you going to do to get her out of it alive?"

"I don't know yet."

"We have less than an hour to figure it out," Jack said.

"There," Arnold said. "Do you see that?"

Declan, Mustang, Cole and Mack crowded around the monitor.

"I don't see anything but treetops and a tin roof," Declan said.

Arnold pointed to the right of the tin roof at the top of a tree. "See the white angles making corners on the edges of the green tree?"

Jack shoved his way through the men gathered around and stared at what Arnold pointed at. "That could be the van."

A movement beside the house caught their attention. A man stepped out from beneath the porch and walked to the tree, where he opened what was clearly the door of a vehicle.

"That's it," Jack said. "Where are they from here?"

Arnold pulled his phone from his pocket and touched an icon. A map opened up, with a blue dot and a green dot. "We're the green dot. The blue dot is the location of the drone." Arnold glanced at Declan. "Drive the SUV. I'll fly the drone."

"We can't go storming in. The Trinity operatives will kill their captives and disappear into the woods," CJ said.

"We'll get close and go the rest of the way in by foot," Jack said.

With that plan in mind, the men piled back into the SUV and followed the directions on Arnold's phone app.

CJ brought up the rear on her motorcycle.

When they were within half a mile of the location, they pulled the SUV off the road and hid it in the brush. Declan's Defenders got out. Arnold opened the rear of the SUV and handed them a variety of weapons, including three AR-15 semiautomatic assault rifles with scopes, two 9 mm Glocks, a couple of smoke grenades, a small brick of C-4 plastic explosives and two detonators.

"Are we going to war?" CJ asked.

"We don't know how many there are of them," Jack said, as he fitted a full magazine into the pistol he held. "And you're damn straight we're going to war. They infiltrated the White House, set off an explosion, and they're holding Anne and the vice president of the United States hostage. I consider what they've done an attack on this country."

CJ nodded. "Point made."

Declan stepped forward. "Secret Service, FBI, other agents are aware the VP has been taken. They'll be searching soon, following leads. My guess is this battle will be joined soon enough by more forces."

"Are you armed?" Jack asked CJ.

She nodded. "I have what I need. But I thought you would want me to offer myself up in exchange before you go storming in and risk getting them killed."

Jack shook his head. "Everything we've learned about Trinity is that they don't negotiate, and they don't let anyone live who might be able to identify them."

"You've got it right," CJ said. "I'm letting you know now, though, I would willingly let you trade me for the hostages if I thought it would do any good."

"It won't," Declan said and slammed his magazine into the Glock he'd chosen to carry. "Let's go. We're wasting time."

They moved out, slipping through the woods, paralleling the road in to the small farmhouse.

As they neared the house, they stopped and assessed the situation.

Two men stood on the porch.

From what Jack could see, someone was moving around inside. He couldn't see Anne or the vice president. He assumed the man moving around inside was guarding the two hostages.

Declan held up three fingers.

Jack nodded.

Declan gestured to Mack, who carried one of the AR-15 rifles. He motioned for Mack to cover them.

Mack moved to a better position, dropped to the ground and pointed his rifle at the men on the porch.

Cole held up the C-4 explosives and indicated the van.

Declan nodded and pointed to his watch, then held up five fingers, giving Cole five minutes to set the charges and give them time to get in position.

Which left Mack, Mustang, Declan, CJ and Jack to get in, take down the bad guys and rescue Anne and the vice president.

They circled the house and came at it from the back, where the trees and brush grew closer to the structure.

Jack prayed they were doing the right thing by going on the offensive versus attempting a trade.

Either way, someone was going to die that day. And he hoped it wasn't going to be Anne or the vice president of the United States.

Chapter Fourteen

Anne slowly worked her way into the corner with the old wooden crate. Two of her three captors had stepped out of the house, leaving only one to watch over her and the vice president.

The man inside was the guy who'd been watching the rear of the van as they raced out of DC. Now, he looked like he was bored, and paced the floor.

Every time he turned away from her, Anne pushed herself backward, sliding on her bottom toward the crate. When he spun and paced back in her direction, she froze.

Finally, she made it to the crate. She rubbed the tape across the rough corner of the wooden crate. One by one, she could feel she was tearing through the layers of tape until the last piece ripped and she was able to pull her wrists free.

Her captor spun and walked toward her.

Anne held her breath, afraid the man had noticed she'd moved and was coming to ask her why.

But then, he seemed to change his mind, as if he was too preoccupied by something else, and he stepped out the door.

Quickly, while he was out of the house, she peeled the tape off her ankles, leaving a piece across the top to fool the assassins into thinking she was still bound.

The three men all entered the house together.

"Time's running out," Tully said. He hit Redial on his cell phone and punched the speaker button.

The phone rang and rang, finally going to Jack's voice mail.

Tully growled low in his chest. "I've decided. I'm shooting the girl first." He punched the end button and glared at Anne. "Guess he wasn't that interested if he's willing to let you go first." He raised his pistol and aimed it at Anne's head.

"I'm going outside." The man who'd been pacing stepped out of the house. The other shrugged and joined him.

Which left Terrence with his gun still pointing at Anne's head.

"Why do you suppose your boyfriend didn't answer his phone?"

"How do I know?" Anne said. "He might be in a dead zone."

"I can tell you who is going to be in a dead zone."

"Don't." The vice president spoke up. "Don't shoot her. If someone has to go first, let it be me."

"Sorry, dude," Tully said with an evil smile. "You're our ticket out of here alive. Once we have our defector, we'll need leverage. You're a big-ticket item that will buy us a chopper out of this." His smile turned to a sneer. "No, the lady is expendable. You're not."

Anne bunched her muscles. With Tully staring at her, she didn't stand much of a chance of getting away, but she'd be damned if she sat still and waited for a bullet to blow through her head.

Just as she was about to throw herself at him, an explosion shook the little house. Sheetrock crumbled and fell from the ceiling. Part of the tin roof flew off, exposing the inside of the building to laden skies.

Tully dropped to the floor, cursing. "What the hell was that?"

As he staggered to his feet, Anne took the opportunity she needed and threw herself into him, hitting him like a football linebacker. Since he didn't have his balance, yet, he fell backward, landing hard on his back. His gun hit the ground and slid across the floor.

The sound of shots being fired outside made Anne duck automatically.

When her captor reached for his weapon, Anne beat him to it and kicked it out of range. He grabbed her ankle and pulled hard.

Anne twisted but fell to her knees. She kicked and kicked again, but his grip was too strong. Then she turned and aimed her kicks at his face, catching him in the nose. He yelped, let go of her ankle and pressed his hand to his face.

Anne crawled across the floor and reached for the gun.

"Drop it or I'll shoot the vice president," someone said behind her.

Anne rolled to her back, the gun in her hand aimed at the door.

The man who'd been in the van's passenger seat during their ride stood leaning heavily on the doorframe, blood dripping from a wound to his left shoulder. He held a pistol in his right hand, aimed at the vice president.

"Don't shoot him. I'll drop it," she called out, setting the gun on the floor beside her.

The wounded man shifted his aim to her. "I should have killed you first."

Anne refused to close her eyes. Refused to show her fear. If the man was going to shoot her, he would have to look her in the eye, knowing he was a bastard.

The sharp report of gunfire sounded.

Anne waited for the impact, the pain and the bleeding.

When none of that came to pass, she touched a hand to her chest and watched as the man holding the gun on her dropped to the floor.

Jack stepped into the doorframe, a handgun

gripped in his fist. His gaze swept the room. When it landed on Anne, the tension seemed to melt from his body. "Anne."

A movement out of the corner of her eye made Anne turn away from the best thing that ever happened to her.

Tully was scrambling across the floor, toward the gun the dead man had dropped.

Anne swept the weapon she'd dropped from the floor, sat up and pulled the trigger. The kick surprised her. But her aim was true.

Tully dropped where he was and lay still.

Jack collected the guns from the floor and stuck them into his pockets. Then he went to Anne and drew her to her feet and into his arms. "I didn't know what I would find. I'm so glad I found you alive."

She captured his face between her palms and kissed him hard. "Hold that thought." Then she broke free of his embrace and dropped to her knees beside the vice president. "Sir, are you all right?" She removed the tape from around his wrists while Jack freed his ankles.

"Yes." The VP laughed, the sound cracking. "I am now." He sat up and rubbed the raw skin on his wrist. "And I have you to thank for that."

At that moment, Declan entered the little house. "We took care of the guy out front." He and Jack helped the vice president to his feet and out onto the porch.

Arnold drove the SUV up to the house and ushered the vice president into the front passenger seat as Anne and Jack walked down off the porch, hand in hand.

"You don't know glad I was to see you," Anne said. "How in the world did you find us?"

"Your earbud had a GPS tracker in it."

"But the driver tossed it from the van back on the main highway."

Jack grinned. "And they lost us. But we have our secret weapon." He tipped his head toward Arnold. "Charlie's butler is a man of many talents. He had a drone and an arsenal in the back of the SUV. The drone we used to locate the white van, and the weapons...well you know the outcome of that."

A woman wearing a black leather jacket and matching pants approached them. Her long auburn hair fell down around her shoulders like a fiery curtain. "Anne Bellamy," she said and held out her hand.

Anne stared at the hand. "I know that voice."

"I'm CJ Grainger, former Trinity operative."

Anne took the hand and pulled the woman close, frowning. "You show up now? After all we've been through?"

CJ nodded. "I'm sorry. Had I shown up earlier, I'd be dead, and these guys would still be active in the White House. Trinity is down three operatives."

"Make that four," Declan corrected. "Gus caught the one who set off the explosives in the West Wing."

Anne let go of CJ's hand, the frown easing. "Forgive me if I'm not so grateful. It's been a tough day."

CJ smiled and touched Anne's arm. "I'm sorry I brought you into it, but I had to have someone on the inside to look out for the others." She nodded toward the vice president. "If I thought you would have survived a trade, I would have done it in a heartbeat. But I know how Trinity works. They don't leave witnesses."

"What are you going to do, now that we know who you are and what you look like?" Jack asked.

CJ shrugged. "I guess I'm going to have to re-engage. I can't disappear completely. Trinity will never leave me alone as long as it's still in existence."

"Then you'll help us bring Trinity down?" Declan asked.

CJ nodded. "It's good to know I won't have to do it alone."

"Come on," Declan said. "We need to get the VP back to DC before they mobilize the military."

Two F-35 fighter planes flew overhead.

Mack laughed. "Too late."

"I'm sure they scrambled as soon as the explosion went off in the West Wing," Cole said. "And I'll bet the president was hustled out of the White House onto the Marine One helicopter and taken to Andrews and Air Force One."

A larger airplane flew overhead.

All eyes turned to the sky.

Jack chuckled. "Good call, Cole. That's Air Force One." He handed his cell phone to Anne. "You better call your boss and let him know you're all right and you have the vice president with you."

Anne did just that, thankful that she was able to report the good news. Things could have turned out a lot different had Jack not given her that earbud and if Arnold hadn't brought along a drone. She hadn't known how lucky she was going to be when that man on a motorcycle appeared outside a bar in DC to whisk her away to safety.

When she was done with the call, she reported to Declan. "They're sending a helicopter out to pick up the vice president. We're about to be bombarded with federal investigators, county sheriff, state police and every other law enforcement agency in the area." She turned to CJ. "Now would be a good time to disappear."

CJ nodded. "I'll meet up with you soon."

"Come to the Halverson estate," Declan said. "Charlie will want to meet you."

CJ smiled. "I look forward to it. She's filling a big pair of shoes her husband left behind. John Halverson was a good man with good intentions. I'm glad to see she's carrying on with his legacy." She drew in a deep breath. "Thank you all for helping me smoke out the trouble in the White House." CJ gave a mock salute, turned on her black bootheels and vanished into the woods.

Anne slipped her arm around her hero and leaned into him. "I guess we can't leave yet, can we?" She sighed. "It's been a long day."

"And it will be a lot longer before we get back to Charlie's." He hugged her close. "But I'm okay with that. As long as you're here with me."

"Same."

The day slipped into evening. A helicopter arrived, landing in a field near the small farmhouse. The president had armed the helicopter with a press secretary. A slew of law enforcement personnel came, questioned and went. And the reporters... they swarmed to the location almost as quickly as the agents.

The press secretary fielded all the questions and reassured the country that the president and vice president were well, and on their way back to DC. It would be business as usual in the White House come Monday morning. No, it wasn't a foreign terrorist attack, but a homegrown terrorist strike. No mention was made of Trinity.

Anne was okay with that. She didn't want the bad guys to get all the attention. And with Declan's Defenders on to them, it was only a matter of time before they were neutralized.

When they got back to the Halverson estate, it was close to midnight.

Charlie met them at the front entrance and hugged every one of them. Carl had food prepared in the kitchen. Everyone ate in silence, promising to de-brief in the morning.

Anne ducked into the shower, rinsing off the dust and grime from the explosion and the abandoned farmhouse. Standing in front of the mirror, she tallied the new bruises and counted herself lucky that bruises were all she'd acquired.

She entered her bedroom and stood at the door in the T-shirt she'd been using as a nightgown. How many days had it been since she'd first met Jack? It hadn't been many, but it seemed like a lifetime.

And though she'd spent the past eight hours with him, she couldn't wait to see him again. Leaving her room, she went to the one next door and knocked lightly.

The door opened immediately. Jack took her hand and drew her through. He'd had his shower before her, and his hair was still wet. He looked so good and strong it made her heart swell.

"I wish I'd known all I had to do was get attacked to meet a man like you, Jack Snow. I would have done it years ago."

"Years ago, it might not have been me."

"Good point. I'm glad I wasn't attacked until recently. And I'm even more grateful my hero turned out to be you."

He tipped her chin up and stared down into her eyes. "If I recall correctly, you're my hero. Seems you shot a man to save my life."

She shrugged. "If I hadn't shot him, you would have."

"I don't know. I was so glad to see you I didn't see him going for that gun."

"We make a good team." She leaned up on her toes and linked her hands behind his head, bringing his face down to hers. "Enough talk about heroes. I'm more interest in making love with you."

"Yes, ma'am. That's a much better use of our time." He swept her up in his arms and carried her to the bed, where he proceeded to make mad, passionate love to her.

Anne fell asleep in Jack's arms, happy to prove to herself that love could come to a person a second time in life. And Jack was the man who'd helped her realize it.

Epilogue

Jack sat at the conference table in the war room below John Halverson's study, having slept in until eight o'clock. Anne sat beside him, holding his hand beneath the table. All was better with the world, but not quite good enough.

Yes, he had the woman of his dreams beside him. She was well and alive after a frightening attempt by Trinity to kill her. Which brought him to the conclusion something had to be done about Trinity.

Declan stood at the end of the conference table, a cup of coffee in his hand. He looked tired, like all of them felt. "I've been trying to figure out what the vaccination deaths in Syria had to do with the explosion in the West Wing," he said. "We learned this morning that Waylon Pharmaceuticals completed a sale of one of its divisions this morning. It happens to be the one doing the research on the nanotechnology-based cancer vaccination. If sanctions had been voted in, that sale would not have taken place. Maybe it's adding one plus one and coming up with three, but we think the explosion delayed implementing sanctions long enough to complete the sale. We think they only wanted to delay a decision on imposing Russian sanctions. At the same time it gave Trinity the cover they needed to kidnap the vice president and Anne so they could lure CJ out of hiding."

"Seems like a lot of trouble for those two goals," Jack said.

"The sale netted close to a billion dollars," Declan said.

Mustang and Gus emitted low whistles.

"That might be worth disrupting an NSC meeting," Jack admitted.

"That brings us to why we're all here this morning." Declan took a deep breath and continued, "Though I never had the pleasure of meeting John Halverson, I feel as though I've gotten to know him through the people whose lives he touched and the work he was doing to bring down a mafia-like organization that has the potential to rot our great country from the inside out."

Jack nodded, his lips pressing together.

"You all know Jasmine, aka Jane Doe, a former member of Trinity." He nodded toward Jasmine, who sat beside Gus at the conference table. "And most of you got to meet the latest addition to our little team yesterday at a little farmhouse in the Virginia countryside." He waved a hand toward the auburn-haired woman who stood near the door.

She had politely refused to take a seat, as if being in an enclosed room made her nervous.

"CJ is with us because she wants the same thing we do. The destruction of Trinity. We've managed to eliminate some of the operatives, but there will always be more where they came from, as long as the organization remains intact."

"We need to cut off the head of the snake," Jack said.

Declan nodded. "In order to effect change, we have to neutralize their leadership. We hope that between CJ and Jasmine we can learn more about the inner workings of Trinity so that we can find the leader of the organization and take him down."

Charlie sat at the other end of the table, her hands folded together on the surface. "My husband died trying to do what you all are about to undertake. I hope you succeed where he did not. And I pray you all survive the effort. If anyone feels they've done enough and want out, now's the time to go. No hard feelings. I will understand and stand by your decision."

Declan raised his eyebrows. "Anyone want out?"

As one, the men of Declan's Defenders responded with a resounding, "Hell no."

"Okay then," Declan clapped his hands together. "Let's make it happen."

He turned to CJ. "You've put yourself at risk by joining forces with us. You need someone to have your back and look out for you."

CJ shook her head. "I don't need a bodyguard, if that's what you're suggesting."

"I'm not suggesting that," Declan said. "Cole is more like the eyes in the back of your head, an extension of your abilities."

CJ frowned. "Cole?" She looked around the room at the men. "Which one of you is Cole?"

Cole lifted a hand.

She snorted. "Again, I don't need a babysitter or bodyguard. I've managed to survive on my own for over a year since I left Trinity. If I have someone following me around, that leaves me even more exposed."

Cole lifted his shoulders. "It's your choice. But it helps to have another set of eyes watching your back. We've been a team for a long time. Each man on this team has saved my life at least once, and I've saved theirs."

"I'll think about it," CJ said. "And if I agree to this arrangement, it will be on my terms. For now, I've got work to do to figure out who the leader is of Trinity. Thank you for inviting me to come here today. It is nice to know I'm not alone." She turned and started for the stairs leading out of the basement. She'd only gone three steps when she turned back. "Cole, I'll be in touch."

"Do you need my phone number?" he asked.

"No need. I'll find you," she said confidently and left.

Jack chuckled at the look of irritation on Cole's face. "Cole, I suspect you will have your hands full with that one."

Cole's brow creased. "I suspect you're correct in that assumption." He drew in a deep breath and let it out. "Well, let's get this party started.

* * * * *

YOU HAVE JUST READ A
HARLEQUIN®
INTRIGUE®
BOOK

If you were **captivated** by the **gripping, page-turning romantic suspense,** be sure to look for all six Harlequin® Intrigue® books every month.

COMING NEXT MONTH FROM

(H) HARLEQUIN

INTRIGUE

Available January 21, 2020

#1905 WITNESS PROTECTION WIDOW
A Winchester, Tennessee Thriller • by Debra Webb
In witness protection under a new name, Allison James, aka the Widow, must work together with her ex-boyfriend, US Marshal Jaxson Stevens, to outsmart her deceased husband's powerful crime family and bring justice to the group.

#1906 DISRUPTIVE FORCE
A Declan's Defenders Novel • by Elle James
Assassin CJ Grainger has insider knowledge about the terrorist organization Trinity after escaping the group. With help from Cole McCastlain, a member of Declan's Defenders, can she stop Trinity before its plan to murder government officials is executed?

#1907 CONFLICTING EVIDENCE
The Mighty McKenzies Series • by Lena Diaz
Peyton Sterling knows she can only prove her brother's innocence by working with US Marshal Colin McKenzie, even though he helped put her brother in jail. Yet in their search for the truth, they'll unearth secrets that are more dangerous than they could have imagined...

#1908 MISSING IN THE MOUNTAINS
A Fortress Defense Case • by Julie Anne Lindsey
Emma Hart knows her ex-boyfriend's security firm is the only group she can trust to help her find her abducted sister. But she's shocked when her ex, Sawyer Lance, is the one who comes to her aid.

#1909 HER ASSASSIN FOR HIRE
A Stealth Novel • by Danica Winters
When Zoey Martin's brother goes missing, she asks her ex, black ops assassin Eli Wayne, for help. With a multimillion-dollar bounty on Zoey's brother's head, they won't be the only ones looking for him, and some people would kill for that much money...

#1910 THE FINAL SECRET
by Cassie Miles
On her first assignment as a bodyguard for ARC Security, former army corps member Genevieve "Gennie" Fox and her boss, former SEAL Noah Sheridan, must solve the murder he has been framed for.

YOU CAN FIND MORE INFORMATION ON UPCOMING HARLEQUIN TITLES, FREE EXCERPTS AND MORE AT HARLEQUIN.COM.

HICNM0120

Four Days Until Trial

Sunday, February 2
Winchester, Tennessee
It was colder now.

The meteorologist had warned that it might snow on
Monday. The temperature was already dropping. She
didn't mind. She had no appointments, no deadlines and
no place to be—except *here*.

Four days.

Four more days until *the* day.

If she lived that long.

She stopped and surveyed the thick woods around her,
making a full three-sixty turn. Nothing but trees and this
one trail for as far as the eye could see. The fading sun
trickled through the bare limbs. This place had taken her
through the last of summer and then fall, and now winter
was nearing an end. In all that time she had seen only

"Life," he said after a moment, his accent thicker than it should have been, almost as if his temper was high, which wasn't in the least bit rational, "is all about compromise."

"Really?" she asked. Her eyes searched his, and she looked somewhere between amused and genuinely baffled, which somehow made it worse. "How would you know?"

Cayo tossed back the rest of his espresso and decided he was tired, that was all. There was no deeper reason for any of this. How could there be? He hadn't slept. That was why his head was so muddled. Why he could not seem to sort through his own thoughts, his own motivations. Nor even his own reactions.

"I am finding it difficult to track all of your accusations," he said after a moment, his tone dry. Almost conversational. "You believe I am a sociopath, yet last night you told me I am also afraid. Today I am unfamiliar with compromise. Before, I was Godzilla, was I not?" He was fascinated by the color that rose in her cheeks, and then equally intrigued by the way she squared her shoulders, as if withstanding an attack. "I believe I take your meaning, Miss Bennett. I am a monster without equal."

Monster. It was only a word, he told himself then, as it seemed to echo hard in him, recalling that white-washed village high in the Spanish mountains, his grandfather's harsh pleasure on his eighteenth birthday. *It is just a word. It means nothing.*

"You are a man who assumes that his will is sufficient permission to do anything he likes," Drusilla said slowly, as if she were considering each word carefully. "There are no consequences for the things you do." She reached for her tea, and poured a stream of the hot liquid into the delicate cup before her. Her gaze flicked to his, then away. "It would never occur to you to care."

He wanted to touch her with a new kind of fury, so intense was his desire to feel her skin against his. To take that mouth of hers and learn it, own it, make it his. To follow her down onto the nearest flat surface and lose himself inside her, at last.

But he did nothing of the kind. He held on to his control by the faintest, thinnest thread. Again.

"Of course not," he said coldly, as if there was nothing steaming up the air between them, as if there were no tension at all, no desire, no *need.* He reached for the *Financial Times* folded beside his plate and told himself he was dismissing her as he'd always done before, without thought. Without a single care, as accused. "That's what I pay you for."

It was a remarkably long trip.

I didn't want you to leave, he'd said.

Dru couldn't stop replaying it in her head, again and again. She handled the packing, the delivery of appropriate clothes for Cayo from the Milan ateliers he preferred and her own hurried selections from La Rinascente, the city's premier department store hardly a stone's throw from the Duomo. She sent out a flurry of emails, made the day's series of phone calls, and carried out the usual duties of her job, accustomed as she was to performing it wherever she happened to find herself.

But she couldn't seem to get last night out of her mind. The chill of the air, the inky dark and his hand so soft against her cheek. That storm in his midnight gaze that had crashed through her, too. That still did. Why should a few quiet words and a couple of touches affect her so? Why should she feel as if everything was different, when nothing seemed to have changed at all?

They boarded one of Cayo's jets in Milan late that evening, and Dru made her way to her usual bedchamber. She stretched out on the bed and dared not let herself succumb to the turmoil inside herself, not when there was still the rest of her two weeks to live through. She couldn't let herself crack so soon. She'd never survive.

When she woke hours later, they simply went to work as if they were in the Vila Group's London headquarters rather than on a plane headed across the planet. She sat right there at his side in the area set apart for business. She queued up his calls, handling the many details of each, presenting him with the necessary documents and background materials he needed, and reminding him of anything he might have forgot or overlooked as the calls wore on. She prepped the various people who rang in, alerting them to Cayo's shifting moods and often suggesting ways to combat them. Between calls, they discussed various strategies to employ or different approaches to take to tackle each new issue or person.

"I'm tired of his games," Cayo said of one mutinous board member at one point, raking his hands through his hair in agitation. "I want to end him."

"That's one approach." Dru removed a stack of documents from in front of him and replaced them with another, larger stack. "Another might be to simply work around him the way you did with the Argentina project last year. Isolate him. Who will he play his games with then?"

Cayo eyed her for a moment, an approving gleam in his dark gaze that should not have given her so much pleasure.

"Who indeed?" he asked softly.

Dru made sure his coffee was always hot and fixed to his taste, and insisted that he eat something substantial after a certain span of time, simply serving him a meal if he refused to step away from the work at hand. When his voice took on that particularly icy edge that boded only ill, she calmly suggested he repair to the master suite to either rest or work out his temper on the exercise equipment that flew with him everywhere. She was on top of their travel plans, too; making certain that there was not the smallest chance that Cayo Vila should find himself inconvenienced in any small way, no matter where he was in the world or what he had to do. All of which she'd done a million times before.

But it wasn't the same.

Something really had changed last night, and it permeated even their most simple exchanges. The very air between them seemed electric, charged. Her hand brushed his and they both froze. She looked up from her tablet to find him watching her, a brooding sort of expression in those dark eyes of his, the gold in them gleaming in a way she didn't recognize. But she *felt* it. In her breasts, deep in her belly. In her limbs that were too heavy today, her breath that she couldn't quite catch.

It made her wonder. It made her too hot, too shivery, *too aware*. It made her want—again, anew—what she could never have.

Some seventeen hours into the almost twenty-four-hour trip, plus refueling stops, and they had worked roughly nine of them. Hardly half a day's work in Cayo's book, Dru knew. They took a break, sitting in the common area of the plane. Dru sipped at her water and knew better than to ask why Cayo was watching her with that new, disconcerting light in his eyes. Dark and considering, as if he had never seen her before. As if that strange, dream-like conversation on the terrace in Milan really had shifted something fundamental between them. That, she was sure, was why she felt almost watery, insubstantial. Needy and breathless. Unable to think about anything but Cayo, in all the ways she shouldn't.

"Why Bora Bora?" he asked. "When I suggested you take a holiday, I assumed you'd go to Spain. Portugal, perhaps. This seems like something of a reach."

Dru rolled the water bottle between her palms, letting the cold glass soothe her, letting the sound of the engines wash over her like white noise.

"Why *not* Bora Bora?" she asked lightly. "If working for you has taught me nothing else, it's to demand the best in all things."

"Indeed." Some fire flared there, in that golden topaz gaze, and for a moment she couldn't look away. Then his lips quirked into a hard sort of smile, sardonic and faintly amused. "I'm delighted to discover you take indolence as seriously as you take everything else."

"Perhaps all I want from life is to sit under a palm tree and stare at the sea," she said, though the very thought was faintly unnerving, somehow.

"And be waited upon hand and foot?" he asked, a note in his voice she couldn't decipher.

She thought of Dominic's ashes, packed away in the tin that functioned as an urn and sat in the center of her bookshelf back in London. And of the promises she'd made, to him and to herself. That she would let him go into the wind, the water. The least she could do was honor the man he might have been, had he made different choices, or been stronger against his own demons.

And she knew that she needed it, too. The closure. The ceremony. A way to let go, once and for all.

"Something like that," she said now, not quite meeting Cayo's eyes.

He didn't believe her. She could see it in the way he shifted in his deep leather seat, as he scraped that thick, black hair back from his brow.

"How debaucherous." It was a taunt. And it hit hard, though she should have been impervious to him.

"I leave that kind of thing to you, Mr. Vila," she snapped.

Unwisely.

Everything seemed to pull taut. There was no air, no sound. Dru had the panicked sense that the plane had dropped from the sky—but no, Cayo did not move a muscle, it was only in her head. She felt her heart thud hard against her chest, then slow, and she could not seem to look away from him, from that hard mouth of his that she could not pretend she didn't crave. From that dangerous light in his eyes as he stared back at her.

"Is that a challenge, Miss Bennett?" he asked softly, that voice rolling through her, turning all of that need into an ache, insistent and sweet, burning her from the inside out. His cruel mouth moved into a hard smile, and she felt it like a caress. "I will endeavor to live up to your fantasies."

Did he know? Dru felt herself flush. Did he know what kept her awake—what tormented her, what she could see all too clearly even now—that delicious fusion of what had happened in Cadiz and on the yacht and what she imagined came next—

"But first," he continued in that silky, supremely dangerous tone, his gaze narrow on hers even as he gestured toward his phone again, "let's close this deal in Taiwan."

Dru felt hollowed out and more than a little light-headed with jet lag, not to mention her own much too vivid imagination, when they finally made it to what she assumed was Bora Bora, but which could have been anywhere for all she was able to discern in the thick, heavy dark.

The helicopter they'd taken after their landing in Ta-hiti set down in a small field lit with tall tiki torches. The night was close and warm, sultry against her skin. She could smell the sea and the deep green of wild, fra-grant growing things. The sweetness of flowers hung heavy, like perfume against the dark, and when she tipped her head back to watch the helicopter fly away again, she had to stifle a gasp at the brilliance of the stars that crowded the night sky. The roar of the heli-copter faded, leaving only a deep tropical hush behind. It seemed to arrow into her soul.

"Come," Cayo ordered her impatiently, and strode off.

Porters appeared from the darkness to handle the bags, and Dru followed Cayo over a wooden walkway, lit with more torches and hemmed in on all sides with lush greenery. Even in the dark, Dru could all but taste the burst of *jungle* all around her. Cayo was ahead of her, his long legs eating up the distance and before she knew it, she was hurrying—matching her stride to his, just as she'd always done.

Just like the dog on a leash he'd threatened to make her, a small voice inside of her pointed out. She shook it off.

Cayo stopped walking before a large Polynesian-style house with high, arched rooftops and wide, open windows that stretched the length and width of the walls, featuring pulled-back sliding shutters and unobstructed views.

And on the other side of the walkway was water. Nothing but dark water, lapping gently against the shore, and off in the distance, a smattering of low lights. Dawn was coming, bluing the inky night. Dru could make out a mountain in front of her, off on its own island across the water, black and high.

"This is the villa," Cayo said.

He looked down at her as she drew closer to him, his ruthless face softened, somehow, by the soft tropical dark. Or perhaps she was only being fanciful. The torch lights surrounded them in a halo of golden light, and somehow made it seem as if they were standing even closer together than they were. As if there was nothing else in the world but the two of them, adrift in all this lushness.

"I don't know why you would ever leave a place like this," she said, trying to shift the focus back to the place. Away from the two of them. She smiled, but suspected it looked as nervous, as unsettled, as she felt. Still, she pushed on. "But perhaps it takes a different kind of imagination to conquer the world from this far-off little corner of it."

And suddenly he was too close, though she hadn't seen him move. He loomed above her, his shoulders wider than they should have been and his chest too broad, and he was too close for Dru to breathe, too close for her to do anything but lose herself in the dangerous amber of his gaze.

Her pulse went crazy beneath her skin. Her mouth went dry. And she felt that long, low ache between her legs.

His hard gaze slammed into hers, as if he meant to hold her there with the force of it. And sure enough, Dru found she couldn't move.

"Don't speak to me like I'm another one of those investors," he said fiercely. Almost angrily. "Don't expect me to dance to your tune simply because you make a bit of cocktail conversation."

He was right, she had been doing exactly that—and she hated that he'd seen it so clearly. That he'd seen *her*. She'd always thought she'd wanted that but the truth of it terrified her. It was her job to read him, not the other way around. Never the other way around!

"My apologies," she bit out. "I won't point out your lack of imagination again."

He didn't speak. He only reached over and dragged his thumb across her lips, testing their shape, and it wasn't a soft touch, a lover's caress. It was starkly, undeniably sexual. If she hadn't known better, if it hadn't been impossible and unthinkable, Dru would have said he was staking his claim. Imprinting her with his touch, as he might brand cattle or stamp a logo onto a product. Leaving his mark.

She should have slapped his hand away. Instead, she burned. Long and slow and deep.

The way she always had. The way she always would.

"Believe me," he said, and his voice was so soft and still so demanding. So consuming. A thread of sound in the sultry night, surrounded by flickering golden light and the wild, incapacitating staccato of her own heartbeat. "My imagination grows more vivid by the hour."

Dru's lips felt as if they were on fire, and she could feel his touch all through her body, coursing through her veins, even after he dropped his hand and eased away. Her heart didn't stop its frantic beating. Her mouth was

still so dry, her stomach in a knot. She felt him everywhere. And for a long moment, he only looked at her,
his dark eyes hot and shrewd and that cruel mouth im-
passive.

And even that felt like a touch, and with the same
result.

Cayo turned then to greet the smiling man who approached them, from inside the villa Dru realized she'd
forgot about entirely. When he looked back at her, his
gaze was too dark to read.

I didn't want you to leave, he'd said on the terrace in
Milan, half a world away now. And still it rang in her,
through her, like a bell. *I still don't.*

She wanted that to mean something. She *wanted.*
And she could still feel his touch moving through her,
making her his as surely as if he'd tattooed his name
on her skin in the blackest ink.

You're tired and overwrought, she told herself, fighting back another surge of heat behind her eyes. *Nothing
will feel like this in the morning. It can't.*

"You look exhausted," Cayo said, his gaze moving
over her face, making her imagine he could read her
every thought that easily. He nodded, as if coming to
some kind of decision, and the way his mouth curved
then looked self-mocking. "Frederic will show you to
your rooms."

And then he walked away, disappearing into the
thick night.

Leaving her to make sense of what was happening
to her—to them—on her own.

Fighting off emotions she couldn't understand, much
less process, Dru obediently followed Frederic through
the villa. There were tall, vaulted ceilings and the same
rich, dark wood she'd seen outside. Airy, spacious

rooms without proper windows, simply cut-out spaces in the walls to let in paradise on all sides. Bright-colored wall hangings, low and inviting sofas in magentas and creams. Polynesian artifacts on built-in shelves in the walls, and glorious flowers scattered across ornamental tables. She followed Frederic down a level and then outside again. They walked along another, far shorter path that delivered her to a private bungalow splayed out over its own private pier. Here, too, the walls were open to the night, letting the softest of breezes into the expansive suite. Dru couldn't seem to breathe deeply enough to take it all in.

And again—still—all she wanted to do was dissolve into the tears she knew were waiting for her and cry herself dry. Cry until she couldn't feel this anymore, whatever this was: Cayo and the dark and that touch, imprinted on her skin. Claiming her.

With a smile, Frederic showed her the glass floor hidden away beneath a rug in the sitting area.

"In the day," he promised, "you will see many fish. Even turtles."

"Thank you," she whispered, summoning her smile from somewhere.

"Sleep now," the man said kindly. "It will be better when you sleep."

And she wanted to believe him. She did.

Everything felt too huge, too unwieldy, she thought when he left. Her own head. This place. Cayo, of course. Cayo most of all. It all felt impossible, and painful. It hurt from the inside out. She moved over to the opening across from the four-poster bed draped in filmy mosquito netting from high above, and looked out at the water and the smudge of orange light behind the mountain in the distance. Daybreak was coming. And she was in paradise with the devil, and she burned for him as if she'd already fallen. Perhaps she had. Perhaps that was why this had hurt so much from the start.

There was no reason at all she should cry now. She wiped away the tear that tracked its way down her cheek. And then all the ones that followed. She felt her face crumple in on itself, and had to pull on reserves she hadn't known she had to breathe through it—to fight back the sobs that she knew lurked *just there* and would be the end of her.

She must not give in. *She must not start.* It was only two weeks, and less than that now. She needed to be strong only a little while longer.

Oh, Dominic, she thought as she crawled on to the bed, not even bothering to change out of the clothes she'd been wearing across several continents and more time zones than she could count. *I wish you could see this place. It's even better than you dreamed.*

Her last thought as she drifted off into blessed unconsciousness was of Cayo. That mesmerizing curve of his hard, impossible mouth. The touch of his hand in the cold, wet dark, so hot against her chilled skin. That unquenchable fire that burned ever hotter, ever brighter by the day, no matter how she tried to deny it. No matter how hard she fought. He would destroy her. She knew it. She'd always known it—it was one of the foremost reasons she had to leave him.

So there was no reason at all that she should be smiling against the soft white pillows as she drifted off into oblivion.

CHAPTER SIX

DRU WOKE TO sunshine on all sides. It streamed in the open windows of her room, bathing her in light and the sweet, fragrant breeze. It felt like some kind of blessing, chasing away what shadows remained from the long night before. She stretched luxuriously on the soft mattress and told herself she was fine now. Fully restored. Cayo's touch, his talk of debauchery, that fire that only seemed to build between them—it was all part of a darkness dispelled. She was sure of it.

She rose from her bed and dressed slowly, in deference to the sultry weather. She pulled on a loose and flowing pair of linen trousers and paired them with a strappy black vest. Then she swept all of her hair up into as sleek a ponytail as was possible in this climate. The result, she thought, frowning at herself in the mirror, was as close to tropical and yet professional as she was likely to get. She slipped on a pair of thonged sandals and stepped outside, where it appeared to be well into a perfect afternoon.

Dru blinked in the brightness and took in her surroundings. There was another pier down from her bungalow with a selection of small watercraft drawn up to it and on the shore nearby. She could see water in all directions, a darker blue on the far side of the island and that stunning turquoise beneath her bungalow in what must be the famous Bora Bora Lagoon.

She walked back into the villa and was struck anew by the beauty she'd only partially registered last night. The dark wood, the high ceilings to draw up the day's heat, all of it exposed to the tropical paradise and thus a part of it, too. The jungle pressed in on all sides, with the sea just beyond. It felt as wild as it did welcoming, and made something in her seem to ease as she stood there.

When she finished eating a simple meal of toast and tea out on one of the many terraces overlooking the water, she felt restless. Cayo typically did not expect her to rush to work after a long-haul flight unless he had explicitly stated otherwise, so she didn't feel she had to seek him out at once. She assured herself any employee would feel the same—that it had nothing to do with all the churning emotion he'd stirred in her the night before. *Nothing at all.* Instead, she wandered down to the wooden path and followed it. It ran down to the pier, then on, making its lazy way down to the farthest point of the island and then looping back around.

Palm trees rustled over her head and bright flowers bloomed jubilantly on either side of the tidy boardwalk. She could hear birds up above and the waves against the shore. It made perfect sense to her that Dominic would have wanted this to be his final resting place. The sun was warm on her face, the breeze a caress against her skin. She felt serene. At peace.

All you needed was a good night's sleep, she told herself firmly.

As the villa came into view again, perched up over its own gleaming white beach, she saw there was a whole section of it she'd yet to explore. It was not until she left the path and climbed up for a closer look that she realized that what looked like a separate wing was, in fact, Cayo's master suite.

The wide-open walls meant she could step inside too easily and so, giving in to an urge she didn't recognize, she stepped into the first of the rooms, and then sucked in a sharp breath. It was an airy space appointed with deft masculine touches, bold colors and clean lines, but the centerpiece was the massive bed that dominated the room. *Cayo slept here last night,* a little voice whispered. Or perhaps more recently, as it was still unmade, the snowy white coverlet tossed to one side, the pillows dented.

And suddenly, Dru went hot all over. Then cold. Almost as if she was feverish.

She reached over and traced the indentation in the nearest pillow with a fingertip. She imagined him naked and dark against the crisp sheets, that perfect, impossible body on display, her own body softening and melting at the pictures in her head—

It was clearly time to find the man—her boss, she reminded herself sharply—and concentrate on what remained of her time in this job, not on her incurable madness where he was concerned. Not on the way she burned.

She glanced at the art and small collections of statues and carvings as she made her way down the hall, peering into each room as she passed. There was a library fitted with a wall of books, a seating area within and a covered lanai outside with a plush loveseat and two armchairs—perfect for a read in the shade. There was a private lounge with a flat-screen television on one wall and a fire pit with a dramatic chimney on the other, and what looked like a built-in bar in the corner.

And then an office suite, kitted out with computers and other equipment, sleek modern furniture—and Cayo.

Dru stopped in the doorway, watching him as he frowned down at his laptop with his mobile clamped to his ear, as usual. His hair looked unruly, as if he'd spent hours raking it back with his fingers, and he'd neglected to shave. It made him look even more dark and sexy than usual. Unpredictable, somehow. Edgy.

"You misunderstand me," he was saying in cold, deadly French into his mobile. "It is no matter to me whether we ever open a plant in Singapore. But I suspect it is of great importance to you. Perhaps you'd like to rethink your tactics?"

He looked absurdly beautiful, as if someone had carved him into being from the finest stone and set him among lesser statues. He fairly gleamed in the golden sunlight streaming in behind him. He looked terrible and great the way the old gods might have, dangerous and mighty, and if he'd announced that he could command the weather at his whim, she would have believed it. The storm within her howled into being anew, the fever and the yearning, and he was to blame.

He raised his head then and met her gaze. Her stomach dropped and she stopped kidding herself about *serenity* and *a good night's sleep.* It was as if he was inside her, provoking her, making her ache and burn.

He looked at her as if she were naked and beneath him. And Dru couldn't help but wish she was, no matter how much she hated herself for her own eternal weakness.

Cayo sat back in his chair, his eyes on her as he finished the call with an abruptness that she knew must have made the man on the other end wince. He tossed his mobile on to the desktop in front of him and then regarded her, his golden eyes narrow and much too shrewd. His olive skin seemed darker against the loose white shirt he wore, making it impossible not to notice his lean, muscled arms and that perfect chest. Her breasts swelled against her vest. Her palms felt damp. And there was that same familiar ache, blooming into life so low in her belly.

Sleep or no sleep, she was doomed.

"Henri is still giving you trouble?" she asked, determined to ignore what was happening to her, what she felt. Desperate to concentrate on business instead.

"He remains unclear on the chain of command," Cayo replied, though the way he looked at her made her think he was not thinking of Henri or the Singapore project at all. "I think he has already convinced himself that I am not, in fact, the majority shareholder now."

"You expected that," Dru reminded him. She reached out a hand and touched the door frame next to her, running her finger over the dark wooden beam. The slightly rough texture made her feel even warmer, somehow, as if she was touching him instead. "You felt his personal connection with the employees and his decades of company loyalty far outweighed any tussles over authority you might have to have."

"So I did." He leaned against the arm of his chair and propped up his jaw in his hand, eyeing her in a way that made her keenly aware that he was one of the most powerful men in the world and she was…the only person she knew who had tried to defy him. "How do you find Bora Bora? Is it living up to your expectations?"

Dru couldn't seem to hold his gaze for more than a second at a time, and had no idea why. She felt…fluttery. It was as if he really had branded her last night with that odd, small touch in the dark, and she didn't know how to regain her equilibrium. Not when he was in front of her like this. Her lips seemed to tingle all over again, as if remembering. *Yearning.*

"I don't understand you," she said.

"That is hardly a breaking news item," he said dryly. "What is it you feel you need to understand? I am a simple man, when all is said and done. I like what I like." His hard mouth curved, his dark eyes gleamed gold. "I want what I want."

She ignored the way his voice lowered so suggestively, the images that it conjured before her and the wildfires it sent spinning over her skin. She dropped her hand to her side and nodded at the view behind him. An infinity pool lay on the far side of the patio, the water as smooth as glass, surrounded by more of the smooth dark wood, and beyond it, the endless sea. Yet Cayo sat with his back to it, more interested in his laptop computer, the documents spread out before him on the desk, the television on the wall tuned, as ever, to the financial news.

"You haven't been here in years." She knew she should walk to the desk, sit down, act appropriately and do her job, but she couldn't bring herself to move that close to him. Not so soon after the last two nights of all that savage intensity. Not yet. "Not in as long as I've worked for you."

"It was eight years ago, I believe," he agreed, that lean body much too still, as if he was deliberately leashing all of his power as he sat and watched her. As he *waited.* "When I bought the place from some Saudi prince or another."

Dru bit at her lip, that fluttery feeling twisting and suddenly too close to another surge of what felt like tears. As if it was impossible to be around him without all of this emotion welling up in her. She was afraid she might simply burst.

"I don't understand the point of owning beautiful things you never see." Her voice should have sounded casual. Easy. Not…raw. Wounded. She was supposed to be so good at this kind of thing! "And now that you're here for the first time in almost a decade, you're sitting inside in an office, working. Moving all your money and power about like an endless game of chess. Why bother collecting all these little pieces of paradise if you never plan to let yourself enjoy them?"

He looked at her for a beat, then another. And then that same look she'd seen the night before, as if he'd come to some kind of decision, gleamed in his eyes. A little chill snaked down Dru's back. Cayo moved from his chair, rising to his feet and prowling toward her.

Dru had to fight to stand still—not to break and run. He stopped when he was a foot or so away, and that cruel mouth of his, brutally sensual and entirely too dangerous, quirked slightly in the corner. Dru felt it like another touch, like the hand he'd pressed against her cheek in Milan, like his thumb across her mouth last night. Her blood seemed too hot in her veins, her skin felt too tight across her body, and when she reached over to grab the doorjamb again, it was because her legs were too weak to hold her upright.

And still, he only looked at her. Through her. Making the fire inside her leap high, burn white.

"I appreciate your concern," he said in that silky voice that teased along her oversensitive skin, moved like a shiver down her spine, and then made even her bones ache. "It's too bad you insist upon leaving me. We could play chess with my properties together."

"What a lovely idea," she said with a great insincerity she took no pains to conceal, and which made him look something close enough to amused. "But I am terrible at chess."

"I find that hard to believe." She thought he nearly smiled then, gazing down at her. "You are always at least six moves ahead. You'd excel at it."

She had the oddest sense of déjà vu for a moment and then it came to her—he was talking to her like a person. Not as his employee, but as another human being. Someone he actually knew. The last time he'd done this, he'd teased her in just this way. They'd smiled. They'd told stories, shared parts of themselves over small dishes of food and large glasses of wine. Or she'd thought they had. That had been that long dinner in Cadiz, before their fateful walk home, and Dru couldn't stand her own treacherous heart, the way it softened for him anew, as if she didn't know exactly where moments like this led. Precisely nowhere, with a three-year detour through infatuated subservience.

She could not let him reel her in. Not again.

"I'm not here to play games," she said quietly, hoping he couldn't hear the unevenness in her voice, that clash between what was good for her and what she wanted. "I'm here to be your personal assistant. The only other offer on the table was to be your dog. On a leash. Isn't that what you said? Is that what you'd prefer?"

His gaze heated, becoming so molten she could hardly bear it, though she didn't look away. His mouth twisted. She remembered belatedly that he was much too close, his potent masculinity and all of that restless, brilliant power of his bright and brilliant between them, making her swallow hard. Making her feel too hot, too weak, all at once.

"If you want to be my pet you must sit," he growled at her. Daring her. Commanding her. "Stay. *Surrender.*"

And the worst part was, she very nearly obeyed.

"I do appreciate the offer," Dru whispered when she could speak, but she hardly heard her own voice, lost as it was in the thunder of her heartbeat, the shriek and clamor of the storm only gaining strength inside her. "But I think I'll pass."

She should have moved—but she didn't. She only stood there, paralyzed, as Cayo closed the distance between them and stretched an arm up, over his head, to brace himself against the doorjamb and look down directly into her face.

She thought of old gods again, stunning and unpredictable, implacable and fierce. Something deep inside her seemed to go very, very still. He leaned there, propped up in the doorway, dark eyes and that sinful body, exuding the ruthlessness and command that made him who he was.

Worse than that, he looked at her as if he knew her at least as well as she knew him. As if he could read her as easily as she'd learned to read him. And the very notion was as terrifying—as impossible—as it had been before.

"Tell me," he said, his voice even lower, his golden amber eyes so hot she worried they might blister her skin or consume her whole. "What are *you* hiding from?"

For a moment, she looked almost as if he'd punched her in the stomach. But then she blinked, the mask Cayo had come to hate descended, and she even produced a strained sort of smile.

That might have irritated him, but he was done with this. He'd decided he would have her no matter what games she played, and he would lick that wall away if he had to. He looked forward to it.

"The only thing I've been hiding from today is our workload," she said brightly. Hiding, he knew. Right there in front of him. "Perhaps we should get to it."

"Forget about work," he growled, a sentence that had never crossed his lips before, perhaps not ever. And he didn't allow himself to consider the ramifications of that—all he could seem to concentrate on was the confusing woman in front of him. And how very much he wanted her, despite all the reasons he knew that was a bad idea. "We're in Bora Bora. Work can wait."

"I beg your pardon?" She looked unduly horrified.

"What's the point of being the boss if I can't decree a holiday on a whim?" he asked, striving for a lighter tone and, if that look on her face was any indication, failing. "Didn't you suggest I enjoy myself in paradise not five minutes ago?"

"To hell with the consequences, is that it?" she asked, throwing that back at him, and her eyes flashed as if she was angry with him. Which grated.

He didn't understand any of this. He didn't understand what was happening to him, and he certainly didn't understand why everything he said made her so unhappy, or so furious. Or both at once. Why she leaped from boats to escape him, then looked at him on a dark Italian terrace with all the world in her eyes and spoke of *punishment,* making him feel small three years later.

He was not a man who dealt well in uncertainties.

But what he did know was passion. Sex and desire. He had built his life around what he wanted. He knew *want.* And much as she claimed to hate him, much as she threw words or shoes at his head, he knew she wanted him as much as he wanted her. He could see it.

He'd always seen it, if he was honest with himself. And he was tired of fighting off the only thing that made sense in all of this.

"Consequences are for lesser men," he said.

He'd already decided. When he'd walked away from her last night despite the way he burned to take her, when he'd found himself handling his own brutal need alone in his shower, he'd known he was done with this. She was leaving him anyway. There was only so much complication that could occur in the time she had left. Why was he denying himself? He was not the kind of man who did without the things he wanted.

She blinked at his arrogance, but that was better. He didn't want the threat of tears, the sting of her temper. And he certainly didn't want that neutral wall of hers, designed to keep the world at an icy remove. He wanted heat. He wanted that fire again, and who cared anymore what burned?

"Come," he said. It was an order. He didn't pretend otherwise. "Kiss me."

Drusilla's eyes flew wide. One hand went to her throat. He imagined he could feel her pulse there, imagined it kicking against his own hand instead of hers. He wanted to press his mouth to her skin and taste her excitement for himself.

"What did you say?" Her voice was no more than a whisper.

"You heard me."

"I am not going to kiss you," she said, coming over all flustered and something like prim then, her gray eyes brimming with outrage.

Yet behind it, mixed in with it, that consuming, distracting heat that matched his. That called to him. That meant, he knew, that he already had her. It was only a matter of time.

"But you will, Drusilla," he promised her. "Trust me."

Dru didn't know why she wasn't running away from him.

Her heart pounded so hard it made her feel faint, everything inside her seemed to be in revolt, and yet she only stood there. Gazing back at him, while uncertainty and longing howled and fought and pooled between her legs in a hot pulse of desire.

"Don't call me that," she said instead of all the other things she could have said—*should* have said. What was the matter with her? Why couldn't she seem to summon the will to protect herself the way she should?

"Your name?" His eyes gleamed like gold. He was so close, so arrogant and sure, and it was harder and harder to remember all the reasons she shouldn't let herself fall over this particular cliff. All the reasons she shouldn't jump headfirst, for that matter.

"My mother is the only person who ever called me Drusilla," she found herself telling him as if she were not standing in this doorway torn apart by tension, while her body clamored for things she was afraid to look at too closely. And far more afraid to do. Or not do. She wasn't sure which scared her more. "And I have not laid eyes on that woman in at least ten years."

"Dru, then," he said, and it moved through her like honey, her name in his mouth. It set fires in her in places she hardly knew existed. It felt like a lock falling open, but she knew better than to give in to that. She knew better than to trust herself around this man. Look at what a kiss had wrought! "And I think you want to be on my leash, after all. Don't you?"

There was no denying the sensual intent behind that question. Or the frank appraisal in his eyes.

Or what it did to her.

The hall fell away. The world with it. There was only him. Only Cayo. Nothing but the exquisite tautness that wound around them, stealing her breath, making his eyes seem to glow. There were scarcely two feet between them and yet all she could focus on was his mouth and that carnal knowledge, that masculine certainty, in the way he looked at her.

She should have said something. Anything.

When she only gazed at him, fighting for breath, unable to speak, his eyes went dark with a need she was afraid she recognized all too well.

"Then come." Another order, which should have enraged her. His mouth curved into something sardonic—and impossibly sexy. Those wicked brows rose in challenge. "Heel."

She felt the words sizzle through her, white-hot and life-altering, and that was when she knew with a sharp burst of clarity that there was only one way this would end. She knew him, didn't she? Cayo's attention span when it came to the women who shared his bed was famously short. If she really wanted to leave him, if she really wanted to be free of this hold he seemed to have on her, then this was the way to do it. This was a one-way street. No turning back.

No matter what it cost her.

"Well?" he asked softly, taunting her.

Dru swallowed, hard. She held his gaze for a long moment, understanding that this was a line she could never uncross. That she had no idea, really, what giving in to this kind of inferno might do to her—the damage it might cause. She'd spent three years recovering from a kiss, after all. She couldn't imagine what this would do.

But it didn't matter now. He looked at her with that certainty in his eyes, that sheer male confidence and stark carnal promise, and she knew that she didn't have it in her to walk away from this. Not when she'd spent so long imagining it, fantasizing about it. Yearning for it with everything she had.

Who cares how you have him, so long as you do? a greedy voice inside her asked, and she didn't have it in her to disagree. She'd lost her will to fight somewhere high above the Pacific Ocean. She didn't have to lose herself, too. She wouldn't, she promised herself. This was a strategy, not a surrender.

She closed the distance between them, watching the light in his fascinating eyes burn ever brighter the closer she came. She slid her hands over the taut planes of his chest, reveling in his heat, his bold strength. There was no going back—but there was no way forward, either, without this. And the truth was that she wanted him. She always had. This way she could have everything— she could have Cayo in the way she'd dreamed of since Cadiz, and then her freedom in a little over a week. In every way that mattered, this was a victory.

It was, she assured herself, her gaze searching his. *It was*. But what she felt was that wild flame searing into her, burning through her, making all these things she clung to, all these things she told herself, so much ash.

"Please do not tell me that you intend to do all of this in tedious slow motion," Cayo said, that curve in his mouth telling her he was teasing her again and connecting hard to all the places that longed for him like this, for his touch, turning her fever for him ever higher. "I believe that is far more entertaining in films than in real life."

"For God's sake," she said, no longer his assistant, not in a moment like this. Not when they were changing everything, no doubt for the worse, and she couldn't even pretend to care about that as she should. "Shut up."

And then Dru stretched up onto her toes, plastered herself against the length of him, and doomed herself forever by pressing her mouth to his.

CHAPTER SEVEN

SHE TASTED THE way he remembered. Better. So hot and good and *his*.

Cayo's arms came around her, pulling her against him, into him, needing to feel the weight of her breasts against his chest, the softness of her belly against the thrust of his hardness, the gentle swell of her hips against his. He kissed her again and again, reveling in the punch of it. The kick.

And she met him. Her arms wrapped around his neck, her mouth moved against his with the same urgency, the same demand. He thought she said his name. He wasn't sure he could speak or if he did, what language he might use, or if it would all come out as nonsense. He didn't care.

She was intoxicating, and he could finally let himself indulge in her as he wished.

At last, he sank his hands into her dark hair, exulting in the feel of it, the scent. Warm silk and the faint hint of vanilla. He pulled out the band that held her hair and let the mass of waves fall around her shoulders. He angled his mouth for a better fit, gathering her closer, taking what he wanted, at last.

He smoothed his hands down the sensual curve of her back, then tested her pert bottom, making them both groan when he moved her against the thrust of his arousal. It wasn't enough. It was barely a start. He took and he took until she was gasping his name, breathing hard, and he had to rein himself in. Or have her right there in the hallway—and he had no intention of going too quickly.

Not with this woman. Not with Dru. Not when it felt as if he'd waited lifetimes for this. For her.

He moved to taste, briefly, the freckles the sun had already raised across the bridge of her nose, then traced the line of her cheekbone, her satiny cheek, her stubborn jaw. She smelled of coconut and flowers, and tasted like magic, and he could not seem to get close enough.

She made a small noise in the back of her throat, like a purr, and it nearly undid him. *Mine,* he thought, with a surge of possessive triumph. *All mine.*

He took her hand in his, marveling at how delicate she was, how perfectly formed. He led her down the hall, the afternoon sun still golden and shining through the windows of the rooms they passed, and he couldn't pretend he didn't feel victory thump through him like a drumbeat when she simply followed him like this, those gray eyes dizzy with want—very much like the docile, biddable female she had pretended to be for so many years, but wasn't. The surrender of a strong woman, he thought with pure male satisfaction, was so much more exciting than that of a weak one. He intended to revel in hers.

Once in his bedroom, he pulled her to him again, luxuriating in the feel of her in his arms. *Finally.*

He took her mouth again, kissing her anew as he maneuvered her toward the bed. When the back of her knees hit the mattress she pulled away and looked up at him, her breath coming too fast, her fathomless gray eyes dark now and dazed with need, her pretty face soft and flushed and *his*.

She was his.

Cayo didn't speak. He didn't counter his own uncharacteristic possessiveness, or even try. Nothing about Dru had made sense so far, not since that rainy morning in London when she'd changed everything he took for granted. Why should this? He tugged the vest up over her head, sliding it over all of that long, dark hair, and smiled when he saw her royal blue bra and the round breasts he'd only glimpsed through her wet blouse before now.

"Perfecto," he murmured, and leaned down to press his mouth against the crest of one breast, sucking on it through the thin, glossy material. Dru gasped, and so he did the same with the other, waiting until her head was thrown back and her eyes closed before he reached around and unhooked the bra. She reached to pull it from her arms and he bent and licked the closest nipple, pulling it into his mouth.

And Dru went wild.

Cayo got lost in it then, in her. In her heat, her softness, her beautiful cries. He stripped her trousers from her long, sleek legs, then that other scrap of satin and lace. He hardly noticed as he shrugged out of his own clothes, because it wasn't fast enough, it meant he wasn't touching her, and it took entirely too long before he was naked and she was sprawled across his bed the way he wanted her, the way he'd wanted her for longer than he'd been aware of it. This was no new need that roared in him, demanding he take her again and again until they were both sated. What moved in him felt old and complicated, as if he'd hidden it from himself. But he wasn't hiding any longer. He stretched out beside her, propping himself up on one arm, fiercely satisfied to see her nipples were hard and her tattletale English skin was pink and rosy.

His.

She rolled as if she meant to begin exploring him herself, but he pressed her back down.

"But I want—"

"Sit," he murmured, tracing a finger down to her breast and toying with its peak, making Dru arch from the bed with a moan.

He bent to replace his fingers with his lips, and she cried out again, writhing beneath him as he tugged her nipple into the heat of his mouth even as he cupped her other breast in his hand. Then he kissed his way down the gentle swell of her abdomen, licking over her navel and the gentle curve of her hips. He learned she had a trio of small birthmarks near her left hip bone, and that she couldn't keep her hips still, especially when he held them between his hands and then curved his fingers around to test the shape and sweet, silken perfection of her bottom.

And then he parted her thighs and kissed his way even lower.

"Cayo—" she started again, naked passion in that voice, so full of *want* it made his hardness ache in response.

"Stay," he ordered her, and licked his way into her molten core, exulting in the fresh, hot taste of her desire.

She arched from the bed again, her hips rising to meet his mouth as he took her, tasted her, made her his. Unequivocally. And then she exploded all around him, sobbing out his name as she fell off the side of the world.

And it was not nearly enough.

He moved back up the bed, and pulled her to him,

then rolled them both, sitting up and lifting her so she sat astride him. He wanted to see her. He wanted to see everything.

"Cayo…" She whispered his name, her eyes fluttering open, to gaze at him as he pressed against the core of her.

She was wet and hot and soft, and he wanted her so badly he nearly shook with it. He held her bottom in his hands, lifted her, and watched as she shivered in turn when he slid himself along the entrance to her core, teasing her. Her gray eyes darkened again. She pulled her perfect lower lip between her teeth. She lifted her arms and wrapped them around his shoulders, bringing her breasts flush against his chest.

"Surrender," he whispered, and then he drove into her, and there was nothing at all but fire.

That perfect, encompassing fire. It roared through him, into him. It incinerated everything he thought, everything he knew, until there was nothing at all but Dru. And she was supple and curvy and draped all around him. She began to move her hips and he groaned, too close to the edge.

He wrapped his hands around her hips to slow her down, then set his own pace. Slow. Deliberate. Torturing them both. Hot and endless strokes that made him grit his teeth and made her drop her head to his neck and sob out her pleasure. He moved her up and down as he thrust into her, again and again, wanting it never to end. Wanting to stay balanced in all this lush perfection forever. Wanting to breathe her in like this, so deep inside her he hardly knew which one of them was which.

She lifted her head then and her gaze locked with his. Held. He felt her breath on his face, her legs tight around him, and still he moved, building that fire into a raging blaze, making her moan even louder, watching those gray eyes of hers glaze over with the same incomparable passion that stormed through him. Taking him over. Making him want nothing more than to burn in it, over and over, too hot to bear, until there was nothing left of him.

This is Dru, he thought, unable to stop looking at her, touching her, feeling her in every part of him. *And this is mine.*

And he understood then that he had no intention of ever letting her go. Whatever that might mean.

She closed her eyes and threw back her head, her lovely back arching toward the setting sun through the windows behind her, the fading light casting her lush body in oranges and golds.

Like some kind of pagan goddess, and all of her his.

She started to shudder again, wild and untamed in his arms, and when she called out his name this time, he followed her over the edge. At last.

Dru lay tangled with him in the wide bed and watched the sun drip down toward the sea, then melt away.

She could not seem to form coherent thoughts. There was only the buzzing in her limbs and under her skin, like some kind of high-voltage live wire, still sending out sparks. She felt Cayo's hard shoulder beneath her cheek. She felt the heat of his skin and the way his chest rose and fell. She did not think. She wasn't sure she wanted to think. She watched the sky instead.

Cayo stirred beside her when the sun dropped below the horizon, as if roused by the twilight. He turned to face her, his eyes dark and once again unreadable in the deep shadows of his chamber.

He slid his hand up to hold her cheek and then

brought her face to his. For a moment he only gazed at
her, and she felt a great stillness inside her, a kind of
hush. As if she was waiting for something, poised on
the edge of another high cliff while all the rest of her
seemed to shiver.

The clock is already ticking, a voice whispered inside her head, ruthlessly practical when Dru felt anything but. *He's already gone.*

But as if he could hear her, he kissed her. Deep and
slow. Sweet. Addicting. And then the fire kicked in. As
if it could never be quenched. As if none of this would
ever be enough. She had been a terrible fool, she acknowledged as his hand moved over her face, angling
her mouth closer to his for a better fit, a deeper kick. She
should have known better than to think she could handle
this. She would leave him as planned, she understood
then in some deep, primitive way, but then she would
mourn him, and she might never stop. She had walked
right into this, and there was nothing for her but Miss
Havisham and regret on the other side of it. And still
she kissed him, unable to help herself. Unable to stop
what she'd already started, what she'd already done.

No sense borrowing trouble, she thought then, in
some desperation. It would come no matter what she
did. It would hurt. Maybe she'd always known that.

He rose over her in the bed and settled himself between her legs, and Dru let go of a future that seemed
far away from this moment, too far away to matter. He
settled his weight on his hands and looked down at her,
still watching her with those too-shrewd eyes of his.

"Dru," he said. Just her name. As if he was tasting it.

"Cayo," she replied in kind, feeling far too vulnerable. She didn't know what he saw when he looked down
at her like that. She didn't know how to prevent him

from seeing everything, all of her hopes and fears and terrors, not when she had abandoned herself so completely to be with him like this.

But he simply twisted his hips and thrust into her. Slick. Hot.

And she stopped caring what he saw. What he knew. She concentrated instead on the sleek perfection of this age old dance between them. As if she'd been made to fit him, just like this.

He moved slowly, hypnotically. As if he did not wish to build that fire between them this time so much as encourage it to burn high on its own. She matched his lazy rhythm, her hips rising to meet his, every part of her exulting in the way they fit together. In the way they moved together. Slow and easy and devastating.

She told herself it was the only thing that mattered.

This time, she could reach up and explore the sheer beauty of his lean, smooth torso. She ran her hands over his hard pectorals, then trailed her way down that mouthwatering abdomen. Smooth skin stretched across steel. Hard male beauty unlike any other. Ferocious and proud. Fierce and demanding. She pulled herself up from the bed to kiss his chest, to taste the bold heat of him, the incomparable strength. The delectable power.

The pace began to change, then, the fire burning ever hotter. Cayo's shoulders blocked out the world, and she forgot everything but this. Everything but him. Everything but the wildness they made here, and the way it stormed through her, tearing her apart from within.

He slid down to pull her close and she loved it. The full, hard weight of him against her, pressing her into the bed, making her feel somehow small and yet cherished, all at once. She could feel his breath in her ear, and then he began to murmur words she didn't know in

Spanish, crooning against the length of her neck while still he thrust into her, over and over and over again. She wrapped her legs around his hips and clung to him, mindless and wanton, entirely at his command. And when he reached between them and pressed his fingers against the heart of her need, she burst into a million pieces. Again.

He kept on as she shattered around him, until he shouted out her name and shuddered against her, burying his face into the crook between her neck and her shoulder. And even broken into too many pieces to count, even thrown as she was off the side of a very high cliff and still floating her way down to earth, Dru understood that nothing was ever going to be the same again. Especially not her.

Cayo's version of enjoying himself in paradise, Dru was not greatly surprised to learn, involved cutting down his business hours to something like six or eight hours per day instead of more than twice that.

"What a great sacrifice this must be," she murmured toward the end of one such "holiday" afternoon as she took more dictation, her fingers flying across the keyboard when she would have preferred to explore him instead, not that he had asked. "To abandon yourself so hedonistically into a normal person's version of a workday."

Cayo eyed her, his dark eyes as hot as they were amused. In deference to the fact he'd decreed this a vacation—and, perhaps, all that had changed between them—he wore a white shirt he had not bothered to button, displaying his mouthwatering physique and olive complexion and making Dru glad she was so adept at touch-typing. She could stare at him without missing a single word. His feet were even propped up on the desk in front of him, completing the picture. He would have looked like indolence incarnate had he not been sitting in his office suite, composing lists of commands for his fleet of vice presidents the world over to obey as soon as Dru pressed Send.

"You are always welcome to distract me," he said after a moment.

She opened her mouth to offer a knee-jerk sort of demurral, but stopped herself. What was there to lose? Cayo's business would storm ahead the way it always did when these strange days were over, when she was gone. But she would never get another chance to have him like this. She had the sense again, as she had repeatedly since that first day here, that she was gathering up all these white-hot, deliriously passionate moments to hoard later, when she was alone. When she was free. When she had nothing but memories to hold on to.

"If you insist, Mr. Vila," she said now, watching that fierce light blaze in his eyes. She slid out of the chair she'd pulled up next to his desk and onto the floor, smiling slightly as his hard face tightened with desire.

Slowly, holding his gaze, she crawled between his legs.

"Is this a new form of taking dictation, Miss Bennett?" he asked, that dark amusement in his low voice, though she could hear the faint rasp in it that hinted at the fire within him, and she smiled, running her hands over his hard thighs, his taut abdomen. His legs thudded down on either side of her, caging her right where she wanted to be. "I'm a fan."

Then she reached into his soft trousers, lifting out the hard, smooth length of him and taking him deep in her mouth.

He groaned. And Dru worshipped him, tasting the velvet smoothness of him, loving him with her mouth, her tongue, her hands and her lips, bringing him to a roaring finish with his hands gripped tight in her hair.

It was these moments she was collecting, she told herself as he lifted her into his lap and kissed her hungrily, his heartbeat pounding hard beneath her as he held her against his chest. These moments when she could kid herself and pretend that he was hers.

They fell into a kind of pattern as the days passed. Cayo was still her boss, despite the dramatic change in their relationship, and Dru did not dispute that. What might have been untenable if she hadn't already planned to leave him was really more like a game when it was only her heart, not her career, at stake. So she was happy enough to continue performing her duties, with only cosmetic alterations.

"Don't do that thing with your hair," Cayo said one morning as she stepped out of the massive, glass-enclosed shower, complete with a window overlooking the ocean, that was its own room in the master suite's bath.

He stood in the door that led out into his bedroom, his dark eyes burning as they tracked over her, watching as she wrapped herself in a towel. He'd pulled on another pair of the linen trousers he favored in the warm weather, but no shirt, and all of that muscled masculine perfection on display made her feel overheated. Again.

They'd woken at dawn and gone for a swim in the quiet lagoon. He'd lifted her against him where he stood, simply pulled her bikini bottoms to the side and slid inside her, rocking them both to mindlessness in the clear, warm water, as the sun began to light the perfect sky above them.

She was still trembling slightly from the aftereffects.

"Don't do what with my hair?" she asked. It couldn't be healthy, wanting someone like this. She'd imagined sleeping with him would be a single act, a fix, the end of all that yearning and infatuation.

But instead, you made it worse, that voice inside was quick to remind her. As if she didn't know.

He made a vague gesture toward the back of his head. "That twist," he said. A strange expression crossed his face then, something she might have called vulnerability on another man—but that was impossible. This was Cayo. "I like it down around your shoulders," he said gruffly. "I like my hands in it."

And he'd turned and disappeared, leaving Dru to make of that what she would.

She pulled on the cheerful, bright blue-and-yellow maxidress she'd adopted as her uniform here, and ran her fingers through her hair as it settled around her shoulders in damp waves. She stared at herself in the large mirror that dominated the nearest wall, and hardly recognized herself. The exposure to the sun had brought out her freckles, and that sheen to her skin. Her eyes were bright, her mouth soft, somehow. And her dark hair tumbled all around her, still wet from her shower, giving her a sensual and sultry sort of look. She was poles apart from the image of Dru Bennett she'd prided herself on embodying in her five years at the Vila Group: impeccably, quietly fashionable. Professional above all else.

She could lie and tell herself that it was the islands doing this to her, turning her into a different person, but she knew better. It was Cayo.

She just had to remember that it was temporary.

Back in London, Dru would never dress this way.

Just as she would never interrupt a dictation session as she had the other day, or wear her hair down because a man demanded it. Just as she would never sleep with her boss, no matter how much she might have wanted him, and then carry on working for him. But this was Bora Bora, and it was as if what she did here didn't count.

It's only a handful of days, she reminded herself now as she walked to meet him in the office. *It will be like none of this happened when I get back home.*

She told herself that the twisting feeling in her stomach was joy. That it was happiness that she was letting herself do this, experience this, live in the moment here, when it was so unlike her. She had her whole life in front of her to regret this, after all. There was no sense starting now.

But it was as if Cayo knew that there was something she wasn't telling him—or perhaps he felt the pressure of the temporary nature of this as well. Sometimes he merely picked her up and held her against the nearest wall when he wanted her, his expression so fierce as he thrust within her, as if he saw the same painful future before him. Or he woke her again and again in the night, to taste her, to touch her, to send her flying over the edge. As if to prove he could. As if to make sure it was real.

One afternoon, after he'd ended their workday, he found her on the lanai outside the library. He stood in the entryway for a long moment, watching her, until Dru set her crime novel aside and gave him her full attention.

"Did you need something?" she asked, and smiled at him, ready for another series of commands. Plans for the next day's business, perhaps.

"I don't know how you do it." His voice was dark

and low. It made a shiver of unease snake along the back of her neck.

"Read?" she asked mildly.

He ignored that.

"Your words, your smiles." He ran a hand along the jaw he shaved irregularly here, and looked not unlike a pirate as he gazed down at her, rakish and unapologetically lethal. But she didn't recognize that look in his eyes. "Even in my bed. There are a thousand places for you to hide, aren't there? And you do."

Her heart thudded hard against her ribs. And there was a kind of ringing in her ears, as if alarms were going off all around them. But she knew that wasn't true—there was only the sound of the waves as they crashed against the sand. The birds singing in the trees. The wind dancing through the chimes out on the terrace.

"I don't know what you mean."

"Do you know, I almost believe you."

He didn't look angry, or upset in any way. She could have handled either of those without blinking. He looked almost…resigned. All of that clever attention of his focused on her, and growing darker by the moment. And it was making her feel panicky. Desperate. Afraid, again, of what he might see.

"I'm not hiding." She stood, then opened up her arms, proving it. "I'm right here."

He smiled, and it had the usual effect of rendering her breathless, for all it was shaded as much with regret as with desire. She didn't want to know why.

"Are you, Dru?" he asked. But he closed the distance between them as if he found her as difficult to resist as she did him, and pulled her against him. "Are you really?"

Dru didn't answer. She kissed him instead. Hot. Desperate. With everything she was capable of giving him.

He didn't speak again.

He had her kneel on the small sofa, then took her from behind, his hands on her hips and his hard chest at her back as he thrust into her, making her sob out his name with only the glittering sea before them as witness.

And when he bent his head to her neck, spent in the aftermath of their passion, she murmured soothing words and told herself it was another victory. Another memory; hers to hoard.

CHAPTER EIGHT

THEY SAT OUT on one of the patios one evening, surrounded by softly flickering candles, with the canopy of stars bright and astonishing above them. Dru leaned back in her chair and stared up at them, aware on some level that time was passing even in moments like this one, when she felt outside of time altogether.

Don't forget what temporary means, she advised herself. *Don't pretend that any of this can last.*

Across from her, Cayo was finishing a call with a CFO at one of his New York companies. He frowned out toward the dark ocean as he talked, his voice growing increasingly more impatient. Dru sipped at her wine and watched him, imprinting that impossible face into her memory, making sure she had memories enough to spare. That blade of a nose, that granite jaw. Her boss become her lover. Now that it had happened, it felt inevitable. As if they had always been headed here. As if the three years in between Cadiz and now had been part of some grander plan.

Just as she had always intended to leave him, eventually. Lest she forget her own plans. Her promises.

Victory, she chanted quietly in her own head. *This is a victory. I'll go home the winner at the end, and do exactly as I planned to do two weeks ago.*

But she wasn't sure she believed her own cheering squad.

The staff brought out plates of tuna tartare to start, and Dru took a bite, sighing with pleasure at the burst of flavor, the excruciatingly fresh taste. She took a sip of her wine. She smiled when Cayo ended his call and ignored the way he looked at her, so dark and brooding.

"It's fantastic," she told him. "You should have some."

"Are you working tonight, Dru?" His tone was cold, brusque. It lanced into her, as no doubt he intended it to do. "I thought we agreed that business ended at half five today. When I want you to perform in your role as perfect assistant, capable of any measure of small talk under any and all circumstances, I will let you know."

"Or don't have any," she said blandly. "More for me."

His mouth moved into a hard kind of curve, too intense to be a smile.

More courses appeared before them. Parrotfish stuffed with crab. Mahi-mahi in a sweet coconut curry. A platter of grilled shrimp and scallops, and another of artfully arranged sushi. The table was bright with all the colors, and the food looked almost too pretty to eat. Almost.

"Tell me something about you," he said when their plates were full, and there had been no sound for some time save the clink of silver against china and the ever-present crash of the ocean against the shore. "Something I don't know." He shook his head impatiently when she opened her mouth. "I don't mean anything on your CV, which you trot out by rote and which I know is stellar or I wouldn't have hired you."

Dru put down her fork and regarded him calmly for a moment, while that same alarm inside her shrieked anew. There was no reason he should want to "know something" about her. She needed to change the subject, redirect his attention. He had enough weapons to use against her as it was. Why add to his arsenal?

"What is it you want to know?" she asked, warily. She picked up her wine, pressed the glass to her lips and then decided she already felt too unbalanced. There was no need to throw alcohol in the mix and make it that much worse. "Is this when we discuss our lists of past lovers? Mine is shorter than yours. Obviously."

His dark amber eyes gleamed, as if he appreciated her attempt to focus the conversation back on him, and what was, she was all too aware, an impressive and lengthy list indeed. But he didn't take the bait. He only smiled slightly, and speared a plump shrimp on the sharp tines of his fork.

"You personally witnessed the ignoble end of my family, such as it was," he said, his voice as low as his gaze was intent, and something about it shivered through her, making her ache for him in a different way. "What of yours? You never speak of them. I assume you did not spring full-grown from an office-supply warehouse, brandishing one of those gray suits of yours like a weapon."

The expression on his face said he wasn't entirely sure about that. Dru cleared her throat and recognized that she was stalling. She couldn't seem to help it. There had been a time when she would have been thrilled to encourage his interest in her—any interest at all. But not now. Not when she had a much greater sense of how hard it was going to be to leave him already. What would it be like if he really knew all of her? How would she survive losing him then?

"Did you encourage personal chatter about the office

all these years and I missed it?" she asked lightly. He inclined his head, awarding her the point, but he still waited expectantly. He was still not distracted from his question. *Damn him.* She set her wine back on the glass-topped table, feeling jerky and uneven. Unduly defensive. "We lived in Shropshire, in a village outside Shrewsbury, until my father died. Dominic and I were barely five years old." She saw his brows knit together and nodded. "Twins, yes. We moved around a good bit after that. In the end, it was a relief to go to university and stay in one place for a few years."

"Why did you move around so much?" he asked. If she didn't know better, she would think he was fascinated. That he really wanted to know the answer. And maybe that was why she told him—because, despite everything, she wanted to believe that he could want that, and that trumped even her heightened sense of self-preservation. To say nothing of her sense, full stop.

"My mum had a lot of boyfriends," she said, which was more than she usually told anyone. It was amazing how easy it was to strip all those hard, dark years of the fear and the tears and simply cram it all into one little sentence that barely hinted at either. "Some became stepfathers."

She had no intention of telling him anything further. But when she dared meet his gaze again, he was looking back at her the way he always did. Dark eyes in that warrior's face, brooding and *intent.* As if she was a mystery he wanted to puzzle out. And would.

"My mother also remarried, I suppose you could say," he said then, in that dry way of his that hinted at a dark humor she'd never imagined he could possess. Or had thought she'd only imagined lurked in him on that one night in Cadiz. She would miss it. She could tell. "But as she is now a bride of Christ we are not meant to complain."

Dru couldn't help but smile, and his eyes warmed in return, and she knew then that she was going to tell him things she'd never breathed to another soul. Because she still wanted him to know her, despite how temporary this was. Despite the very real fear that it would give him too much power over her. She wanted to imagine, when he was on to his next assistant, ensconced on one of his yachts with his next blonde supermodel, that he would remember her, too. And when he did—*if* he did—she wanted this to have mattered. And that meant sharing parts of herself she'd never let anyone else see.

"They were always violent." She was surprised how little her voice shook, and how easy it was to look at him and forget what she'd been through. How safe he made her feel, simply by not looking away. As if that simple act shared the burden of it, somehow. "To Mum, and then increasingly to Dominic. I was quite good at not being seen."

"I believe you," he said, an undercurrent in his voice. "You still are."

"But then I got older," she said. She was far too captivated by the way he watched her, as if he was supporting her that simply, that completely, to respond to the strange thing he said. She filed it away. "And they started to notice me more." She swallowed, then shook her head slightly, as if to shake away the memories. His gaze darkened. Hardened. "There was one named Harold who was the worst. Always trying to get me alone. Always quick to stick his hands where he shouldn't. But when I told Mum she slapped my face and called me a liar and a whore." Dru shrugged, almost as if that memory didn't still sting. Almost as if she was so tough it hardly registered, when the truth was, she'd never said that out loud before. Not like that. "So when I could, I left. The last time I saw her I was nineteen."

The only other person she'd shared her dark history with was Dominic, and they'd always used their own shorthand—never quite mentioning the facts of what had happened so much as the effects. She'd never told any of her mates at university, or even the small handful of boyfriends she'd had back when she'd still had time for a social life. It had seemed so private, and so terribly shameful, and her mates had all been about having a laugh, not dredging up the horrors of Dru's childhood. She'd enjoyed them precisely *because* they weren't the sort for intimate confidences or bared souls. It meant hers were safe.

She jerked her gaze away from Cayo's now, reaching blindly for her wine, no longer caring what it might do to her. It was better than what *he* was doing to her simply by listening. By making her feel safe when there was no such thing. She knew that better than most.

"And your brother?" Cayo asked after a moment. "Your twin? You're not close with him either?"

It shocked her. It felt like a kick in the stomach, an attack, and her first reaction was pure, unadulterated fury. And then, if she was honest, a lot of it was that same old, terrible guilt she always felt where Dominic was concerned.

"Not as such, thanks," she snapped at Cayo, not caring if she was being unfair. "As he's dead."

And then she hated herself. So deeply and so comprehensively it made her feel ill. She slid the wineglass back onto the table and wrapped her arms around her middle, certain she needed help to keep herself together.

Cayo didn't look away. He gave no indication that he minded that she'd snapped at him like that, out of nowhere. He simply sat much too still and much too close across the table, watching her fall apart.

"I'm sorry," he began after a moment, his voice calm.

"No," she interrupted him, her words feeling thick in her mouth. "I'm sorry. I shouldn't have said it like that. How would you know? Only it was rather recent and I've still not managed to figure out how to talk about it. About him."

"Recent?" Cayo frowned then. He looked as close to confused as she'd ever seen him. "What do you mean by recent? I don't recall you taking any time off."

In the past five years. He didn't have to say that part. It was understood.

"Time off?" She shook her head, then let out a hollow little sound, not really a laugh at all. "It's not as if you give out any personal time, Cayo. I can't imagine even having asked for time off. Look how you reacted to my resignation."

That muscle leapt in his jaw, betraying his temper. His eyes went black with something that looked again like pain. Tortured and grim, the way he'd looked that night in Milan. It made her want to reach over and touch him, soothe him. And once more, she deeply regretted her words the moment they hung in the sweet night air between them, but she couldn't seem to stop herself. And she couldn't take them back.

"Yes," he said after a moment in a deep, rough voice she hardly recognized. "Of course. I am such a heartless monster that I would keep you from your brother's funeral, purely out of spite."

Her own heart seemed to tighten at that, and she shook her head. "That's not what I meant."

"After all," he continued in the same dark and bitter tone that made her want to weep and to protect him, somehow, from whatever made him sound that way, even if it was her, "what do I know of family? You are the only person in the world who knows how little regard my own grandfather held for me. You heard him. You are also the only person in the world who has maintained any kind of close relationship with me for any length of time." His smile then hurt to see. "You would certainly know how little qualified I am to speak on the subject of families."

She felt awful, and it moved in her like heat. Like fear. And she couldn't stand it.

"Don't be an idiot," she said, almost crossly.

He froze. His dark eyes widened.

"I said I doubted you would give me time off," she said, very distinctly. "You are a demanding boss, Cayo. You insist on round-the-clock availability and access. I had no reason to think you would greet the news that I even *had* a personal life with anything but horror."

"You have no idea what I would do," he replied tightly.

"I know exactly what you would do," she retorted. "It's what you pay me for. What you offered me three times my salary and the private island of my choice for, if memory serves."

For a moment he only looked at her. The moment stretched out between them, and despite what she'd just told him, Dru had no idea how he would react. None at all.

And then, impossibly, proving how little she knew him after all, he threw back his head and laughed.

She'd never known he *could* laugh. It was an infectious sound. Joy moved across his hard, fierce face, the laughter lighting him up, changing him, changing *her*—

The truth slammed into her, stealing her breath, making her head spin. The scales fell from her eyes, and hard—so hard they seemed to bruise her on their way down.

She was in love with him.

And quite clearly, she had been for a very long time.

Once again, she'd been fooling herself. She'd called it an "infatuation," called it her "feelings for him." She'd minimized it in her own head, worrying only that this trip would take recovering from. She hadn't dared so much as think the truth. Meanwhile, she'd chosen to lose herself in his life. She'd never thought to ask why she'd been passed over for that other job three years ago even though she'd known perfectly well she'd been qualified for it. Worse, she'd chosen to keep her distance from her brother—when he'd died, but even before, if she was honest. It was easier to send money from afar than it was to roll around in the messes Dominic had made, though it hurt her to admit she'd done exactly that. She'd done all of it.

All to cater to and care for a man who would never love her back. Who hadn't the slightest idea what love *was*.

Then again, came that voice inside her, brutal and unflinching, *do you?*

The world seemed to tilt around her wildly, sickeningly, as if she'd found herself trapped on some carnival fun ride. She felt a terrible shame wash through her, scalding her. She'd wanted her damaged, selfish mother to love her as she should have done. She'd wanted all of those stepfathers to love her like a daughter. She'd wanted Dominic to love her more than his addictions.

And Cayo... He couldn't love anything, could he? So she'd settled for making him *need* her instead. And she'd thought he valued her for that, if nothing else.

Was that what she'd wanted, in his office that day that seemed so long ago now? Had some part of her believed she would fling her resignation at him, still smarting from the printed email she'd found, and he would leap to his feet and declare his love for her?

Of course he hadn't. No one ever had, and Cayo wouldn't know how, even if he did feel the things she did. Her entire life was a great and complicated monument to deeply pathetic, sadly epic, and wholly unrequited love.

She was such a fool.

And he was watching her now, that unexpected laughter still on his face, making him more than simply beautiful in that hard, fierce way—making him handsome, too. Almost approachable.

It broke what was left of her heart.

"Are you all right?" he asked, his eyes still bright as they searched hers, sharpening as they saw whatever must have been there—the truth, she feared. The terrible truth she could never, ever let him know.

She didn't know how she did it.

"I'm fine," she managed to say. He frowned, no doubt at that shaky note in her voice that made her sound anything at all but *fine,* so she gestured at her mouth, and lied. "I've bit my tongue, that's all."

Time, it turned out, was the one thing Cayo couldn't control.

It was the afternoon of her final day—which neither one of them had mentioned directly yet, though it hung there between them no matter how many times he'd taken her the night before, or this morning—and he could not bring himself to pay attention to the conference call that she was participating in as his representative. He sat next to her at the small table in the office, his legs stretched out before him, and found he could do nothing at all but watch her as she spoke into the speaker phone in the center of the table.

"I'll be certain to bring that to Mr. Vila's attention," she said, in that smooth and capable voice of hers that, now he knew what lay behind it, made him burn. "But in the meantime, I think we need to take another look at those figures before we jump to any conclusions."

Maybe it was that he could see her, when the rest of the people on the call could not. No doubt they pictured the usual Dru, in her sleek suits and dangerous heels, her hair tamed and twisted out of view. But he saw the real Dru. Wild hair and that hint of color on her pale skin, the dusting of freckles across her nose and shoulders. Bare feet and a turquoise sarong wrapped around a hot pink bikini. Not in the least bit professional, not that anyone could have told that from her cool voice.

She was magnificent. She was his. And she was going to leave him.

He didn't know what he was going to do about that, he only knew he couldn't allow it. He wouldn't.

But he also knew he'd run out of options.

She propped her head up with one hand as she listened to the call, the various executives talking over each other, all of them completely unaware that Cayo was listening to them dither and bicker. He'd found that it could be highly educational to use Dru in this way, to make them think they were talking to someone far more approachable than Cayo ever was. He'd found it helped ferret out all manner of truths.

He wished the same could be said of Dru herself.

"Mr. Vila prefers to be offered potential solutions when presented with problems, Barney," she said into the speaker. "I can certainly raise your concerns to him, but I suspect he's going to give you a similar reply. Only he won't be quite as polite."

There was some laughter, and she glanced over to smile at him, her gray eyes sparkling nearly silver. *Real,* he thought with satisfaction. Not one of her work smiles she trotted out to placate or soothe him from time to time, all of which he'd come to hate. But even so, he knew she was still hiding from him. He didn't know what, or why, but he could see the secrets in her eyes. Even now.

Perversely, it only made him want her more.

He'd told her that she was the only person he'd ever had any kind of close relationship with, and the stark truth of that haunted him. She was the only person alive that he had ever trusted. He had allowed her unparalleled access to all parts of his life. To him. No employee had ever been so entrenched in his personal life before and he had certainly never allowed one of his women anywhere near his business. Only Dru bridged those worlds. Only Dru.

And his time with her was almost up.

Giving in to an urge he hardly understood, as if it might ease the sudden heaviness in his chest, Cayo reached over and took her hand. Her eyes flew to his, but he concentrated on the slide of her fingers against his. The way they fitted together so well, even here. He brought her hand up to his lips and pressed a kiss to the back of it. She curved her palm to better fit against his mouth, his jaw, as if she was holding him too, and something shifted inside him. A wall he hadn't known was there tumbled down, and he knew, then, what he must do.

There was one way to keep her. One strategy he hadn't tried. It would keep her close. With him. And so what if it wouldn't be precisely as it had been? It was good enough. He might even like having her as his family, whatever that word really meant. She was the closest thing to it he'd ever known.

He just had to get her to say yes.

"The helicopter will be here in two hours," Dru said the following morning, careful to sound calm. Matter-of-fact. "The plane will be ready to go once we get to Tahiti."

Cayo stood at the end of the pier, with his back to her. He looked remote, forbidding and still, she wanted to lean into all of that broad strength, rest her head against his shoulder blade. She wanted to let the pure, male scent of him surround her. She wanted to soak in his heat like the sun. Her bare toes curled into the smooth, warm wood beneath her feet and she told herself she was fine. That she felt nothing but relief that it was all almost over, with only the long plane ride left to survive. *Perfectly fine.*

They had woken up at dawn, wrapped around each other in Cayo's huge bed. He had pulled her over him before she was wholly awake, sliding into her so smoothly she'd wondered whether it was real or a dream. *Or goodbye,* a harsher voice in her head had suggested. She'd ignored it, leaned down to him and kissed him.

Slowly, they'd explored each other. Long, drugging kisses and endless touches, building a different kind of flame. One that burned long and sweet. One that danced and seduced and drew out the perfection of each caress. One that made them both sigh out their pleasure when it turned white-hot and wild all around them.

Dru felt the glowing embers of that same fire inside her, even now. She'd almost been afraid to track Cayo down after she'd confirmed their arrangements—as if she thought he could see straight through her to that place that would never stop burning for him. That place he could ignite with so little effort—a look, a touch. Would that ever fade? Would time without him dim it? Somehow, she doubted it.

"I suppose no one can stay in paradise forever, can they?" she asked brightly when he didn't turn to face her, trying to make conversation—anything to cover her own nervousness. Anything to pretend it didn't hurt.

"Don't." It was hard. Fierce.

"It's so lovely here." She felt helpless. Unable to stop. "But it's not real, is it?"

He turned then, so dark and ruthless, dressed in no more than a pair of white loose trousers and still, so dangerous. She almost took a step back to keep him from looming over her, but she restrained herself. His eyes slammed into hers.

"But this is?" His accent was more pronounced than usual, and she felt it inside, like an echo. "Your deliberately inane chatter? Surely you know by now that it won't work on me."

That might have stung—it did—but Dru couldn't let herself fall into that trap. There would be no fighting that led to kissing, no explosions of temper or passion or anything else. No shoes. No jumping from the pier. She wouldn't let him sabotage her departure. More importantly, she wouldn't let herself do the same.

"You are far too busy to spend any more time hiding away from the world," she said, and that wasn't idle conversation or flattery. It was the simple truth. He was who he was. "Even here."

"As you pointed out to me only last night," he said gruffly, "the point of hiring the best people in the world is occasionally to delegate responsibilities to them."

"I did say that." She smiled, but it felt hollow. He didn't return it. And last night felt so far away now. As if it belonged to other people. "Cayo…"

She bit her lip and watched his dark amber eyes turn nearly black with a mixture of pain and passion, and her heart seemed to squeeze tight in her chest. If she started crying now, she worried she would never stop. She tried to shove that dangerous ache away.

"Don't make this harder than it has to be," she whispered.

Still, he only stared back at her, as if he were hewn from stone. He looked powerful beyond measure, ruthless and fierce and she thought it might kill her to leave him. That thing inside her that had no pride, no respect, no boundaries whatsoever, might physically take her down as she tried to walk away. Her little masochist within, who wanted him and only him, however she could have him. Whatever that meant.

However much it hurt.

"It doesn't have to be hard," he said then.

His voice was low, and there was an intense light deep in the dark of his gaze. He reached over and traced a lazy pattern just above the waistband of her linen trousers, where there was a gap between them and her top. She sucked in a breath, so attuned to him that even that faintest touch unleashed the fire in her, made her body ready itself for him, as if on command. When he looked at her again, there was gold in his eyes and the faintest curve on that cruel mouth of his.

"I think you should marry me," he said.

The world stopped.

No breath. No sound. No air.

But somehow, she didn't faint. She didn't fall. She only stood there, staring back at him. "What did you just say?"

"Don't play that game." He took her chin in his hand, his gaze piercing into her, seeing far too much—and she couldn't allow that. She wouldn't survive it if he knew she loved him. Dru jerked her head back, and he let go, but not without reminding them both, wordlessly, that he'd allowed it.

"You can't be serious," she said, her breath, her voice—all of her ragged. Uneven. Trembling as if what he'd said was some kind of earthquake and she was still swaying in the aftermath.

"I have never been more serious in my life," he grated out, his dark eyes flashing.

And this, she found, hurt worst of all. It was everything she'd ever wanted—more than she'd dreamed possible—but not like this. Never like this. Two weeks ago he'd tricked her onto that plane, claiming they were bound for Zurich. This was no different.

It just hurt more.

"No," she said, her voice barely a whisper. "I can't."

"Why not?" It was the voice he used to do business, to make deals. To convince whoever dared say no to him that they should change their answer—and they usually did.

Dru felt bruised. Battered. Torn apart by what she knew was the right thing to do, and that treacherous part of her that wanted him however she could get him. Why couldn't she simply jump at this chance, her masochistic side wondered. He might learn to love her. Maybe he already did, in as much as he was able. And wasn't *maybe* good enough?

But there was another voice in there now, a new one. Fragile and tiny, but hers.

"I deserve better," she heard herself say.

The effect on Cayo was immediate and dramatic, though he didn't seem to move. It was as if all that power, all that ferocity, was suddenly burning in his exotic eyes while the rest of him went terribly, alarmingly still. As if she'd wounded him beyond measure.

"'Better'?" he echoed.

Dru's hands shot out, as if to touch him, to hold him, but at the final moment she found she didn't dare. Her throat was thick with grief, her chest hurt, and there was nothing she could do. She couldn't make this better—and he was making it worse.

"I have a promise to keep to my brother," she whispered. "Nothing is more important than that."

Not even you, she thought miserably, while everything inside her revolted.

"Marry me." But it was less a command than a plea, wrapped up though it was in his ruthless delivery. "It's the only solution." When she only stared back at him through eyes that grew blurrier by the moment, he looked almost desperate. "I don't know how to lose you," he said, his voice near a whisper. "I can't."

"You'll have to learn," she managed to push out past the constriction in her throat.

"Dru—"

"I can't settle, Cayo." She threw that out, through the riot inside of her, through the tears that threatened. And it just kept hurting more. "Not even for you."

"Dru."

Even the way he said her name hurt. As if she was the one who'd mortally wounded him. He reached over and took her face in his hands, and that was when she noticed the tears wetting her cheeks, despite her best efforts.

But he didn't love her. He didn't even pretend. Not even now, to marry her. To keep her. *He didn't love her.* So she could tear herself into pieces by leaving now, or she could stay with him and marry him and fall apart by degrees, year by loveless year, until she really did hate him the way she'd only wished she could two weeks ago.

"I am not the monster you think I am," he said, soft and dark and straight into her heart, like a knife.

"Your two weeks are up, Cayo." It was the hardest thing she'd ever done. The greatest sacrifice she'd ever made. She stepped back, watched his hands drop away, and knew she would never be whole again. "You have to let me go."

CHAPTER NINE

IF THIS WAS what it was like to *care,* Cayo thought some weeks after he'd returned from Bora Bora and Dru had left him on the tarmac without a backward glance, he had been right to discourage the practice for the whole of his adult life.

When I decide to sabotage you, she had told him once, *there will be nothing the least bit passive about it.* He couldn't help but wonder if this was what she'd meant. This…aching sense of loss that colored everything a dull gray.

He hated it.

He glared at one of his many vice presidents across the wide expanse of his London desk, and managed, somehow, to refrain from wringing the man's neck.

"I don't understand why I'm having this conversation," he said coldly. The other man winced. Cayo drummed his fingers on the glossy expanse of his desktop. "Surely I hired you to make decisions at this level yourself."

He was being far kinder than he felt. Personable, even. But he knew he was measuring himself against the kind of results Dru could have wrung out of this man with a few smiles and a supportive word or two and, by that tally, he was a failure.

That was something he was getting used to, however
gracelessly. And she still wasn't here. She had disappeared completely after his plane had touched down
on British soil, just as she'd promised she would. He
supposed he hadn't believed it would happen, that she
would really do it. He still didn't.

"Of course, of course, I would be happy—" the vice
president in front of him stammered out. "It's only that
you always wanted to hear every detail of every potential negotiation before—"

"That was before," Cayo said, and sighed. He rubbed
at his temples and tried to stop glaring. "If there's nothing else…?"

He sat back in his mighty chair behind his massive
desk and watched the other man sprint for the safety
of the outer office. And then, like clockwork, his new
assistant appeared in the doorway to update him on his
schedule and his messages.

Claire was everything anyone could want in a personal assistant, he thought then, eyeing her. The agency
had placed her the day he'd arrived back from French
Polynesia, and she'd acquitted herself beautifully in the
weeks since. She was a quick learner. She was eager
to please and yet didn't tremble every time he spoke,
like so many of his executives. She was even pleasant
enough to look at, in a very blond and vaguely Nordic
sort of way, which he knew always put the potential
investors and various clients at ease. She'd been with
him a month now and he had yet to detect a single flaw.

Save one. She wasn't Dru. She hardly knew how
he took his coffee, much less how to finesse his frac-
tious and demanding board of directors with seeming
ease and nonchalance. He didn't ask for her thoughts
on delicate business negotiations. He would never trust

her to have his interests at heart while tending to long calls filled with unhappy executives. Claire was, he supposed, a perfectly decent personal assistant.

Which forced him to consider the fact that Dru had been far more than that. She'd been more like a partner. And she was gone now, as if she'd never been at Vila Group at all. As if she'd never been with him.

What had he expected? He kept asking himself the same question, and there was never any answer. *Dru hated him.* She'd told him so. Had he really believed that sex could change that? Or that it might change who he was—who he had always been? This monster who did not even know when he was crushing the life out of the only thing he'd ever really cared about?

"Mr. Vila?" Claire asked. A note in her voice suggested it was not the first time she'd said his name. "Shall I get Mr. Young on the phone for you?"

He was not himself. He had not been for some weeks now, and well did he know it.

"Yes," Cayo muttered. It wasn't her fault she wasn't Dru. He had to keep reminding himself of this. Several times a day. "Fine."

He dealt with the call with his usual lack of tact or mercy and when it was done, found himself at the great wall of windows that looked out over the City. He had been scowling out at the depressingly typical British rain for several minutes before it occurred to him that he'd been doing too much of this lately. Brooding like a moody adolescent.

He was disgusted with himself. Had he moped when his grandfather had tossed him out? He had not. After an initial moment to absorb what had happened, he had walked off that mountain and built a life for himself. He hadn't mourned. He hadn't *brooded.* He'd focused and he'd worked hard, and in time, he'd come to think of his grandfather's betrayal as the best thing that had happened to him. Where would he be without it?

But, of course, he knew. He would have been a cobbler like his grandfather in that pretty little whitewashed town, living out a simple life beneath the red roofs, smiling at the tourists who snapped pictures and paid too much for their restaurant meals. Suffering through the whispers and the gossip that would never have subsided, no matter how diligently he worked to combat them, no matter what he did. Paying and paying for his mother's sins, forever and ever without end. He let out a derisive snort at the thought.

I am better off, he told himself. Then told himself he believed it. *Then and now.*

But even so, he stared out the window and saw Dru instead.

They'd sprawled on a blanket on the sandy beach together one night in Bora Bora, wearing nothing but the bright, full moon beaming down from above them. Dru had been nestled against his shoulder, her breath still uneven from the heady passion they'd indulged in, scattering their clothes across the beach in their haste. Their insatiable need.

"I'll admit it," Cayo had said. "I never had a pet quite like you before."

"No?" He'd heard laughter in her voice, though he could only see the top of her head. "Do I sit and stay better than all the rest?"

"I was thinking how much I enjoy it when you surrender," he'd murmured. Hadn't he had her sobbing out his name only a few moments before? He'd been teasing her—something he'd only just realized was reserved for her alone, but when she'd shifted position so she could look at him, her gaze had been serious.

"Careful what you wish for," she'd said softly, in a voice that didn't match the look in her eyes.

"I don't know what you mean," he'd said, reaching out to curl a dark wave of her hair behind her ear, reveling in the thick silk of it between his fingers. "There is nothing wrong with surrender. Particularly to me."

"Easy for you to say." Her voice had been wry. "You've never had the pleasure."

He'd smiled, but then the moment had seemed darker, somehow. Or more honest, perhaps.

"Is that what you're afraid of?" he'd asked quietly.

She'd let out a small sound, as if she'd almost laughed, and then looked away.

"My brother was an addict," she'd said, her voice small, but determined. "I don't know why it feels like I'm betraying him to tell you that. It's true."

Cayo had said nothing. He'd only stroked her back, held her close, and listened. She'd told him about Dominic's attempts at recovery, about his inevitable falls from grace. She'd told him about the way it had been before, when she'd worked in other jobs, and had dropped them to rush to Dominic's side, only to find herself heartbroken and lied to, again and again. And occasionally sacked, to boot. She'd told him about the good times peppered in with the bad. About how close she'd been to her twin once, how for a long time the only thing they'd had in the world had been each other.

"But that wasn't quite true, because he also had his addictions," she'd said. "And he always surrendered to them, eventually. No matter how much he claimed he didn't want to. And then one day he just couldn't come back."

He'd turned then, rolling her over to her back so he could gaze down at her, searching her face, her eyes. But she'd been as unreadable as ever. Still hiding in plain sight, her gray eyes shadowed tonight, and darker than they should have been.

She'd reached out, then, carefully, as if he was something precious to her. She'd traced the line of his jaw, his nose, even the shape of his brows with her fingertips, then run them over his lips, her mouth curving slightly when he'd nipped at her.

"I wonder what that's like?" she'd whispered then, and he'd seen something like agony in her eyes, there and then gone. "Unable to resist the very thing you know will destroy you. Drawn to it, despite yourself."

"Dru," he'd said, frowning down at her. "Surely you can't think—"

But she hadn't let him finish. She'd silenced him with a searingly hot kiss and then moved against him, seducing him that easily. He'd forgotten all about it, until now.

Had she been warning him? Had she known that she would get into his blood like this, poisoning him from the inside out, making him a stranger to himself? Cayo frowned out the window now, through the rain lashing across the glass. For the first time in almost twenty years, he wondered if it was worth it, this great empire he'd built and on which he focused to the exclusion of all else. Lately he wondered if, given the chance, he would trade it in. If he would take her instead.

Not that she'd offered him any such choice.

His intercom buzzed loudly behind him. He didn't move. He didn't know, anymore, if he was furious or if he was simply the wreckage of the man he'd been. And he didn't like it, either way.

It took everything he had not to sic his team of investigators on her, not to have her every move reported back to him, wherever she was now, like the jealous, obsessive fool she'd once accused him of being. He'd been fighting the same near-overwhelming urge for weeks. She'd told him he needed to learn how to lose her, and he'd found it was not a lesson he was at all interested in mastering. The truth was, Cayo had never been any good at losing.

You have to let me go, she'd said. And he had, though it had nearly killed him, kept him up at nights and ruined his days. She was the one thing he'd ever given up on. The one thing he'd let slip through his hands.

And that felt like the greatest failure of all.

Cayo couldn't forgive himself. For any of it. Or her, for doing this to him. For turning him into this weak, destroyed creature, not at all who he'd believed himself to be, before.

Worst of all, for making him *care.*

Dru hadn't had time to collapse into the fetal position under her duvet once she'd made it back to her tiny bedsit in Clapham from the rainy tarmac where she'd last seen Cayo, despite the fact that was all she wanted to do.

Her already-booked flight straight back to Bora Bora had been leaving in two days' time. She'd met with Cayo's studiously blank-faced attorneys on the morning before her flight, and she'd signed whatever they'd put in front of her, not caring if it took blood and her firstborn, so long as it ensured her freedom. Finally. It had been the last necessary step.

And more than that, it had meant he was letting her go.

Some part of her had imagined he might pull his Godzilla routine. Roar and smash, grab and hoard. De-

mand another two weeks. Trap her into that marriage
he'd proposed. *Something.* But he'd let her walk away
from him at the airport. There had been nothing but a
look in his eyes that she'd never seen before, turning all
of that dark amber nearly black and eating her alive inside. The cold, dull, gray English day around them had
been so depressingly *real life* she'd almost wondered
if Bora Bora, the yacht in the Adriatic, Milan, and everything that had happened between them had been no
more than a fevered dream.

The attorneys had been real, however, sliding papers at her one after the next in the Costa Coffee near
Clapham Junction. She'd signed the last five years of
her life away with every pen stroke. At his command.
With his blessing.

Cayo Vila, who never gave in, who had never heard
the word *no,* had let her go, at last.

Just as she'd told him to do, she'd reminded herself.
Just as she'd asked.

And then she'd gone back home, carefully taken the
tin that held Dominic's ashes, taped it shut and wrapped
it up, and packed it away in her checked bag.

The trip had been brutal. When she'd finally staggered into her hotel on the southern part of Bora Bora's
main island, far away from Cayo's private island, it had
been impossible not to notice the differences. She'd told
herself she didn't care. That she'd come for a specific
reason and to perform a specific task, and when had
she become such a princess that she found her rather
smallish room that faced a bit of garden *depressing?* It
was still a garden in Bora Bora.

She'd been furious with herself—and with Cayo—
for spoiling her so thoroughly. She'd become used to all
of the luxury he surrounded himself with, apparently. It

had only served to make her that much more appalled at herself and all the many ways she'd let herself down.

It had taken her a week to get up her nerve—and, if she was honest, to recover a little bit from those two intense weeks she'd spent with Cayo. But finally she'd been ready. One evening, at sunset, she'd taken one of the kayaks out and brought Dominic's ashes with her. As the sky exploded in oranges and pinks, she'd tipped his ashes out into the beautiful, peaceful lagoon.

And while she'd kept her promise to the first man she'd ever loved, and always would, she'd talked to him.

"I wish I could have saved you," she'd whispered to the water, the sky, the sea beyond. "I wish I'd tried harder."

She'd remembered her brother's delighted laughter that she'd never heard enough of. She'd thought of his wickedly amused gray eyes, so much brighter and more alive than hers—and then, sometimes, so much duller. She thought of his too-lean form, his shaggy dark hair, his poet's hands, and the tattoo on his shoulder of two hummingbirds that was, he'd once said with his cheeky grin, meant to represent the two of them. Free and in flight, forever.

"I wish I knew what happened to that picture of us as babies," she'd said, smiling at the memory of the old photograph. "I still don't know which one of us was which."

She'd mourned. She'd thought of their mother, so terrified of being on her own that any man had done, no matter how vicious. She'd thought of all those years when it had been Dominic and Dru against the world, and how much she'd miss that for the rest of her life. He'd taken something from her she could never get back, and as she floated out there with jagged Mount

Otemanu before her and the world she knew so far away, she'd let herself weep for the family she'd lost, her potential children who would never know their uncle, the whole rest of her life stretching out before her with nothing of her twin in it except what she carried with her. In her.

Which wasn't enough, she'd thought then, bitterly. It would never be enough.

"You took part of me with you, Dominic," she'd told him as the inky darkness fell. "And I'll never forget you. I promise."

And when all his ashes were gone she'd made her way back to her hotel, where, finally, she'd curled up on the bed, pulled the duvet over her head, and fallen apart.

She'd stayed there for days. She'd cried until she'd felt blinded by her own tears, until she'd made herself retch from the force of her sobs. She'd let it all out, at last, the terrible storm she'd been carrying with her all this time. The grief of so many years, the pain and the fury and all the lies she'd told herself about her motivations. How much she'd loved Dominic and yes, to her shame, how much she'd sometimes hated him, too. His excuses and his promises, his grand plans that never amounted to anything and his pretty, pretty lies that she'd so desperately wanted to believe. She'd wept for everything she'd lost, and how alone she was, and how little she knew what to do with herself now that she had nothing left to survive, no purpose to fulfill, no great sacrifice remaining to build her life around.

But one day she sat up, and opened all the windows. She let the breeze in, sweet with flowers and the sea. She breathed in, deeply. She had her tea out on the hotel's pretty beach, and felt born again. Made new. As if she really had put Dominic to rest.

Which meant it was time to face the truth about her feelings for Cayo.

"Am I so scary?" he'd asked so long ago that night in Cadiz. The restaurant had been noisy and crowded, and his arm had brushed against hers as they sat so close together at the tiny table. His unforgettable eyes had still been so sad, but there was a curve to that cruel mouth of his, and Dru had felt giddy, somehow. As if they were both lit up with the magic of this night when everything, she'd been sure, was changing.

"I think you take pride in being as scary as possible," she'd replied, smiling. "You have a reputation to uphold, after all."

"I am certain that somewhere beneath it all, I am nothing but clay, waiting to be molded by whoever happens along," he'd said, that near-smile deepening at the absurdity of a man like him being swayed by anything at all save his own inclination.

"Metal that might, under certain circumstances, be welded, perhaps," she'd said, laughing. "Never clay."

"I bow to your superior knowledge," he'd said, swirling his sherry in his glass, his gaze oddly intent on hers. She'd felt herself flush with heat, and had felt out of control. Reckless. Yet it had felt right, even so. More right than she could remember anything else feeling, maybe ever. He'd leaned close, then murmured close to her ear. "What would I do without you?"

She knew what he'd do without her, Dru thought now, staring up at the perfect sky and the glorious lagoon, neither of which seemed to be as bright as they'd been before. Without Cayo. He was probably doing it right now—carrying on being Cayo Vila, scary by design, taking whatever he wanted and expanding his holdings on a whim.

But she was distorted by his absence. Disfigured. And it didn't seem to get any better, no matter how many days passed.

She sat in her cramped seat on an Air Vila flight from Los Angeles to London, staring at the picture of him on the back of the in-flight magazine, and she thought her heart might tear itself apart in her chest.

I can't do this, she thought then, scraping away the tears before they fell on her snoring seatmate. She couldn't live out whatever life it was she thought she ought to live, knowing that he was out there, knowing that she would only ever see him in these painful, far-away glimpses. On the telly, perhaps. In the magazines. But never again right in front of her. Never again close enough to touch, to taste, to tease.

She'd been in love with him for so long. She was still in love with him, however hard she wished it away. It hadn't changed. She was starting to believe it never would. She felt minimized. Diminished, somehow, without him. As if she'd depended on him just as much as he'd depended on her all this time.

Back in her bedsit in London, she tried to tell herself that her whole life was ahead of her. That she need only pick a path to follow and the world was hers. She woke the morning after her return and scanned the papers, looking for clues to her next chapter—but it all seemed cold and empty. Pointless.

She was haunted by Cayo even now, in a tiny flat he'd never visited, on a bright morning that shouldn't have had anything at all to do with him. Her eyes drifted shut as she stood at her small refrigerator, and she saw him. Dark amber eyes. That fierce, ruthless face, with that blade of a nose and his cruel, impossible mouth. She *felt* him. She couldn't breathe without imagining his hands on her skin, his smile, the sound of his voice as he said her name. And that same old fire still burned within her, stubborn and hot, even now.

Did it really matter how he wanted her, as long as he did? Dru found herself pacing the small space that was her kitchen in agitation. She wished he'd handled it differently back in Bora Bora. She wished he'd lied and told her he wanted her, needed her—and not only as his assistant. She might not have believed him, but she'd have wanted to. And maybe it would have been enough.

But she couldn't marry him when he couldn't even pretend to love her. It turned out that was her line in the sand. Her single remaining boundary.

"A girl has to have some standards," she said out loud, shaking her head at herself. At the things she'd clung to all her life, like her belief that she would never be like her mother—and here she was, alone in her flat, halfway to Miss Havisham, arguing her way back to a man who could never love her the way she deserved to be loved.

But that was the problem. Dru didn't simply want to be loved. She wanted to be loved *by Cayo*. And she couldn't see how it made any kind of sense to do without him entirely. Maybe a sliver of Cayo really was better than nothing at all—because nothing else would do. The thought of another man was laughable. What would be the point? Another man wouldn't be Cayo.

Why couldn't they continue as they'd been? She considered it now, scowling fiercely into her sink basin, and the truth was, she couldn't even remember why she'd been so angry with him. Or why she'd been so desperate to get away from him. These weeks were the longest she'd gone without seeing him since she'd started to work for him five years ago. And she hated it. She craved the simple solace of his dark gaze, his impatient voice. Him. She missed *him*.

He might not want her the way she wished he could. He might only have proposed to her as some last-ditch effort to hold on to something he didn't want to lose, the same way he might feel about a particularly limited-edition racecar, for example. Dru understood that. And it wasn't that it didn't hurt. It was that being without him hurt more.

She wanted him more than she wanted her self-respect, it turned out, whatever that made her. A fool. Her mother. A very sad woman destined for a sad life of *slivers*. She supposed she would spend the rest of her life dealing with the fallout of this choice she couldn't seem to help making today. One way or the other.

But in the meantime, she knew exactly what she had to do.

Dru strode back into his life, and into the center of his office, on an otherwise unremarkable Wednesday afternoon.

She looked casual and chic in tight black trousers tucked into high, gleaming boots with dangerous heels and a very complicated sort of burgundy jumper that tied like a scarf and was somehow carelessly elegant. Her glorious hair was swept back into a low ponytail. She'd clearly spent more time in the sun, and it suited her. She had a healthy glow about her, and her eyes were clear as they met his.

Mine, he thought, with a nearly vicious surge of desire.

He wanted his mouth on her. He wanted to be inside her. He wanted her with a savagery that should have taken him out at the knees. Instead, Cayo thrust his hands into his pockets and stood there behind his desk, watching her, as the fury he'd been tamping down began to boil.

"I know how little you like it when people drop in on you without appointments," Dru said in that calm, easy voice of hers that had been haunting him for weeks. "I apologize." She smiled that damned smile of hers. The one he hated. "Your new assistant seems lovely."

"She is perfect in every way," Cayo agreed, his voice all but a growl. "A paragon, in fact. Truly the best personal assistant I've ever had."

"I'm delighted to hear that," she said, so very pleasantly. As if he was just another rich man she had to placate. As if she was working. "Though, if memory serves, you are a bit free with that particular bit of praise. It does render it rather meaningless, I'd say."

He didn't say anything. He couldn't.

"I went back to Bora Bora, as planned," she told him quietly, her gaze searching his, though he didn't know for what.

"I hope your flight was pleasant." He couldn't help his sardonic tone, or the way his brow lifted. "Fly commercial, did you?"

"It took over forty hours." There was the hint of a rueful smile on her lips, which was closer, at least, to something real.

He was meant to respond to that, he knew. He should have. Her eyes met his as if she was encouraging him simply to talk to her, as he might have done before. But he couldn't do it. She'd wrecked him in ways he still didn't understand. She'd left him. He'd let her leave. He still couldn't comprehend either one of those things.

And beyond all that, he wanted her. Pure and simple. Despite knowing exactly how much wanting her destroyed him.

"Dru." He said her name with all the fury and betrayal and longing inside him, letting it pour out of him, not even caring how it hit her. "Why are you here?"

He watched her swallow, hard, as if she was nervous. It became physically painful that he still wasn't touching her.

"I've come to interview," she said, and her voice didn't quite shake but still, he heard emotion there beneath it. A better man might not have taken that as some kind of victory—but he had no such pretensions.

"Interview?" he echoed. He could hear the chill in his own voice. "For what?"

Her chin rose, those gray eyes of hers glittered, and once more, she was hiding from him. He could see it.

"My old position, of course."

He'd dreamed of this. Exactly this. He couldn't help but smile, and he didn't have to see her reaction to know it wasn't a very nice smile at all.

But she didn't break. Not his Dru.

"I'd like my old job back," she said, very distinctly. Politely. She folded her hands in front of her like the passive and obedient underling she had only ever pretended she was, and walked straight into his hands with her head held high. "I've come to beg for it, if necessary."

CHAPTER TEN

HE LOOKED AS though he wanted to take her apart with his teeth. Dru fought to control herself—her pounding heart, her galloping pulse, that heaviness in her stomach that couldn't decide if it was desire or anxiety. Or some combination of both.

"If you would like to beg, don't let me stop you," Cayo bit out after a long moment, though his midnight amber eyes gleamed. "You can begin on your knees."

She remembered that day in Bora Bora with picture-perfect clarity. She remembered crawling to him across the polished wood floor, smiling up at him from between his strong legs. Wanting him more than her next breath. She still did. Heat flashed over her, and she was afraid she turned bright red. His eyes were narrow and hot, and she knew beyond a shadow of a doubt that he was remembering the same thing.

"Sweet memories," he said, deliberately provoking her, but she couldn't seem to react the way she might have before. She couldn't seem to breathe past the sheer *force* of him. It was if she'd dulled the intensity of him in her memory, to protect herself. He was shocking and bold, dark gold eyes and jet-black hair, and all that mouthwatering muscle and masculine grace. His suit was perfectly tailored and made him look sleek. Predatory. But not at all tamed. Not Cayo.

And now she knew what he could do with every last inch of that beautiful body. She found she'd lost her voice completely.

His eyes gleamed even more molten gold than before. He stepped out from behind his desk and roamed around to the front, leaning back against it so he was only a foot or two away from her. She schooled herself not to react, not to step away or show anything on her face, even as the back of her neck prickled in warning. In desperate, mindless want.

"Tell me," he said in that soft, supremely dangerous voice of his. "What would possess you to reapply for this job you wanted so desperately to leave? What will it look like the next time you decide you hate me, do you think? What will you throw at me then?"

"Perhaps I was hasty," she managed to say, before she lost what remained of her sense and begged him to take her, however he wanted her. "I may have let my grief over the loss of my brother affect my better judgment."

He eyed her for a long, chilly moment.

"The position is already filled." Cold. Harsh. Absolute. "You were correct," he continued, and there was so much Spanish in his voice that her breath caught. "It was ridiculously easy to replace you. It took a single phone call."

"Oh, I see," she said then, pretending she was as strong as she made herself sound. "You feel I deserve you at your scariest. Vicious and cutting. Is this my latest punishment?"

"What would I possibly punish you for?" he demanded, his voice low and dark. It connected hard with her belly. "It seems that I was nothing more than a convenient way for you to scratch that itch. Just as I told you to do." His smile then should have drawn blood. "What happened, exactly, that I should feel you need punishing?"

Maybe he *had* drawn blood. Maybe this was her, unable to move, bleeding out where she stood and all too aware it was her own fault. She should have left well enough alone. She should have figured out how to survive it—after all, she'd known going into it that getting closer to Cayo would end like this. Exactly like this. Perhaps she shouldn't have been so cavalier.

"Nothing," she said, and it was just as well that she was already so close to numb, already so worn out from all the heartbreak and the grief, that it was only a quiet sort of storm that shook through her then. Only a little bit of rain and another gray sky. No need for any commotion. "Nothing happened at all."

She inclined her head at him and then she turned and started for the door. It had been a mistake to come here. Cayo was a bell that could never be unrung. She had to move on, no matter how much it hurt. In time, she'd recover sufficiently from all of this. Of course she would. She'd stop thinking about him. People recovered from heartbreak all the time, all the world over.

She would, too, she vowed. *She would.*

"There is still one position that remains open, however," he said from behind her, and the dark, almost satisfied tone he used made goose bumps break out all over her skin.

Dru stopped walking, and hated herself for it. *You are no better than a junkie,* her inner voice castigated. *No better than your brother—and just like your mother. You'd take any punishment he doled out.*

The masochist inside preened, and she did nothing to prove either one wrong.

"What position is that?" she asked, her voice cool. Disembodied, perhaps, as if she was somewhere else, far from here. Watching from a distance while people other than her were cut to pieces. "Your personal punching bag?"

"My wife."

It was another slap, just as it had been on his island, and this time, she was already so weak. She had already broken down enough to come here. This was just another blow. For a moment she thought she might succumb to the tears that threatened to spill from her eyes—but she blinked them away, furiously, and then turned back to him.

They stared at each other. His dark, wicked brows were raised high, challenge and command. All of the tension and pain, all of the hurt and longing, everything he was to her no matter how she fought against it seemed to hang there and draw tight between them. He looked like thunder. His eyes blazed. And she couldn't seem to summon the pride or self-preservation that might have let her laugh at his twisted version of a proposal. She could only endeavor to keep her tears at bay just a little while longer.

He didn't say that he needed her, that he wanted her. That he longed for *her*. He didn't say that this was hard for him. He looked the way he always looked. Untouchable. Impossibly ruthless. And the most dangerous man she'd ever met.

"Your wife," she said, as if she barely recognized the word. She could hardly speak past the lump in her throat. "And what would that position entail, exactly?"

That predatory gleam shone in his gaze, and his

lean body was so tense, rippling with tension, that she thought he really might pounce. Behind him, rain began to lash at the windows and the sky was dark, and there he stood in the middle of all that, more elemental by far.

"I'm sure we'll think of something," he said, in a voice that made her imagine him thrusting into her: that slick, perfect fit. The electricity. The wildness that made her forget herself completely.

"And when that fades?" she asked, her voice thick. "You are not known for your attention span, are you?"

He pushed away from the desk and started toward her, like a lethal weapon aimed directly at her, and Dru had to fight herself to stand still. Not to run in the opposite direction. Or toward him.

"I have thought of very little else but you since the day you walked in here and quit," he said, moving far too close, forcing her to look up at him. "I never wanted you to leave in the first place. It's not my attention span that's at issue here, is it?"

"I can't marry you." She bit that out, final and sure. Desperate.

His dark brows lowered. "Are you holding out for someone richer, Dru? More powerful?" He didn't laugh as he said it. He didn't have to. His voice dropped, even as his mouth curved into that cold, mocking facsimile of a smile. "Better in bed?"

"Love," she heard herself say, to her utter horror. But there was no unsaying it, even when he looked at her as if she'd thrown another shoe at his head—and had hit her target this time. "There's no point marrying without love."

"Of course," he breathed, and she had never seen that look on his face. Remote and terrible, and if he'd been someone else she'd think she'd ripped his heart from his chest. But this was Cayo. His mouth twisted. "You have already made clear your opinion on my character. Who indeed could marry a monster such as me?"

But though his words were the bitterest she'd ever heard, so much so they made her flinch in reaction, he still moved closer. He reached over and ran his hand down the sleek end of her ponytail, drawing it forward to drape over one shoulder, the gentle touch at odds with the way his gaze burned into hers, fierce and uncompromising. And she remembered, then, that night on the chilly terrace in Milan, when he'd done the same thing. When he'd made her heart ache. When he'd made her believe there was more to this than simply that wildfire.

She remembered treading water in the sea, how she'd ducked under the waves and felt, for a moment, that she might simply let herself sink. How that had seemed better than facing this man who cast such a shadow over her whole life. Who she could not seem to do without, however much she thought she should.

Who had accused her of hiding from him, time and again, and here she was, hiding the most important truth of all from him. When really, what was she protecting? She had nothing and no one. She was wholly alone. She had nothing to lose.

But it was still so hard, so overwhelming, that spots danced before her eyes.

"I don't think you're a monster, Cayo," she whispered. And maybe she had nothing to lose, but it still felt like leaping from a very high cliff into nothingness. "I love you."

He went terrifyingly still, his eyes turning to poured gold.

"And you like to collect things," she continued, not caring about how scratchy her voice sounded, or how many unshed tears pressed against her throat. "You're good at it. You obsess for a time and then you forget all about it while you chase your next obsession." She shook her head, and stepped back from him. "I can't even blame you for that. I saw what your grandfather was like. But how can I marry you when you don't love me back? When you can't?"

"Dru—" he started, but it was a stranger's voice, and he was looking at her as if she'd become a ghost again, right there in front of him, and she knew that it was time to leave. That she should never have come. That she had betrayed herself once again.

"You don't have to say anything," she said softly, and she meant it. She did. "I should have stayed away. I'm sorry."

And then she turned back around and walked away from him. For the last time.

He tracked her back to a converted townhouse in a part of Clapham that was a world away from his three-story penthouse at the top of an old Victorian warehouse perched at the edge of the Thames. This was what she preferred to him, he told himself as he caught the door from one of her neighbors and climbed the narrow, grimy stairs to her second-floor flat—this dingy little place and the dim little life that went with it.

He was so angry with her, Cayo thought it might actually burn off the top of his head.

He pounded on her door, not even pretending to be polite.

"I know you're in there," he growled through the door. "I saw you enter the building not five minutes ago."

He heard the rattle of her locks and then she swung the door open and stood there, scowling up at him, and his curse was that he felt her prettiness like a punch to his gut. Her cheeks were flushed with emotion, making her gray eyes gleam, and he was tired of playing nice. Or trying to. He'd let her go, hadn't he? What else was he meant to do? And she'd been the one to come back and make it perfectly clear that he'd been a fool to do so. That he should have ignored what she'd told him. That he shouldn't have let her go in the first place.

"You are not welcome here," she told him in that cold voice that only made him want her more. It made him think about what best melted all of that ice, and he was certain she could see it on his face when he saw her eyes widen. "Go away."

"I can't do that," he said. He stepped toward her and she leapt back, terrified, he suspected, that he might touch her and prove what a liar she was. He simply shouldered his way inside the flat and kicked the door shut behind him.

And then they were all alone. No brand-new personal assistant in the outer office. And he was blocking the only exit. Cayo could see precisely when that occurred to her, and he smiled.

It was a laughably tiny little place, a bedsit indeed, all in white with a few accent colors—a wooden headboard, the pop of scarlet pillows on her bed—to suggest the idea of space without actually having any. She kept it scrupulously neat, and that was why it seemed slightly bigger than it was—but only slightly.

To his right, a wardrobe and a double bed jutted out into the small, fitted kitchen. Her laptop lay there, on a café table next to what looked like an abandoned cup of tea, and something about the sight made his chest feel tight. He could imagine her there, dressed in whatever she slept in, her glorious hair knotted on the back of her head as she scrolled through the internet with her morning tea. To his left, when he wrenched his gaze away from her laptop and his imagination, was the smallest version of a living room he'd ever seen, featuring only a plush white armchair, a small trunk and a little shelf with a television sat on it.

This was where she slept. Dreamed. Imagined her life without him. Lived it. Even while claiming she was in love with him.

She would pay for that, too, he promised himself. And dearly.

"This is my space," she fumed at him. "It's not one of the many things that belong to you, that you can storm in and out of as you please. I get to decide what happens here, and I want you to leave."

"I'm not leaving." He leveled a dark look at her. "Nor am I planning to run away if things become intense, unlike some."

He moved farther into the room, grimly amused at the way she skittered away from him, or tried to, as there was nowhere left to go. He picked up one of the handful of framed photographs that sat on the narrow bookshelf at the top of her headboard. A younger Dru and a pale, skinny boy who looked just like her, the same dark hair, those same unfathomable gray eyes. Dru was staring into the camera, mischief in her eyes and a slight smile on her lips, while her brother slung an arm around her neck and laughed. They looked happy, he thought. Truly happy. The constriction in his chest pulled taut.

"I did not *run away*," she was protesting. She reached over and snatched the picture from his hand, holding it against her chest for a moment before replacing it. "There was no point continuing that conversation. There still isn't. It hurts too much."

"All you do is run away," he contradicted her, not even attempting to temper the harshness in his voice. "You jumped off the damned yacht. You demanded I let you go. You walked out of my office. And that's not counting the numerous ways you run away without ever leaving the room."

"That's not running away," she hissed at him. "That's called the survival instinct. I'll do whatever I have to do to survive, Cayo, including climb out this window and down the side of this—"

"I promise you that if you attempt to run away from me again," he cut her off, his gaze hard on hers, his voice brooking no argument, "I will lock you up in the nearest tower and throw away the key."

"Another excellent threat," she retorted, unfazed, if that glint in her eyes was any indication. "With shades of Rapunzel, no less. Sadly, not a single one of your sixteen properties features a tower."

"Then I'll buy one that does."

They glared at each other for a long moment, while everything inside him rioted. What was it about this woman? How did she do this to him? Even now, all he wanted was to sling her over his shoulder and then onto the bed, and who cared what she thought about that? He knew how she'd *feel,* and it was rapidly becoming the only thing that mattered to him. She stood in her small living area, her arms crossed over her chest, her sleek boots kicked off next to the armchair so it was only Dru in her stocking feet with too much color in her cheeks.

And he wanted her so badly it was painful.

"What do you want, Cayo?" she asked then, her voice soft, as if it really did hurt her. And he hated that, but there was no other way.

"I want you," he said, gravely. Deliberately holding

her gaze. "That hasn't changed, Dru. I don't believe it will."

She held herself even tighter, while her cheeks paled and she bit down on her lower lip. And he wanted his hands on her. He wanted to bury his face in her hair and inhale the sweet fragrance of it. He wanted to hold her slender shoulders in his hands. He wanted to be what chased her pain away, not what caused it. But he had never known how to do such things. He'd never tried. He didn't know how to start, and all she ever did was leave.

But she loved him. And that was like a bright light where there had never been anything but dark. It was everything.

"I meant what I said in your office," she whispered. "I shouldn't have come back. I should have stayed gone. If you leave now, you'll never see me again."

"I believe you." He kept himself from touching her, but barely. "But I'm not prepared to watch you martyr yourself. Not for me."

Dru felt as if he'd kicked her.

"I'm no martyr," she said in a low voice, her mind reeling.

"Are you certain?" His voice was like silk, danger and demand. And he didn't back down so much as an inch. "I can almost see the flames dance around you as you burn yourself at the stake of your choosing."

She couldn't handle this. He was so much larger than life and standing in the middle of her tiny flat, taking it over, as if the space could not contain him. As if it groaned around him, near enough to bursting at the seams with the effort of holding the force of him within these walls. She couldn't seem to make sense of it. Or breathe past the knot in her stomach.

"I have no idea what you're talking about," she said, but she hardly sounded like herself.

He started toward her, backing her up against the cold windows on the far side of the room. It took all of three steps, and then the cold glass was at her back and Cayo was a wall in front of her, big and tempting and more dangerous to her than anything else in the world.

"What have you told yourself?" he asked in that smooth way that made her look around wildly for some escape route. "Have you cried over me, Dru? The man who cannot love you back? Have you forgotten I know you, too?"

"Are you mocking me?" She was incredulous. Not sure if that was anger or agony that surged inside of her, she focused on that fiercely cruel face of his and asked herself why she'd expected anything else. "Are you really that much of a monster, after all?"

His dark amber eyes glowed with something that was not quite malice—something that shivered through her and made her catch her breath. Temper. Fury. And that simmering, unquenchable desire that had ensnared them in this in the first place.

"How convenient for you," he said, his voice no less deadly for all it was so soft, like a lover's. "To find yourself someone else you can love so bravely, and from afar."

His words slammed into her like blows. Dru heard herself make some kind of horrible squeaking sound, and thought her legs would give out. She staggered back against the windowsill, while Cayo only stood there, pitiless, and watched.

"You only love what can never love you back," he

told her in that same way, so calmly, as if he didn't know how devastating it was. As if he couldn't see what it was doing to her—or more likely, didn't care. "You arrange your life around distant objects that you can circle but never approach. You thrive on it."

"You…" She could hardly speak. She felt winded. "You don't know what you're talking about."

"Don't I?" She saw the shadows in his eyes, the darkness that lurked there. "Do you love me, Dru? Or do you only think you do because you imagine there's no danger I could ever return it? No chance you might risk yourself, not really. You get to pretend to suffer for your great love while remaining, as ever, completely and utterly alone. Hermetically sealed away. The perfect bloody martyr." He paused, his eyes flashed, and his voice dropped. "Just as you did with your brother."

She lifted a hand as if to stave him off, unable to keep herself from trembling, and sank down against the wall, her legs no longer capable of holding her upright. But he was relentless—he was ruthless down into his bones, and he squatted down before her, his coat flaring around him like a cape, his suit clinging to the hard muscles of his thighs. A perfect and pitiless god, rendering his terrible judgment.

"You," he said, as if she had missed his point, "have no idea what love is."

For what felt like a long time—whole ages, perhaps centuries—Dru could only stare at him, stricken, too deeply shaken even to weep. She felt cracked open, as if she yawned wide and he was the brash, bright light exposing all of her darkness to the air.

And it hurt so much and so deeply that she dimly suspected she hadn't yet got to the real pain—that this was only the shock that preceded it.

"And you do?" she asked eventually. Belligerently, though her voice quaked.

Cayo's eyes were brilliant. Dark and gold and molten fire, burning her alive. He reached over and took her hands in his, and she should have jerked away. But instead, she exulted in the feel of his skin against hers after all this time. It pumped through her like heat, as though her own blood betrayed her, as though there was no part of her that wasn't his no matter what she told herself. Or told him.

"Let me tell you what I know," he told her, his voice low, intense. Urgent. His accent was thick and melodic then, wrapping around her, caressing her. "I want you. I want you in ways that I don't understand. I can live without you, but I don't want to. I don't see the point."

"Cayo—"

"Callate," he ordered her. He shifted back on his heels, dropping her hands though she still felt as if he touched her, as if he surrounded her. She folded her hands over what was left of his heat. "I tried. I let you go. *You came back."* His fierce face looked almost harsh. Stark and serious. "You only love what you cannot have, and I have never been anything but a monster. I've never wanted to be anything but what I am." His cruel mouth moved slightly, hinting at that curve. "Until now."

Something swelled up in the space between them, precarious and new. Dru felt the tears trickle down her cheeks but made no move to wipe them away. She could only see Cayo. And like one of those hummingbirds that Dominic had inked into his skin, she felt something flutter up and hover, skittish and shy, like some kind of gift. *Hope,* she thought, and that great cavern inside her, that terrible emptiness that had eaten her alive for so long, began at last to shrink.

She didn't want pain. She didn't want that masochistic streak. She wanted him. She always had. And she was tired of hiding. It was time to stop. Past time.

This time she was the one who reached out. She sat forward and ran her hands along his severe jaw, then held his fierce, impossible face between her hands. She felt the heat of him moving through her, warming her from the inside out.

"If I am not a martyr," she said, her voice small but strong, "and you are not a monster, then who do you suppose we are?"

"That's the point," he said, his hands coming up to cover hers, his gaze melting into hers, the world shifting all around them and the fire that always burned between them bright and hot and true. Making them something more than they were before. Soldering them together. Welding them, finally, into one. Not clay, but tempered steel. "I want to find out. With you."

"I think we can do that," she whispered, and then she tipped forward and kissed him, like a vow.

He found her sprawled out on one of the loungers on the private deck off the owner's suite on the great yacht, her lovely curves displayed to mouthwatering perfection in a wickedly simple bikini.

She smiled as he approached, but did not set aside her tablet until he lifted her bodily into the air and captured her mouth with his. He had not seen her in almost a full twenty-four hours and felt as desperate as if it had been years.

He set her to her feet carefully, enjoying the slide of her against him.

"What is it?" she asked, her clever eyes moving over his face.

He reached into his pocket and pulled out a long, narrow white box and handed it to her. She looked up at him for a moment, then looked down and opened the box. She gasped. And Cayo tensed, not certain this had been the right thing to do.

Dru pulled the pendant into the air and stared at it, her eyes filling with tears.

"Hummingbirds…" she whispered. Two birds nestled together on the silver chain, in the bright and bold colors that could only be Murano glass. They sparkled in the golden sunlight, looking very nearly alive. And when she looked at him again, her eyes were wet, but she was smiling.

"You won't forget him," Cayo said, his voice rough. "And neither will I."

She threw her arms around him and kissed him then. For a long time. Soft and sweet. Making both of them sigh.

It had been eight months now since that scene in her cramped Clapham bedsit. Eight months of Dru in his life, testing him and changing him, making him wonder how he'd lived without her for so long. He could no longer imagine any possible scenario that did not include this woman, who had somehow made him the man he'd never believed he could be. Flesh and blood. Alive. Not a monster, after all. Not as long as she loved him.

"When are you going to marry me?" he demanded when they were both breathless and she was boneless against him.

"When you deserve it," she said, pulling away from him. She wiped at her eyes and then she looked at him as if she thought that eventuality was highly unlikely, and he laughed.

"Must I bribe you into it?" he asked. "You won't take a house. Land. Atolls or islands."

He waved a hand and she followed the gesture, looking out over the deep blue of the Aegean Sea toward the sunny, green little island that stretched there off the side of the yacht. Private and uninhabited. And his. She had insisted that he visit all of his properties or sell them, and so he had, leaving the minutiae of his affairs more and more in the capable hands of his fleet of vice presidents. *Delegating.* This Greek island, one of the Cyclades not far from Mykonos, was the last on the list. He found he liked it. And the process of exploring them all, with her.

"No," she agreed. "I don't want your property. But…"

"Yes?" She amused him. Fascinated him.

"Perhaps a company." Her gray eyes gleamed as she fastened the pendant around her neck. The hummingbirds seemed to dance and shimmer against her skin. "Just a small one."

"Why am I unsurprised that the life of leisure bores you?"

She only smiled. "You have that boutique advertising agency in New York, don't you, that is currently in dire need of leadership?"

He was aware she knew full well that he did.

"What do you know about managing an advertising agency?" But his tone was indulgent and in any case, he had no doubt that this woman could do anything she chose to do, and well.

"I managed you for five years," she said dryly. "I imagine a company filled with artistic Americans could only be a breeze in comparison. A bit of holiday, really."

"I love you," he said, because he did, and because he could think of nothing that pleased him more than the idea of her doing this *with* him. Building all of this *with* him. Making it their empire, not his. Making it matter. "You can run whatever you want, *mi amor*. But I will have to insist that you marry me."

She only watched him, her gray eyes clear and sparkling, and he reached over to take her hands in his, pulling her to him. The sun spilled all over her, bathing her in light, and still she shone brighter.

"There is a little-known clause in all my contracts," he said softly, pressing kisses to her cheek, to the freckles across her nose, to her sweet mouth. "All Vila Group subsidiaries must be run by a Vila. So you see how it is. My hands are tied."

Dru laughed and threaded her arms around his neck.

"You know how I love a sacrifice," she teased him. "I suppose it's a good thing, then, that I love you enough to make such a huge one."

"It is," he said gruffly, but he smiled, and then kissed her again, sealing it.

And it would be, he thought. A very good thing, and they would spend their whole lives making it better. He had no doubts.

He was Cayo Vila. He didn't take no for an answer, and he didn't know how to fail.

* * * * *

#3205 THE TYCOON'S DELICIOUS DISTRACTION
Maggie Cox

Forced to rely on physio Kit after a skiing accident confines him
to a wheelchair, Hal Treverne has no escape from her intoxicating
presence. But unleashing the simmering desire beneath her
ever-so-professional facade is a challenge this tycoon will relish!

#3206 HIS TEMPORARY MISTRESS
Cathy Williams

Damian Carver wants revenge on the woman who stole from him,
and her sister Violet won't change his mind...until he needs a
temporary mistress, and Violet's perfect! But sweet-natured Violet
soon turns the tables on his sensuous brand of blackmail....

#3207 THE MOST EXPENSIVE LIE OF ALL
Michelle Conder

Champion horse breeder Aspen has never forgotten
Cruz Rodriguez, so when he reappears with a multimillion-dollar
investment offer, Aspen's torn. She may crave his touch, but his
glittering black eyes hide a deception that could prove more costly
than ever before!

#3208 A DEAL WITH BENEFITS
One Night with Consequences
Susanna Carr

Sebastian Cruz has no intention of giving Ashley Jones's family's
island back, but he does want her. He'll agree to her deal, but
with a few clauses of his own—a month at his beck and call...
and in his bed!

REQUEST YOUR
FREE BOOKS!

2 FREE NOVELS PLUS
2 FREE GIFTS!

YES! Please send me 2 FREE Harlequin Presents® novels and my 2 FREE gifts (gifts are worth about $10). After receiving them, if I don't wish to receive any more books, I can return the shipping statement marked "cancel." If I don't cancel, I will receive 6 brand-new novels every month and be billed just $4.30 per book in the U.S. or $4.99 per book in Canada. That's a saving of at least 14% off the cover price! It's quite a bargain! Shipping and handling is just 50¢ per book in the U.S. and 75¢ per book in Canada.* I understand that accepting the 2 free books and gifts places me under no obligation to buy anything. I can always return a shipment and cancel at any time. Even if I never buy another book, the two free books and gifts are mine to keep forever.   106/306 HDN FVRK

Name _____ (PLEASE PRINT) _____

Address _____ Apt. # _____

City _____ State/Prov. _____ Zip/Postal Code _____

Signature (if under 18, a parent or guardian must sign)

Mail to the Harlequin® Reader Service:
IN U.S.A.: P.O. Box 1867, Buffalo, NY 14240-1867
IN CANADA: P.O. Box 609, Fort Erie, Ontario L2A 5X3

Are you a current subscriber to Harlequin Presents books
and want to receive the larger-print edition?
Call 1-800-873-8635 or visit www.ReaderService.com.

* Terms and prices subject to change without notice. Prices do not include applicable taxes. Sales tax applicable in N.Y. Canadian residents will be charged applicable taxes. Offer not valid in Quebec. This offer is limited to one order per household. Not valid for current subscribers to Harlequin Presents books. All orders subject to credit approval. Credit or debit balances in a customer's account(s) may be offset by any other outstanding balance owed by or to the customer. Please allow 4 to 6 weeks for delivery. Offer available while quantities last.

Your Privacy—The Harlequin® Reader Service is committed to protecting your privacy. Our Privacy Policy is available online at www.ReaderService.com or upon request from the Harlequin Reader Service.

We make a portion of our mailing list available to reputable third parties that offer products we believe may interest you. If you prefer that we not exchange your name with third parties, or if you wish to clarify or modify your communication preferences, please visit us at www.ReaderService.com/consumerchoice or write to us at Harlequin Reader Service Preference Service, P.O. Box 9062, Buffalo, NY 14269. Include your complete name and address.

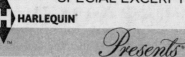
TABBY looked up at him and froze, literally not daring to breathe. That close his eyes were no longer dark but a downright amazing and glorious swirl of honey, gold and caramel tones, enhanced by the spiky black lashes she envied.

His fingers were feathering over hers with a gentleness she had not expected from so big and powerful a man, and little tremors of response were filtering through her, undermining her self-control. She knew she wanted those expert hands on her body, exploring much more secret places, and color rose in her cheeks, because she also knew she was out of her depth and drowning. In an abrupt movement, she wrenched her hands free and turned away, momentarily shutting her eyes in a gesture of angry self-loathing.

"Try on the rest of the clothes," Acheron instructed coolly, not a flicker of lingering awareness in his dark deep voice.

Tension seethed through Acheron. What the hell was the matter with him? He had been on the edge of crushing that soft, luscious mouth beneath his, close to wrecking the non-sexual relationship he envisaged between them. Impersonal would work the best and it shouldn't be that difficult, he reasoned impatiently, for they had nothing in common. She cleaned up incredibly well, he acknowledged grudgingly, gritting his teeth together as his gaze instinctively dropped to the sweet pouting swell of her small breasts beneath the clingy top.

He had done what he had to do, he reminded himself grimly. She was perfect for his purposes, for she had as much riding on the success of their arrangement as he had. Thankfully nothing in his life was going to change in the slightest: he had found the perfect wife, a nonwife....

Two hours later, Acheron opened the safe in his bedroom wall to remove a ring case he hadn't touched in years. The fabled emerald, which had reputedly once adorned a maharajah's crown, had belonged to his late mother and would do duty as an engagement ring. The very thought of putting the priceless jewel on Tabby's finger chilled Acheron's anticommitment gene to the marrow, and he squared his broad shoulders, grateful that the engagement and the marriage that would follow would be 100 percent fake.

* * *

Will sharp-tongued, independent firestorm Tabby Glover accept Greek billionaire Acheron Dimitrakos's outrageous marriage proposal?

Find out in January 2014!

Get 4 FREE REWARDS!

We'll send you 2 FREE Books plus 2 FREE Mystery Gifts.

Harlequin Intrigue® books feature heroes and heroines that confront and survive danger while finding themselves irresistibly drawn to one another.

FREE
Value Over
$20

one other living human. It was best, they said. For her protection, they insisted.

It was true. But she had never felt more alone in her life.

Bob nudged her. She pushed aside the troubling thoughts and looked down at her black Labrador. "I know, boy. I should get moving. It's cold out here."

Allowing herself to get caught out in the woods in the dark—no matter that she knew the way back to the cabin by heart—was a bad idea. She started forward once more. Her hiking boots crunched on the rocks and the few frozen leaves scattered across the trail. Bob trotted beside her, his tail wagging happily. She'd never had a dog before coming to this place. Growing up, her mother's allergies hadn't allowed pets. Later, when she was out on her own, the apartment building hadn't permitted pets.

Even after she married and moved into one of Atlanta's megamansions, she couldn't have a dog. Her husband had hated dogs, cats, any sort of pet. How had she not recognized the evil in him then? Anyone who hated animals so much couldn't be good.

She hugged herself, rubbed her arms. Thinking of him, even in such simple terms, unsettled her. Soon she hoped she would be able to put that part of her life behind her and never look back again.

Never, ever.

"Not soon enough," she muttered.

Don't miss
Witness Protection Widow *by Debra Webb,*
available February 2020 wherever
Harlequin Intrigue books and ebooks are sold.

Harlequin.com